serve

C.W. FARNSWORTH

SERVE

Copyright © 2022 by C.W. Farnsworth

Editing and Proofing:

Britt Tayler, Paperback Proofreader

Alison Evans-Maxwell, Red Leaf Proofing

Cover:

Sarah Hansen, Okay Creations

ALSO BY C.W. FARNSWORTH

Four Months, Three Words

Kiss Now, Lie Later

The Hard Way Home

First Flight, Final Fall

Come Break My Heart Again

The Easy Way Out (The Hard Way Home Book 2)

Famous Last Words

Winning Mr. Wrong

Back Where We Began

Like I Never Said

Fly Bye

Fake Empire

Heartbreak for Two

For Now, Not Forever

CONTENTS

Chapter 1	1
Chapter 2	7
Chapter 3	13
Chapter 4	22
Chapter 5	34
Chapter 6	54
Chapter 7	65
Chapter 8	79
Chapter 9	95
Chapter 10	105
Chapter 11	117
Chapter 12	129
Chapter 13	143
Chapter 14	155
Chapter 15	164
Chapter 16	188
Chapter 17	200
Chapter 18	207
Chapter 19	221
Chapter 20	230
Chapter 21	238
Chapter 22	248
Chapter 23	254
Chapter 24	267
Chapter 25	277
Epilogue	288
Acknowledgments	299
About the Author	301

For the girl who wandered around DC, dreaming up stories.

SYNOPSIS

Georgette Adams is trouble incarnate. Spoiled, sassy, smart…and the First Daughter.

Getting summoned to a meeting at the White House felt like an honor—until I caught the catch.

I'm the newest member of her security detail. Not only for the rest of the summer in DC, but once she leaves for Stanford in the fall as well.

The only place Georgie respects rules is on the tennis court. Her safety is my responsibility.

Our priorities clash and our personalities conflict. Yet somehow, the more time we spend together, the less it feels like work.

But my job description doesn't include making her laugh or enjoying our conversations. And it definitely doesn't involve broken rules or blurred lines.

My only job?

Is to *serve*.

SERVE

C.W. FARNSWORTH

CHAPTER ONE

GEORGIE

I'M STUCK in a sea of dark green.

You might be thinking, *aren't all seas blue?* The ones filled with water, yes.

But I'm not in the middle of a literal ocean.

I'm surrounded by polyester. Hamilton Academy's school colors are green and white. Everyone around me is wearing green, meaning my white robe stands out like a snowdrop planted in a field of grass.

"Hannah Harris!"

My best friend Lucy sighs beside me, then continues picking away at her pink nail polish. Flecks of coral fall to the dark brown, almost black hardwood floor of the auditorium, collecting in a tiny pile like pencil shavings.

"Lucas Jones!"

Luke winks at the two of us seated in the front row as he swaggers across the stage, prompting a drawled "*Damn,*" from Lucy.

I muffle a laugh behind my hand as Headmaster Stewart continues listing off our classmates' names, one by one. Lucy and

I are set to walk last, a nod to our respective roles as salutatorian and valedictorian.

I'm sure most of the audience thinks my father snagged the accomplishment for me, the same way they think one of his award-winning speechwriters constructed the speech I finished delivering fifteen minutes ago.

At the ripe old age of eighteen, I've learned people will think what they like and there isn't much you can do about it. But, God, do I get sick of it.

August Williams crosses the stage to receive his diploma, and then it's just me and Lucy left without them.

"Lucille Drummond."

There are a few muttered words in the audience as Lucy dances across the stage. Possibly about the fact she altered her hem, so that it's several inches higher than everyone else's.

Lucy likes to toe the line. I'm not one to play by the rules incessantly, but in this instance, I knew the repercussions wouldn't be worth the rebellion. Unauthorized adjustments to my graduation attire would have resulted in my mother considering every photo from today ruined. My father would likely have revoked the permission it took two weeks of cajoling to receive from him—attending Elaine Cole's graduation party tonight.

"Georgette Adams."

When my name is announced, there are more whispers than the number that followed Lucy's.

Some are laced with awe, others thick with annoyance. I'm expecting both.

People like to link me with my father's decisions.

It's probably why I'm his harshest critic.

Scratchy polyester swishes around my shins as I stride toward Headmaster Stewart and accept my diploma.

"It's been such an honor, Miss Adams," he tells me.

I suppress the snort that wants to surface. This—the posturing and the politicking—I hate as much as the microscope. I *did* earn the highest GPA in the class on my own—mostly because I despise being wrong and that extends to academics—but I didn't contribute much else to Hamilton Academy.

Headmaster Stewart preferred to turn a blind eye to what I *did* contribute. Any honor tied to my presence has nothing to do with me.

I smile and nod anyway, the response that's been drilled into me since my father first dipped a toe in the political pool over a decade ago.

It's hard to find fault with a smile and nod, but people sure try. A smile can look faked, according to the people who make a living scrutinizing the First Family. Nods can appear dismissive. Haughty.

After I return to my seat, Headmaster Stewart spends another few minutes droning on about...honestly, I'm not listening. I'm more focused on Lucy's leg bouncing. She's anxious to get out of here and start getting ready for tonight. Headmaster Stewart stops speaking eventually, we all throw our caps up into the air, and then we're filing out of the auditorium into the lobby.

The interior of Hamilton Academy is constructed to look like an old European library. It's all dark wood and stained-glass windows and smells like musty old paper. Excited chatter echoes off the high ceiling and the oil paintings that line the walls, depicting portraits of old aristocrats and famous politicians, former alumni who I have just joined the hallowed ranks of.

Families and friends start to filter out into the lobby after the group of graduates. I remain where I am, letting the two people here for me approach rather than going to them. I tap the stiff edge of my diploma against my thigh, watching family members embrace each other.

3

My parents aren't difficult to spot.

Today—attending his only child's high school graduation—was considered a high-risk event for my father. The name of the school I attend isn't difficult to look up, and neither was the date of its graduation ceremony. Confirmed appearances are something the Secret Service tries to avoid, especially at locations with minimal security to start with. Half of downtown DC was blocked off to allow the presidential motorcade to travel here.

The ring of security around my father and mother is comprised of twelve agents. All dressed in black suits, wearing stern-looking expressions, and murmuring into earpieces. And I know there are many more spread around Hamilton Academy's campus, slightly less visible.

When you're the president, flying under the radar isn't often an option.

My parents both love me—I know that. I'm not the show pony daughter they whip out on special occasions for a photo op. But my relationship—with them both, but especially my father—has been stretched and warped over time. Discolored by the demands of public service and the scrutiny of being the most powerful man in the world.

I'm proud of my father. Watching him take the Oath of Office was a surreal moment. And it's a mostly thankless job, with limited power when it matters and a never-ending stream of commentary from those who believe they could meet its many demands better. It's a role my father has tackled with sincerity and integrity.

There are many people who believe he's doing a terrible job of running the country.

I'm not one of them.

But pride is layered within a whole lot of other emotions. The most prominent is resentment. He's given up a lot in order to get where he is. I've sacrificed just as much—maybe more.

And it's moments like these where it really strikes me. When I wish that every single person at my high school graduation didn't have to go through airport-level security just to attend the event. That there weren't snipers on the roof and a police escort plus two ambulances waiting outside.

I'm enveloped in the entourage when it draws near enough. The familiar scent of my mother's honeysuckle perfume surrounds me as she pulls me into a tight hug. "I'm so proud of you, Georgie," she tells me.

She's talking about my valedictorian status, more than anything else. Hamilton Academy is the de facto choice for the children of DC's elite. My fellow classmates are the sons and daughters of senators and Supreme Court justices.

Academic prowess matters to my mother. Before we moved into 1600 Pennsylvania Avenue, she was a philosophy professor at Boston College. Whereas my father is booksmart, he sees school as more of a means to an end, not as an enjoyable experience. He's more interested in my tennis ranking than my test scores.

"Thanks, Mom," I reply, patting her back.

My father embraces me next. "Congrats, Georgie."

"Thanks, Dad."

"Your speech went well."

"Yeah, thanks. Your notes were helpful."

I didn't have the assistance of any speechwriters, but my dad requested to look over a copy of my valedictorian speech last week. I obliged, mostly because it felt like a normal moment between us, which are few and far between these days.

When I was little, my father was the sort of dad who assisted with science fair projects and brought snacks to my tennis matches. That changed. Slowly, at first, then all at once. It's not that he doesn't care, or that *he* changed. His free time just became severely limited when he was elected to the Senate, and pretty much nonexistent when he became President.

One of the agents steps forward and whispers something into my father's ear. Even before his expression turns apologetic, I know what it will mean.

"It's fine, Dad. Lucy wants to head right out so we can get ready for tonight, anyhow."

My mother raises a skeptical brow at that but doesn't ask any questions. It's the middle of the afternoon, so getting ready this early implies more than your average hair and makeup job. It just so happens Lucy bought hair dye to dip dye our hair before the party tonight.

I figure it's one of those situations where it's better to ask for forgiveness than permission.

"Okay," my father replies, waving at someone before turning his attention back to me. "Be careful and have fun."

I mock-salute. "Yes, sir."

A hint of a smile tugs at his lips. I turn to leave, thinking it's the highest note we'll end on.

"Georgie."

I look back. "Yeah?"

"I need to talk to you tomorrow morning. Come to my office at ten, all right?"

If tonight is half as wild as I'm expecting it to be, I'm positive I won't want to be anywhere at ten a.m. tomorrow that isn't my bed. Saying that doesn't feel like an option.

"All right," I agree, internalizing a sigh before turning around and walking away.

CHAPTER TWO

GEORGIE

FIVE TEQUILA SHOTS last night were a choice, I remind myself, as I step out of the elevator that connects the residence to the West Wing.

Not my best decision, I'll willingly admit. But you only graduate from high school once.

The short trip from the elevator to the entrance of the Oval Office feels like an eternity. It smells different up here—*important*. My feet drag and my head pounds as I force my fuzzy sock-clad feet to walk down the carpeted hall past portraits of former presidents. They all look awfully judgmental, but maybe I'm projecting the disapproval I know will be waiting for me.

Margot, my father's secretary, glances up from her desk as I reach my destination. It's a Sunday, yet her hair is pulled back into a neat chignon and she's wearing a pantsuit that doesn't have a single wrinkle.

"Good morning, Miss Adams." She greets me with a polite smile. "Your father is waiting for you, feel free to head straight in."

I grunt a "Thanks" before passing her and opening the door that leads into the round room.

My father is sitting in one of the two upholstered couches placed parallel to the fireplace, wearing his genuine smile, not his staged one. He stands at the sound of the door closing behind me, his mouth quirking with displeasure at my disheveled appearance.

I realize cotton sleep shorts, an oversized, faded *Nantucket* sweatshirt, and strawberry-patterned socks are not what most people would wear to a meeting with the leader of the free world at the White House.

But I'm not here about economic reform or the climate crisis. There won't be any medals handed out during this meeting.

I'm here to talk to my father about what I'm guessing will include restrictions on my summer now that school is no longer in session and taking up most of my time. I'm sure he wishes I was still young enough to get sent off to sleepaway camp.

"You're late," he states.

"It's early," I counter, yawning.

"I'm sure it feels that way, when you've been out half the night." If *unimpressed* were a sound, it would be the tone of my father's voice.

I shrug. "I'm eighteen, I told you and Mom where I was going, and I brought along the whole goon squad."

My father sighs. "Since you've mentioned your *security detail*, I'd like to introduce you to its newest member."

For the first time, my hungover brain registers there is a third person in the Oval Office. My eyes land on the blue-eyed, blond-haired man sitting up straight in one of the two armchairs angled toward the couch where my father was seated when I walked in.

My first thought? *Whoa.*

My second thought? *Jerk.*

"This is Agent Ethan Salisbury," my father tells me. "Effective immediately, he'll be assigned to your detail."

"No."

The suddenness and surety of the word surprises everyone in the room, myself included.

I'm not certain where the conviction comes from.

Maybe it stems from the fact Ethan Salisbury looks like he wandered off the set of an action thriller where he played the handsome hero. Young and good-looking aren't adjectives I'd use to describe any of my other agents.

Or maybe it's the way he's eyeing my pajamas like they're old gum stuck to the bottom of his shoe. Superiority and disapproval radiate off him. He's clearly offended by my choice of casual attire.

Either way, I'm immediately certain having him as part of my security detail is a bad idea.

I have a comfortable arrangement with my current team—I tell them where I'm sneaking off to before I do, and they gloss over certain details in their regular reports to my father.

Agent Ethan Salisbury looks more like the *cross your T's twice, just in case* kind of guy. He's dressed like a Joseph Adams fanboy, right down to the American flag pinned to the lapel of his navy suit. In a contest between loyalty to my father and allowing me to drink at a party, I'm confident which will win.

"I don't want a new suit following me around," I tell my father's pissed-off expression. "I like my current team."

He's taking my rejection of his golden boy worse than Ethan himself, who appears annoyingly serene about the rebuff. Ethan brushes an invisible piece of lint off his tailored pants, not even bothering to make eye contact with me. It's like I'm a movie he's already decided not to watch.

"I'm not asking for your permission, Georgette," my father

states. Full name means business. "Agent Salisbury comes highly recommended and is a new member of the Secret Service. He'll join your team now and will be your head of security once you leave for Stanford in August."

I gape at him. "What? Steve is my head of security."

"*Agent Michaels* is thirty-six. He won't blend in on a college campus, not to mention he has a wife and child here in DC. He'll switch over to your mother's detail once you leave for California."

"How old is *he*?" I don't bother to use Ethan's name, and I don't look over at him as I ask it either.

"Agent Salisbury is twenty-three. He graduated at the top of his class from Dartmouth and passed through his training with flying colors. He's an asset to the Service."

Mini-Joseph looks like he's in shock, hearing my father sing his praises like his favorite tune. I'd love to break it to him—this has nothing to do with Ethan or his credentials. He's just the latest pawn in the power struggle between me and my father. The balance between what I want—a normal life—and my father's decision to take on a role that requires round-the-clock, high security or else threaten democracy.

Am I bitter that my father's aspirations came at the cost of me going anywhere without a squad of heavily armed men?

Yeah, I guess you could say that.

"So you're pawning me off on a rookie with zero experience?" I ask. "Because he's *young*? There are middle-aged men on college campuses, Dad. They're called professors."

My father sighs, heavy and long. "I'm not going to argue with you about this. The decision about who is part of your security detail isn't up to you, Georgie."

"Remind me, Dad, which decisions *are* up to me? Because it's feeling like *none*, right now."

He crosses his arms. "Are you finished?"

"Are *you*? This feels like a *could have been an email* sort of meeting. I have no say in it at all, according to you."

Another lengthy exhale. "Do you have any questions for Agent Salisbury, before he joins your detail?"

"Nope." I pop the P, obnoxiously. "He won't last a week."

My father visibly glowers at the heated prediction. Interestingly, I catch Ethan smirking. It annoys me further, and also intrigues me. "Agent Salisbury and the rest of your team are there for your safety, Georgie. Show some respect. If I hear you're causing problems, you'll be grounded for the summer."

"I'm eighteen, Dad, not eight. And if you hadn't decided saving the world ranked above being a father, we wouldn't be having this conversation."

I'm crossing a line I rarely have. Whatever resentments I've built up toward my father, I don't usually voice them. But something about this moment—the superiority of Ethan, listening to my friends go on about their exciting summer plans last night, the fact I'm overtired and hungover, how I'm a legal adult with minimal control over my own life—is causing some to spill out.

My father looks disappointed, not angry, which is infinitely worse. "I'm doing my best, Georgie."

I look away, pulling the elastic out of my hair and running a hand through the long strands. Too late, I remember why I pulled it into a messy bun before coming down here.

"What on Earth did you do to your hair?"

"I dyed it." I flip the ends up, so he can better see the dark purple coloring the last inch of my light brown hair.

My father sighs. Pinches the bridge of his nose. "Are you going to the club to practice today?"

"No, tomorrow."

Another sigh. "Okay. There's nothing you want to discuss with Agent Salisbury?"

"Like *what*?"

Sigh number five.

"He didn't need to be here, Dad. There's no need to start acting like I have a say in anything when we both know I don't."

I turn and walk away, too annoyed and embarrassed to acknowledge either of the men behind me. There are moments in life, when you know the way you're acting is unreasonable. When you know what you should do or say instead of what you're actually doing or saying.

Right now, I simply don't care. I want to stomp out of the room and shut the door loudly—not a slam, but close —behind me.

So that's exactly what I do.

CHAPTER THREE

ETHAN

COLBY IS SPRAWLED out on the leather couch when I walk into our shared apartment, exactly where I expected to find him. I toss my keys on the counter, drop my gym bag on the floor next to the kitchen island, and grab a beer from the fridge before ambling over toward him.

He mutes the television and glances over at me. "So? What happened?"

I plop down on the couch and stretch my long legs out, resting them on top of the old moving boxes we use as a coffee table. This place is every inch the bachelor pad.

"I got a new assignment."

"Yeah, I figured. The president doesn't call you in just to shoot the shit, Ethan. What's the assignment?"

"His daughter's detail." I crack the can of beer I'm holding open.

"No shit? The First Daughter?"

"Yep." I take a long pull from the can.

"What's she like?"

I laugh, short and unamused. Run my thumb along my lower

lip. "Bratty, spoiled, entitled. She showed up in pajamas, hungover, and threw a fit about having a 'new suit' assigned to her."

Colby chuckles from his seat next to me. "Yeah, Peters said she's a handful."

"When was Peters on her detail?" I ask, surprised.

Colby shrugs and takes a sip of beer. "Dunno. I think he filled in for Wade for a few days last year." He gives me a sly look. "He also said she's hot."

I snort, choosing not to comment. I've never liked Peters and I like him even less now. Talk about acting unprofessional.

"Come on, don't tell me you didn't notice."

"She's an assignment. That's it."

"If she wasn't?"

"She *is*."

He raises both eyebrows at me.

"*Can't get over herself* is not my type."

Colby chuckles. "Please. You *say* you like easy-going women, but you were bored with Stella, and we both know it."

"I never *saw* Stella. That's why we broke up."

"Yeah, sure." Colby takes a long pull from his beer.

His phone buzzes, on the couch between us. He picks it up and glances at the screen. "Fuck. We gotta go. Guys are already at Foggy Bottom."

"That's tonight?" I down most of my beer in one gulp. The arena charges an arm and a leg for alcoholic beverages.

"Yeah. I reminded you last night."

I scrub a hand across my face. "I know. I was distracted." My beer gets finished with one more gulp. "Let me just go change. Two minutes."

"Okay." Colby is already tapping something out on his phone. "Ready to go whenever you are."

I head into my bedroom, which boasts the same lack of decoration as the rest of the apartment. The light gray walls are bare. The only furniture is the black bedframe and a dresser that came with the place.

My t-shirt gets tossed in the hamper, followed by a pair of mesh shorts. I'm glad I showered at the gym earlier, not that I had much of a choice. I was dripping with sweat after the intense workout it took to work off the annoyed aftermath of my meeting this morning. I thought getting summoned to the White House was an honor—until I caught the catch.

You're pawning me off on a rookie with zero experience?

I would never admit this to anyone, let alone Georgie Adams, but her words smart. I've worked my ass off to get where I am. But the protective detail for the First Family usually includes the most senior of agents. My inclusion on the list is an outlier, to say the least.

I'm trying not to focus on the long-term implications. I knew, when I took this job, there was the potential for lengthy assignments I would have no control over. I just didn't expect one of those to be on a college campus. Or in my home state.

There's nothing chaining me to DC. I like it here. It's more where I'll be moving instead that's bothering me.

I change into a pair of jeans and a Capitals t-shirt and then head back into the common space. Colby is rooting through the closet to the right of the front door.

"What the hell are you doing?" I ask him, picking up a stray sneaker he managed to toss halfway toward the couch.

"Looking for my Capitals hat. Have you seen it?"

"Did you check your room?"

Colby emerges from the closet, a tennis racquet in one hand and a winter glove in the other. "Of course I—shit. I think it's on my doorknob."

I roll my eyes as he jogs down the hall that our two bedrooms and shared bathroom jut off from, before shoving my feet into my sneakers and grabbing my keys off the counter.

Colby reappears a few seconds later, black ballcap covering most of his blond hair.

"You're cleaning all this shit up when we get back," I tell him, kicking a baseball glove out of the way so I can open the front door.

"Yeah, yeah," he mutters, following me out into the carpeted hallway.

The temperature change is noticeable and immediate, like opening a refrigerator. Each individual tenant—or tenants—are responsible for paying their unit's heating and cooling bill. But the cost to climate control the communal spaces, the lobby and the hallways, is split between everyone who lives in the fifteen-story building.

For cheapskates like me and Colby, that means the walk to get outside is usually ten degrees different—either warmer or cooler, depending on the season—than the temperature inside our apartment.

We're the only ones in the elevator, but there's a woman with a schnauzer standing in the lobby, talking on the phone.

DC's humid summer heat is waiting outside the glass doors. There's a Metro stop just down the street, one of the main reasons we chose to live in NoMa. The station platform is crowded with the red, white, and blue jerseys of other hockey fans headed to the game.

The Gallery Place/Chinatown stop is packed. It's a fight to reach the escalator, and one of the times being six foot three comes in handy.

By the time Colby and I reach the arena's lobby it's only fifteen minutes until puck drop. Logan and Owen are standing to the left of the metal detectors, both wearing good-natured scowls.

"Nice of you two to show up. With the tickets," Logan grumbles.

Logan is a college buddy of mine who ended up in DC working at the State Department. Owen is Colby's younger brother, a senior at Georgetown University. The four of us get together once or twice a month to hang out. Since the Capitals made the playoffs this year, we sprang for tickets as an early birthday outing for Owen's twenty-second. We're all going out for drinks tomorrow night to celebrate, as well.

"Salisbury has his whole beauty routine, you know." Colby doesn't hesitate to throw me under the bus, even though we both know he was the one holding things up. "That's how he gets all the ladies."

I roll my eyes, slapping hands with Owen and Logan before we get in line to walk through security. Once we're through the metal detectors and the attendant has scanned the tickets on Colby's phone, we take the escalator up to the mezzanine.

We pause at one of the concession stands. Tardiness works in our favor. The line is shorter than usual; most of the people here already having bought their beverages and headed for their seats.

The guys debate what beers to order as the couple in front of us deliberates about getting a hot pretzel or a hot dog.

Logan glances at me. "What are you getting?"

I shove my hands in my pockets. "Nothing. I had a Stella right before we left."

Colby scoffs. "Come on, man. You'll need it, to prepare for tomorrow."

"What's tomorrow?" Owen asks.

"Ethan's first day on the First Daughter's detail," Colby supplies.

Owen's eyes widen. "Really?"

Logan looks confused. "Is that a big deal?"

"No," I answer, at the same time Colby replies "Yes."

"It's *not*," I add, glaring at my roommate and best friend.

"Is it like a prestige thing?" Logan asks, still appearing baffled. "Are you being modest?"

Once again, Colby jumps in. "Guess you've never seen a photo of Georgie Adams."

"Isn't she in high school?"

Owen is already pulling out his phone. Most likely to google exactly what I'm hoping he won't.

"She graduated yesterday," Colby replies. Expressing more knowledge than I thought he had about her. My awareness of the president's only child has been mostly tangential.

I know she exists, and that's about the extent of it. Or that *was* the extent of it, rather. Like it or not—I *don't*, for the record—I'm about to be spending a whole lot of time monitoring her every move.

"Shit," Owen drawls, adding far more syllables than the swear requires. "None of the girls I go to school with look like *that*."

"She's going to Stanford," I respond, for some unknown reason.

I'm uncomfortable. This is one part of being part of the Secret Service I've never appreciated: the interest.

I get it, to a certain degree. From the outside, it looks like a glamorous, exciting career. A chance to see the elitist of DC's many power players up close and personal.

But that has never been the part of the job that's appealed to me.

Colby and Owen grab their beers. I cave to peer pressure and order one as well.

"Shit." Owen curses as he opens his can, wincing as he grabs a few napkins from the stack next to the register to press against the slice on his thumb.

"Look away, Salisbury," Colby jokes.

I roll my eyes but do keep them averted.

I get queasy at the sight of blood, something Colby learned during training. The *one* section he earned a higher mark than me in was emergency medical techniques, so he likes to bring it up at every possible opportunity.

Owen gets the bleeding under control with sustained pressure, Logan and I get our beers, and then we head for our seats.

The players have already left the ice, following their warm-up. We splurged on decent seats with an unobstructed view of the rink. The two Zambonis are doing a final sweep on the ice, removing any shavings or scrapes with a smooth pass of water. An announcer drones in the background, running through the safety procedures and expected conduct during the game.

I settle in the plastic seat and take a long pull of my cold beer. Hockey was never big in the town in Southern California where I grew up. I gained some appreciation for it when I moved east, first at Dartmouth and now here.

Both Colby and Owen are rabid fans, so attending games with them is a regular occurrence. I played tennis in the fall and base-ball in the spring growing up, so my knowledge regarding any intricacies of the sport are what I've absorbed from friends yelling at the screen or at the boards surrounding the ice.

Owen is seated beside me, a Band-Aid wrapped around his thumb courtesy of the Capital One Arena first-aid station.

"Any plans for the summer?" I ask him.

He shrugs. "I'm bartending at Founding Fathers. Started last week."

"That's cool," I reply. Founding Fathers is our usual choice for drinks. The atmosphere is a mix of classy and casual, and the prices are reasonable in comparison to most places. It's where we'll probably end up tomorrow night.

"Yeah. I'm also interviewing for a few internships. We'll see." He shrugs. "Hard to get anywhere in this town without solid connections, and my only one isn't bending over backward to help his little brother out."

"I made my own way, man. You can do the same," Colby replies, from my other side.

Owen scoffs. "Whatever. Sounds like Ethan is the one with the connections, anyway."

I'm the one who scoffs at that. "Hardly. I'm a glorified babysitter."

I say that, then glance around to confirm no one around us is listening—or worse, filming. The Secret Service exists more as an entity than anything else. Aside from high-profile events where threat levels are elevated, our job is to fade into the background as much as possible. We're just an armored suit, standing by. But the last thing I need is for years of work to be wasted thanks to a viral video of me acting like protecting the First Daughter is anything less than an honor.

No one is paying us any attention. They're all focused on the Jumbotron and the ice, where game-winning goals and impressive saves are being projected.

"*Hot girl* sitter, you mean." Owen pulls out his phone and flashes the screen at me. His earlier search is still pulled up and there's a picture of Georgie displayed on the screen.

I stare at the photo for a second too long. Then shrug. Look away. Take a long sip of beer, letting the hoppy liquid sit on my tongue before swallowing.

Owen's eyes are wide with disbelief as he registers my apathy. "Seriously? *Nothing*?"

"Ethan's a tough nut to crack, Owen," Colby says. "You saw

Stella. And *he* broke up with *her*."

"Georgie is hotter than Stella, though."

I roll my eyes. "I'll make sure to tell her you think so."

"Who? Georgie or Stella?"

"Both."

Truth is, I'm not on speaking terms with either of them.

Georgie made it clear I'm nothing but an inconvenience. I could say the same about her. Protecting a member of the president's immediate family is a high honor, but moving back to California, even temporarily, wasn't part of my plan. I already attended college once. Georgie wasn't shy about expressing her disdain for the security following her around. She won't make it easy to guard her.

And Stella? We grew up together. Dated toward the end of high school into our freshman year of college. Broke up. Reconnected on one of my trips back home. Broke up again, under more confrontational circumstances. We haven't spoken since.

I sneak one final glance at the photo on Owen's phone. Honestly, it doesn't do Georgie justice. She's prettier in person. My mind drifts. Instead of looking at a pristine stretch of white ice, I'm picturing a flash of purple. Long legs. Strawberry-patterned socks.

I'm not denying Georgie Adams is gorgeous. I think anyone would find doing so a challenge. But it's the knowledge you can't glean from a photo that is most concerning.

She may be spoiled and entitled, but she's also intriguing. Colby is right—not that I'll ever tell him so. I *was* bored with Stella. We ran out of things to say to each other long before we officially called it quits.

There are a lot of adjectives that come to mind to describe Georgie, following our one and only meeting.

Boring isn't one of them.

CHAPTER FOUR

GEORGIE

THE BLARE of my alarm infiltrates my brain slowly and persistently, an unwelcome melody that jolts me awake.

I silence it and roll over. A couple of minutes later, my phone starts buzzing.

I ignore it until it stops.

Silence.

More buzzing.

With an exasperated sigh, I flip over, so I'm facing my bedside table again. I grab my phone and scroll through the recent notifications. Most of them are texts from Lucy, scattered with missed phone calls, also from her.

Lucy: *Wake up!*

Lucy: *You'd better not still be sleeping.*

Lucy: *I mean it, Georgie.*

Lucy: *Last time, I stood at the court for fifteen minutes like a total loser.*

Lucy: *If you do that to me again, I'm revoking our friendship.*

I roll my eyes and squint at the screen.

Georgie: *Relax, loser.*

Georgie: *I'm awake.*

Georgie: *I won't be late.*

Lucy: *You better not be.*

Lucy: *I'll meet you at court 3.*

With an exaggerated sigh, I toss the covers off and climb out of bed. I use the bathroom and then change into compression shorts, a sports bra, and a tennis dress with a halter style top. Hillside Country Club has a strict dress code.

Since I'm already running late, I toss a granola bar and a bottle of water into my tennis bag rather than stop in the kitchen. I'll probably be able to convince Steve to stop for coffee on our way to Hillside.

I rustle through my bag as I walk down the carpeted hall, trying to quickly check if I have everything that I need.

My flip-flop catches on the edge of the carpet, and I almost fall onto my face, right at the top of the stairs. I hastily grab the railing and decide that anything I forgot will have to stay here. Continuing to rummage feels perilous.

I rush down the carpeted stairs that lead to the first floor. Glance into the treaty room and the private sitting room, both of which appear to be empty. When I walk out of the sitting room and back into the entryway, it's no longer empty.

I'm staring at Agent Ethan Salisbury. Ethan sounds too casual to characterize his stoic expression, even in my own head.

My cheeks flush for two reasons.

Because one, his casual position against the wall makes me think he's been standing there this whole time. That he watched me almost fall down the stairs and then look around the immediate vicinity like an idiot. For the second time in as many meetings, I missed his presence entirely. A dismal record by any standard.

And I'm not sure *how* I missed his presence—aside from the

fact I guess he's good at his job, since the Secret Service prides itself on being as unobtrusive of a presence in our lives as possible.

That's the second reason—he's not the guy you miss. He's the guy you do a double take at. Maybe even a third.

I was sort of hoping I'd exaggerated his appearance in my head. That my hungover, tired brain wasn't taking in details correctly. Turns out, it wasn't. But trending instead in the direction I don't want it to.

He's *better*-looking than I remember. Despite the heat outside, he's dressed in the black suit standard for all agents no matter the time of year. And, boy, is he wearing it. If this were an episode of *Bridgerton*, I'd be fanning myself.

"Where's Steve?" I ask, in what I'm relieved to hear sounds like an entirely indifferent tone.

Ethan straightens, shoving away from the wall and crossing his arms. "*Agent Michaels* is taking the day off."

Cute. He sounds *just like* my dad. I spend more time with these men than with my best friend. A first name basis doesn't seem like a stretch.

"You sound like my dad."

"Thank you."

"That wasn't a compliment."

"You compared me to someone I admire, so I'll respectfully disagree."

I roll my eyes and rest a hand on one hip. "Call Steve. I'm leaving and I want him to drive me."

"No."

I study him, testing his resolve, and am disappointed—but not surprised—when I find it solid. "I can have you fired."

Ethan smirks. *Smirks!* I find it equal parts irritating and intriguing, since most people I encounter are deferential. "Sure. Go right ahead and try."

I pull my phone out of my pocket. "I'll call Steve myself."

Ethan steps forward and grabs my wrist. I want to pull away, but there's a contrary reaction too. One that savors the way it feels, having his callouses grip my arm. One that is very aware of the way my stomach flips and my heart races in response to his proximity.

"Don't you dare," he tells me, tone authoritative and posture menacing.

"Afraid you'll get into trouble for not listening me?" The question is a challenge, a taunt, one I'm confident Ethan won't back down from.

He doesn't disappoint, shaking his head with quick, efficient jerks. "Steve isn't here. He's at his daughter's dance recital. Don't bother him with your *bullshit*." The last word is basically a sneer.

I try to determine if he's lying about Steve's whereabouts. I can't tell, which annoys me further.

"I'm not going anywhere with *you*," I inform him.

He drops my wrist, which feels like a loss. It's a dismissal. "Fine. Sit at home all day and make my job easier."

Ethan shrugs, like he doesn't care what I do or where I go. Of course *he* doesn't. *He* can come and go from the White House grounds as he likes.

A privilege I, a legal adult, do not have.

I don't have a prayer of getting off the grounds without an armed agent accompanying me, even if I made some dramatic break for it. Cameras cover every inch of the property, plus it's gated and patrolled. The element of surprise won't get me very far. Not to mention, the consequences won't be pretty. But I'm tempted—very tempted—for a minute. Just to see the *my way or nothing* confidence on Ethan's face disappear. To shock him and see how he reacts.

"I'm going to talk to my father again," I tell Ethan.

Like a warning.

A threat.

A challenge.

"Go right ahead. He sounded open to reassigning me yesterday."

Ethan deadpans the response we both know means the opposite. I stare at him, taken off-guard by his mocking tone. The agents assigned to me have always been respectful and obliging.

If it came to a question of my safety, I have no doubt they'd put a foot down. But when it comes to everything else, they'll indulge me and cater to my every whim.

I figured that wouldn't be the case with Ethan—it's why I fought this assignment in the first place. But it's different to experience his rancor firsthand.

"You think you're a pretty big deal, huh?" I ask.

"I think you're spoiled."

He crosses his arms, unimpressed.

I stiffen. "Good thing *I don't care* what you think. You're a pawn my father is using to try and keep me under control, nothing more."

Ethan sighs, sounding annoyed he has to listen to me speak. Although annoyance requires some emotion toward someone. Toward *me*, he appears entirely indifferent.

"Are you going out or not?" he asks. "I need to let the gate know."

I'm in what feels like a lose-lose situation. It's not an act; he genuinely doesn't care what I do. Either I go to Hillside Country Club like I was planning to—with Ethan—or I let him throw my day into disarray by staying put. If I choose the latter, Lucy won't actually end our friendship. But she'll be pissed.

Neither option is appealing.

"I'm going out," I grumble, pushing past him and continuing down the hall that leads toward the door.

"Where are you planning to go?" he asks, falling into step beside me.

I quicken my strides. Disappointingly, he keeps up easily. "Why do you care?"

"I care," he drawls. "Because I'll be the one driving."

"What do you mean? Aren't Myles and Kevin coming with us?"

"No. There's an event in the Rose Garden this morning. They're assigned to that."

I've traveled with one agent before. But never one who is a stranger. I met Ethan yesterday. He looks like a male model and has a superiority complex. Lots could go wrong.

"Are you qualified for that?" I snap.

"Yes."

"All you've done is insult me," I remind him. "Excuse me if I'm not *overflowing* with confidence in your ability to protect me."

"You should be."

"Should be what?"

"*Overflowing.*"

I stop walking, just outside the door that leads to the front drive. "Give me a reason."

I'm not expecting him to indulge me.

I'm not expecting him to touch me.

He does both, grabbing my bicep and spinning me toward him, so our faces are inches apart. It's impossible to ignore the intensity burning in his blue eyes. The way my skin sparks is distracting, but not distracting enough.

I'm fully focused on him. On the rough scrape of his calloused fingers and the spicy musk of his cologne. We're closer than we were before. This feels more intimate than when he grabbed my wrist.

"I take my job seriously, Georgie. New agent or not, I'm more than capable of protecting you. All you need to know is that if it ever comes down to being between my life and yours, I'll choose yours. That's what it means to serve. That's why the greater good matters. But you don't care about any of that, do you? Democracy or duty or putting someone else first. All *you* care about is who's hosting the next party. You're throwing a fit because you can."

"You don't know anything about me, *Ethan*."

I think using his first name will annoy him. I wait for him to correct me. To insist that I call him Agent Salisbury.

He doesn't.

He says, "I don't need to," and keeps walking.

Reluctantly, I follow.

The drive to Hillside Country Club takes about twenty minutes. We cross the Potomac and pass into Virginia.

It's a trip spent in total silence.

Aside from me telling him where I'm heading because I had no other choice, if I wanted to make it to Hillside to meet Lucy. I'll be late to meet her, like I promised I wouldn't be. I can hear my phone buzzing in my bag, but I don't answer it.

I alternate between looking at the road and stealing peeks at Ethan.

Ethan is entirely focused on driving. Since he told me he doesn't *need to know* anything about me, he hasn't spoken a word. When I told him I was going to Hillside Country Club, all he did was nod. He did exchange polite pleasantries with the guards at the gate when we drove through, so I know he's capable of acting pleasant, if he wants to. He charmed my father too.

Yet he has no issue pissing *me* off, which is interesting. Ethan clearly takes pride in his job, based on his admiration for my father and his patriotic speech by the parking area. Apparently, his respect doesn't extend past the presidency. He's acting as if I'd *asked* for this, then changed my mind. When in reality, I was handed limitations with a no-return policy.

Ethan isn't relying on any directions to navigate the congested streets, appearing to know the way to Hillside on his own. It feeds a curiosity I refuse to voice.

Has he lived in DC long?

Has he been to Hillside before?

And unrelated, random questions. Why did he join the Secret Service? Is he as unhappy about being assigned to my detail as I am? How did he get the scar on his hand?

The interest is bizarre. I typically consider small talk trite and unappealing. I've never asked any of my agents a personal question before.

To them, I'm a job.

To me, they're an inescapable inconvenience.

Ethan has a magnetism, a forcefield that pulls me in rather than pushes me away. Maybe it's the fact he seems to be so obviously avoiding any rapport with me. If Steve was the one sitting next to me, he'd be cracking jokes as we sipped on our Starbucks. Even Myles or Kevin would be talking about the weather. Flipping between radio stations.

With Ethan, there's *nothing*. Just stifling silence. It makes me want to crack a window, despite the fact it's close to ninety out and the air conditioning is cranking inside the car.

I don't like him; I guess I made that clear.

But he doesn't seem to like me either. It should be a relief. Mutually agreed upon dislike.

Instead, it bothers me.

I think you're spoiled, he'd told me. *All* you *care about is who's hosting the next party.*

Those two sentences echo in my head, running around in circles. Pissing me off more with each pass.

I wish I knew enough about Ethan to hit him back. He has a front-row seat to my life now. To my home. To my relationship with my father. But I barely know anything about him and refuse to ask. Maybe I'll request his file when I get back to the residence. Knowledge is power.

When he pulls up to the front gate of Hillside and reaches toward the glove compartment, I flinch away. Ethan makes a small sound—some mixture between a scoff and a laugh—under his breath as he grabs the members pass. Turns out Agent Salisbury does his homework. It's the only way he could have known where the pass is stored. He's fastidious, something I'm not all that surprised to learn.

Ethan flashes the badge at the gate. It lifts, revealing the winding stretch of cement that leads up to the clubhouse. The White House has its own tennis court. But ever since my family moved to DC, I've preferred to practice here.

Most tennis courts are standard. Chain-link fencing and netting and painted cement. It's easy to pretend you were anywhere. It's harder to do so in the shadow of the Truman Balcony, next to a line of SUVs so reinforced they could drive over a land mine without a scratch in the paint job.

Hillside's parking lot is half-full. Ethan parks near the club-house and we both climb out, leaving the cool confines of the car to step into humid heat. The lingering silence between us feels equally stifling. It rubs at me, an itch I refuse to scratch.

Either Ethan is just as stubborn as me, or he's oblivious to the tension between us. We say nothing as we walk along the brick path that curves past the pool and winds down the hill the club is named for, toward the tennis courts.

Lucy is waiting impatiently, leaning against the chain link that surrounds court three, literally tapping a foot. Ethan continues walking straight as I turn and close the final few feet to the gate that leads onto the court. I ignore him, refusing to pay any atten-tion to where he's going or what he's doing. That's *his* job—to watch *me*. Not the other way around.

"Sorry!" I say, as soon as I reach Lucy. "I know I'm late. Ready?"

My best friend is barely paying me any mind, much less scolding my tardiness.

"Who is *that*?" Lucy asks, twirling her racquet as she looks past me

"Who?" I play dumb.

Membership here is more of a status symbol than anything else. The only people Ethan and I passed on our trip from the parking lot were a couple of women who looked to be in their eighties walking toward the golf course. I don't think Lucy is talking about them.

She slides her sunglasses down her nose like a middle-aged housewife ogling the pool boy. "The blond hottie dressed like James Bond."

I pick up two tennis balls from the basket and shove one into my pocket before glancing over my shoulder to confirm where she's looking.

Ethan is standing at the edge of the patio that surrounds the pool, talking to one of the uniformed members of the country club's staff. The middle-aged man is smiling, which I hope means Ethan isn't requesting some ridiculous security measure that will result in me being politely asked to leave. "Who do you think? He's a new agent assigned to me."

"He's *hot*. Like, wow."

I say nothing, oddly annoyed by her gushing. I take my annoyance out on the tennis ball, squeezing the green felt tightly. Usually, I find Lucy's boycraziness more amusing than anything.

I open the door and step out onto the court, pulling my racquet out of my bag as I walk.

Lucy follows. "How old is he?"

"You want to serve first?"

She ignores my attempt to change the subject. "What's his name?"

"Or we can flip a coin."

She hits my thigh with her racquet. "Georgie! You can't show up with a guy who looks like *that* and not answer my questions."

I sigh. "Agent Salisbury."

"His *first name*, Georgie."

"I forget," I lie, for some unknown reason. "Today is his first day. Can we just play, please?"

Lucy lets out a long-suffering sigh. "Fine. Just saying, if I had a guy like that following me around, *I* would not be focused on tennis."

"Noted. That's probably why I'm the better player," I tease.

She scowls. "Just for that, I'm serving first."

"If you were paying attention instead of drooling over a guy, you'd know I already asked you to."

Lucy flips me off over one shoulder as she saunters toward the line.

I laugh, shove all thoughts of Ethan far away, and head for the opposite end of the court.

CHAPTER FIVE

ETHAN

FOUNDING FATHERS IS CROWDED. I can barely hear the story Logan is telling over the loud chatter and the Coldplay song playing in the background.

We're out celebrating Owen's birthday. I dodged the many questions about my first day on the First Daughter's service by ordering a round of birthday shots to start. Mine is still sitting untouched in front of me. Logan almost knocks it over as he gesticulates wildly.

I settle into the wooden back of the booth, glancing around the busy space. I'm familiar with the interior of this place—the honey wood and the black metal fixtures—I'm not looking for anything, or anyone, in particular.

When I spot Georgie Adams standing by one of the industrial-looking columns with three other girls, I have to do a double take.

This is the *last* place I expected to see her. DC isn't *that* small of a city. And it contains many restaurants much more upscale than this place, where I would expect her to go out to instead. It's a greasy burger, loaded fries, and a beer type of bar. A restaurant, technically, which is the only reason she was allowed inside.

She's young, I have to keep reminding myself. Eighteen. A teenager.

I watch Georgie whisper something to the brunette she played tennis with earlier. The brunette—Lucy, I think—laughs. She flirted with me after their final match.

I'm pretty sure Georgie took a long time to pack up on purpose, leaving me to fend off the advances. She also took the practice a lot more seriously than her friend appeared to. Dedicated and hard-working aren't two adjectives I thought could apply to her. When it comes to tennis, they seem to fit. She's good, too. I played growing up. Even turned down a tennis scholarship to UCLA. I know talent when I see it.

Georgie glances around, same as I did. Spots me, same as I did her. Our gazes meet, holding like there's an invisible string connecting us.

I'm expecting her to look away immediately.

She doesn't.

And I don't either, for some unknown reason.

It's unexpected, after the silent treatment this morning. I figured the arctic conditions would persist between us. They're not thawing, exactly, but her expression doesn't look like ice.

Holding my gaze was unexpected. Seeing her take one step forward—five now—is shocking.

She's coming over here.

A long list of profanities come to mind.

"Fucking hell," I mumble, watching her saunter over toward our table.

My quiet mutter cuts through the conversation at the table, somehow. Owen, Colby, and Logan all follow my gaze to Georgie.

I know what they're all thinking, probably because the same thought crossed my mind when I first saw her, before I really registered that I was checking out the eighteen-year-old I'm somewhat responsible for. Georgie has showered and changed out of the tennis clothes she was wearing earlier. Styled her hair. On a scale to ten, she's an easy eleven.

I make sure to school any appreciation of her appearance from my face, since that's the last thing our uncomfortable dynamic needs.

"Agent Salisbury," Georgie greets, arriving at the table and leaning a casual elbow on the wooden surface, like she intends to stick around a while.

I glance behind her, at Kevin and Myles, who followed Georgie over here. They're both scanning the immediate vicinity, pointedly ignoring this interaction. Or maybe they just don't know what to make of it.

"Georgie," I reply, hoping that will be the end of it and she'll saunter away as quickly as she appeared.

Myles glances at me. He's the next youngest member of her detail, in his late twenties. He gives me a tiny, almost imperceptible shrug, like *what are you going to do?*

She shouldn't be approaching a table of random guys.

I'm surprised by how easily Georgie bends the rules. Then again, looking at her, I guess it's not all that surprising. Standing in front of a group of strangers, she appears entirely at ease.

And she doesn't look the least bit inclined to turn around and leave, the way I was hoping she might.

"I'm Georgie." She leans a hip against the edge of the table and tosses an easy grin around. "Are you guys all loyal patriots as well?"

"Colby. I'm part of the Secret Service too," Colby replies. "Investigative though, not protective. Logan works at the State Department and Owen is my little brother. He's at Georgetown."

He sounds nervous, a little on edge. It's unexpected and entertaining. It also forces me to consider how comfortable I've become around Georgie. Colby views her as the president's daughter—as a precious object on a pedestal. When we were together today, I didn't once think about her in those terms. I simply saw her as a person—one I'm meant to protect and who constantly manages to piss me off.

Georgie smiles at Owen and Logan when Colby introduces them, but otherwise ignores them. They don't ignore her. Logan and Owen both appear to be fixated on details I wish I weren't registering as well. Like how low-cut her dress is.

"There are different divisions of the Secret Service?" she asks Colby.

He nods. "Well, just the two."

"Huh. I had no idea. Don't know much about it, I guess."

"And yet, you have no issue suggesting I don't know how to do my job," I comment, picking at the damp napkin beneath my water glass.

Georgie narrows her eyes at me. "You leave that stick up your ass even when you're off duty, *Agent Salisbury*?"

The guys snicker as I narrow mine right back at her. "We don't all get to enjoy zero responsibility and zero accountability, Georgie. Some of us act like adults."

She leans forward, close enough I can smell the sweet scent of her shampoo. The same smell that invaded the car during the long drive to Hillside and back. "You think I don't—"

"Can I get you guys another round?" The overly attentive female waitress appears to ask. She was here five minutes ago.

"I'll take a vodka soda," Georgie requests.

I glance behind her, between Myles and Kevin, who are both pretending to be too far out of earshot to have heard what she just ordered. *Unbelievable*. How and when did she wrap her entire security detail around one finger?

"She's underage," I say, before the waitress can respond.

Georgie's lips mash into one straight line, but she says nothing as the guys hurry to fill the awkward silence lingering with their orders.

"So, *Colby*, what does the investigative section handle?" Georgie asks, once the waitress has left and it's just the five of us again.

"Fraud, counterfeit, computer hacking, identity theft. All that sexy stuff."

"Do you go through the same training as the rest of the agents?"

"Same basic training for everyone, yeah. Most agents work in investigative unless they're assigned to a specific protective division assignment. Lucky for you, eh Ethan?"

I let out what could be loosely considered a grunt.

"Basic training, like emergency medical techniques?" Georgie asks.

My head snaps in her direction. It's an oddly specific question, and I know *exactly* why she's asking it. I finished first in every single training category for my class, with the exception of one: emergency medical techniques. The sight of blood—even fake blood, in that instance—has always made me queasy. There's only one way she could know that.

She requested my file.

"You requested my file?"

"Reading your middle school report cards were especially entertaining," she replies.

Somewhere, deep, *deep* down, there's a glimmer of respect that she's choosing to own rather than deny. That takes a certain strength of character, one I'm not entirely shocked to learn that Georgie possesses.

Not at all shocked, maybe.

"Those are private records."

She shrugs. "Oops."

I exhale, letting my irritation out long and low. At least I know why she came over here now. This—requesting my file, exchanging small talk with my friends—is her attempt to even the balance of power between us.

Owen leans forward. "Ethan said you're going to Stanford?"

Rather than answer him, Georgie looks to me. For a few seconds, we hold a silent staring contest. Without a winner being determined, she looks away, back at Owen. "Yeah, I am. Are you in college?"

Someone didn't pay very close attention to the introductions. I wonder what distracted her. If *I* distracted her.

"Yep," Owen answers. "Starting my senior year at George-town in the fall."

"Oh. Cool." Georgie glances at me—again—and I can't figure out why I'm keeping track of how many times she does. "What are you majoring in?"

"Business and international affairs."

"Cool," she says again. Georgie doesn't appear to be very invested in the conversation with Owen. But she's still standing here, even though I can see her friends waiting, over by the same column where I first spotted her.

"What made you pick Stanford?" Owen asks.

"I liked their tennis coach the best," she replies.

"You play tennis?" Colby jumps back into the conversation.

"Yep. Ethan didn't mention that either?"

I don't miss how she slips that in. Letting me know she caught Owen's phrasing earlier.

I'd pegged Georgie as too self-absorbed to notice anything that doesn't directly affect her. Wrongly, as it turns out.

"Nope. Did Ethan tell *you* he's got one hell of a backhand?"

That catches her attention. I'm not sure why I notice. Or care. "You play tennis?" she asks me.

"Yes," I answer, and leave it at that.

"Are you good?"

"Yes," I repeat.

"He's better than just good. Ethan got a tennis scholarship to UCLA," Logan boasts.

I wait for the inevitable question that is asked every time that comes up. *Why didn't you take it?*

Georgie doesn't ask it, though. She taps her fingers on the edge of the table and studies me. "You look like a California boy."

At first, I think it's a UCLA reference. Then, I remember what she said about my report cards. She knows I grew up in California, thanks to her snooping.

Georgie may have said she chose Stanford for tennis, but I'm guessing that reason came second to the fact California is as far from DC as physically possible, while remaining in the continental US. In the short time I've known her, it's been obvious that if First Daughter was a position you had to run for, she wouldn't hold it.

Georgie is using college as a means of escape. I think her *California boy* comment is her way of telling me she realizes I did the same.

I didn't think I'd ever be able to say I have anything in common with Georgie Adams. Yet here we are.

When I don't reply, she nods toward the shot glass. "You drinking that?"

"I haven't decided. But no, you can't have it."

She pretends to pout. At least, I *think* she's pretending.

Georgie is an enigma. Every time I think I have her figured out; she proves me wrong. Party girl. Tennis star. Bratty daughter.

Reliable friend. And the harder she is to figure out, the more I want to try to.

Her phone rings, blasting some pop song I could probably name if I really wanted to. She smiles when she sees whatever is on the screen, glancing over one shoulder at her friends. The brunette has a phone up to her ear, obviously the one calling her.

"I'd better go. Nice to meet you guys." She smiles at my friends, glances at me, and then walks away, with Kevin and Myles trailing after her.

"Wow." Logan leans back in his seat. I think that was the longest I've heard him go without speaking. "So that's Georgie Adams."

"Yeah." I grab the shot and down it, savoring the burn of whiskey as it slides down my throat. "That's Georgie Adams."

━━━

Two hours later, Logan and Owen head out. Logan has an early day tomorrow and Owen is going to a club with some of his college buddies.

Usually, I'd be right behind them. Tomorrow is a rare day off for me, but I've never been able to sleep in late. Most mornings, I'm up by six a.m. Each minute I stay here is literally one less I'll stay in bed.

But still, I stay in place, occasionally taking a sip of water. Anyone who was here for dinner has long since cleared out, and while they're still serving food, the bar is far busier than the kitchen.

There's a band performing covers of old eighties songs. They're decent, but I'm not listening to anything they're playing all that closely.

I'm fixated on the dance floor. On Georgie Adams.

Either one of her friends or some guy must have bought her drinks, because she's definitely tipsy. Laughing and dancing with one of her friends as nearby, a group of guys ogle her ass.

Kevin and Myles are both paying close attention, but neither look concerned. They're acting like this is a normal occurrence, which pisses me off for a multitude of reasons.

"She has two agents here. You're off the clock," Colby tells me, glancing at Georgie, then back at me.

"There's no such thing," I tell him.

He shrugs, neither an agreement nor a disagreement. We went through training together. He's seen how obsessive I am—about the responsibility and the potential repercussions. There's a reason becoming an agent is a competitive process and training is intense. You have to be the best of the best.

If the president's daughter got drugged or assaulted when I was in the same room—on duty or off—I'd never forgive myself. Letting my guard down around the person I'm assigned to protect isn't an option.

That's easy to rationalize. To justify, even if it reinforces Colby's complaints I'm too focused on work and need to take some steps back. Suggestions that my new role have made next to impossible.

But there's also something else. A churning in my gut and a tightness in my chest.

I don't like seeing Georgie around other guys, which is not rational in the slightest. The blond closest to her looks harmless, preppy in a blue polo shirt and a dorky grin. He says something that makes her laugh, before she stumbles on nothing but air.

I toss a ten on the table to pay for the beer I only took one sip of. Aside from the one shot of whiskey hours ago, all I've had to drink is water. "Head home without me."

"You're not serious."

"She's my problem, until I'm told otherwise. On duty or not."

Colby groans but doesn't look all that surprised by my insistence. "All right, man." He slides out of the booth at the same time I do, punches my shoulder, shakes his head, and then heads for the door.

When I look back at Georgie, she's staring straight at me. She tracks me, as I leave my table and walk toward Kevin.

"She's drunk," I state in greeting, once I reach him.

Kevin sighs. "She didn't order anything herself. I've been watching."

I scoff. "Even worse. If someone gave it to her, it could have had anything in it."

"Look, man, I know you're new to the team. Eager to prove yourself. This probably seems like a big step in your career. But she's a teenage girl. If we made a big scene every time she snuck some alcohol, she'd just get sneakier about it. At least this way we can keep an eye on her."

"She's testing you." *And you're failing*, I add, silently. Technically, Kevin is my superior. Rubbing in the fact he let Georgie get wasted on his watch isn't going to earn me any favor.

"Georgie is…" His voice trails. "I get it, kid. You're new to the job. This is an important assignment. You're eager to prove yourself, to stand out to the president. Some friendly advice? If you're *really* trying to make a good impression, don't try to micro-manage. It'll have consequences. Georgie is good at getting exactly what she wants."

A flip of purple hair draws my attention. I glance past Kevin, at Georgie. The blond guy is still standing next to her. He's speaking, but she's not paying attention to whatever it is he's saying. She's looking right at *me*, with some mixture of curiosity and a challenge.

Without another word to Kevin, I head straight toward her.

Georgie watches me approach. "Let's go," I tell her.

"Past your bedtime?" Her tone is a taunt.

"You're drunk," I inform her.

"You told me not to drink." That's *it*. That's her full explanation for why she's wasted. There's obstinate, and then there's off-the-rails.

Well, I can be stubborn too.

"We're leaving."

"*We?*" She arches a brow, coyly.

Everything about her feels intentional, all of a sudden. The tilt of her head and the curve of her lips and the way one strap of her top is dangerously close to falling off her shoulder.

I start to second-guess how drunk she really is. The shrewdness in her eyes is impossible to miss. It shines like a beacon of intelligence.

"I'm taking you home."

I expect her to argue. So of course, she doesn't. She glances at her friend from the courts, who's talking to a guy a few feet away. "You good, Lucy?"

"Yep," she replies. "Have fun with Blond Bond."

I grimace internally at the moniker but say nothing. I nod toward the door, silently telling Georgie to go ahead.

"I didn't come up with it," she tells me. Then she starts walking toward the exit. I follow, and a glance behind confirms Myles and Kevin are right behind as well.

I've got no confidence she won't head right back inside if I leave her with them. "Follow us," I tell Myles and Kevin, then hustle Georgie toward the edge of the parking lot. Neither of them argue, just head for the black SUV parked a few cars down from mine.

"Ooh, you're trying to get me alone?"

Georgie looks me up and down, as best she can manage while

I'm literally pulling her across the pavement. She stumbles, so I slow my pace a little. I'm eager to get her out of here before she decides to become less cooperative. Or—God forbid—someone recognizes her, and I have to start doing damage control.

"I don't go further than second base on a first date," Georgie informs me. "I'm not having sex with you."

Not a lot surprises me. I'm naturally even-keeled, and I've gone through intensive training with a bottom line to expect the unexpected. But, this time, *I'm* the one who trips. I regain my footing quickly, blaming a crack in the asphalt, although surprise played the biggest role.

It's far easier to expect the unexpected when you have *some* idea of what it might be. Hearing the word sex in Georgie's sultry, throaty voice was never in the potential realm of possibility on what I thought this evening might entail.

She studies me when we stop at my car. My expression, my body language. Then muses "Interesting," like I'm a piece of art on display before climbing into my SUV.

I want to ask her *what* is interesting, but I don't. Doing so would imply interest, interest I shouldn't have when it comes to Georgie Adams. Her mood isn't any of my business.

Her thoughts, her emotions, her feelings?

None. Of. My. Business.

Her safety is my only concern. I'll protect her body, nothing else.

But fuck if the curiosity doesn't chafe. The suggestion that something about *me* interests *her*.

I don't have an inflated ego, nor am I lacking self-esteem. Ever since I escaped puberty with a deep voice and clear skin, girls have been happy to approach me. But it's been rare—nearly unheard of, actually—for any interest on my part to extend beyond the physical.

I'm not a people person. I'm moody and guarded, have been since I was a kid. It's rare for me to indulge—much less encourage—conversation beyond the necessary and the mundane.

But not knowing what Georgie considers *interesting*? It burrows under my skin and burns. Itches like a scratch I can't reach.

"Back to the prison cell," she grumbles as I climb into the driver's seat and start the ignition.

I roll my eyes. "You've clearly never been to an actual jail, if you consider the White House one."

"Have you?" she asks, surprising me once again.

"Yeah," I reply, as I pull away from the curb.

I feel her eyes on me, and it makes me glad I have the road to focus on. "Why?"

Georgie Adams knows no boundaries—at least with me. She didn't ask any of my friends anything probing earlier. I'm not sure if it's the alcohol talking or if she's hoping she'll ask something sensitive enough to make me quit. "I was a government major in college," I answer. "I did some pro bono work with a local nonprofit."

"Wow. Sounds like you really went *wild* at Dartmouth."

"Well, I never stayed out until four a.m. the night before a meeting with the president, so yeah, I guess I'm tame in comparison to you."

"You pulled my security reports?"

I decide she's not nearly as drunk as I thought, considering it took her seconds to surmise the only way I could have known what time she got home the night before we met. It feels strange, to think of that morning in those terms.

In my memory, it should be logged as the day I met the President of the United States. The day I got the assignment most agents wait their whole careers to receive. That most *never* receive.

Yet I know with complete certainty that every time I think of June seventeenth, it will be recalled as the day I met Georgie Adams.

"*You* requested my file," I say in response.

Not my finest defense. I didn't request her security reports so I could spy on her sleeping habits though. I did it to learn her routine and her habits. To make me a more effective bodyguard. I know Georgie well enough to understand she won't appreciate my attempts at thoroughness, though. She'd ask why I couldn't manage to find anything better to do with my time.

She's quiet for a minute, which is disconcerting after the endless chatter leading up until now. "It's different. He's my dad."

I'm not sure what to say to that, so I opt for nothing. It's not that I don't get what she's saying; I do. It's the wistfulness in her voice that makes me pause, that gives me the impression Georgie's relationship with her father might be more complicated than the rebellious teenager/overprotective father I'd pegged it as.

Suggesting or acknowledging that is a segue into a conversation I'm not sure Georgie wants to have with me, and I'm equally unsure I want to have with her. My job is to keep her safe, not listen to her problems or offer advice. It's annoying, how many times I've already had to remind myself of that.

"What else did you do at college?" she asks, suddenly.

"What do you mean?"

"Aside from graduating at the top of your class and assisting the helpless, what did you do in college? What was it like?"

She's teasing me. But there's also genuine curiosity in her voice.

"It was—it was fun."

"Fun?" She snorts. "I don't think you know the meaning of

47

the word *fun*. You went to parties? Got drunk? Hooked up with girls?"

All of a sudden, this drive feels like it's lasting hours. My skin itches a little more with each question she tosses at me. "I was focused, but that doesn't mean I didn't let loose too."

Truth is, I did all of those things. I'm not nearly as buttoned-up as Georgie seems to think I am.

If she were any other woman, I'd tell her so. Show her so.

"Huh. I can't picture it," she replies.

I say nothing.

"Why were you so focused?"

I shift. "For this, essentially. It's difficult, becoming an agent. It's a competitive process."

"Bet you're regretting not going to more parties right about now."

I *almost* smile.

"Why?" she asks.

"Why what?"

"Why did you want to become an agent? I mean, unless there's a terrorist attack, it seems pretty boring. Myles and Kevin just watched me dance and drink for the last couple of hours."

I doubt they minded.

"My dad," I answer. "I wanted to be a Secret Service agent, like my dad."

I clench the steering wheel a little tighter after I do, shocked at myself. There are many ways I could have replied to her question, some of them true.

Patriotism. Excitement. Purpose.

I had to go with the honest, vulnerable reason.

She pushes, just like I knew she would. And I can't figure out why she does. In the short span of time I've seen Georgie interact with other agents, it's been difficult to imagine her asking their current mood, much less their family history.

"Is he proud of you? Happy you followed in his footsteps?"

"He's dead," I state, bluntly. "So I don't know."

"How did he die?" Georgie asks, just as direct. The question everyone wants to ask in response, yet few do.

"Brain aneurysm. It was sudden."

"How old were you?"

"Four."

"Do you remember him?"

"I like to think so. But it's mostly stories, memories my mom and brothers talk about."

"You have brothers?"

I risk a quick glance over at her. "I guess you didn't read my file all that closely."

"I skimmed parts," she responds. "So?"

I sigh, but I'm not all that annoyed by her questions. More surprised she's bothering to ask at all. "Yeah. Two. One older, one younger."

"Middle child, huh? A lot about you just made more sense. What do your brothers do?"

"Hudson works in construction. Parker is a software developer."

"Do they live nearby?"

"No, they both ended up back in California after college."

"Why didn't you?"

"I wanted to know how my dad felt, I guess. Living here. Working here."

"Is that why you don't want to go to Stanford with me?" she asks. "You want to stay in DC?"

"Who said I don't want to go to Stanford?"

Georgie scoffs. Looks out the window at the passing lights of the city. "It's obvious."

"It's my job. I go where I'm told to, no questions asked."

"Lack of say. I know how that feels."

"You chose Stanford."

I catch movement out of the corner of my eye, as she turns to face me again. "You chose to become an agent."

We're both silent after that, the only sound in the car the quiet hum of the radio. Georgie leans forward after a minute, her hair brushing my arm as she scans through a few stations. She stops on "Hey Jude" and leans back against the seat with a satisfied smile I catch when I glance over.

"Beatles fan?" I ask, surprised. It's not the type of music I expected her to listen to.

"Maybe," she replies. "Why?"

"Just wondering."

"Yeah, right. What, you assumed I listened to boy bands and pop ballads?"

My lips quirk, because yeah, that's exactly what I assumed. "Maybe."

"My favorite song is 'Blackbird'."

"Your code name." All the members of the First Family are assigned codenames beginning with the same letter. President Adams is Bobcat, and the First Lady is Bumblebee

"Yeah. They wouldn't let me use Boss, so…"

An unexpected chuckle leaves my mouth before I can stop it. Georgie takes full advantage, letting out a dramatic gasp. "And here I was, thinking you were incapable of amusement."

"Maybe you should stop making assumptions."

"Maybe you should take your own advice."

It's a fair point, so I don't dispute it.

"Had you been to Hillside before?" she asks after a beat of silence.

"Before today? No."

"How did you know where to go, then?"

I smirk. "You wanted to ask me that this morning, didn't you?"

Georgie rolls her eyes. "Maybe."

"I do my homework. I didn't request your security reports just to figure out what time you stumbled home that night, you know."

She says nothing to that. A yawn escapes me after a glance at the dash reminds me how late it is. I catch Georgie's smirk out of the corner of my eye. "Tired?"

"I'm an early riser. I wake up early no matter what time I go to bed, unfortunately."

"How early?"

"Five thirty. Sometimes six."

"You get up then?"

"Yeah."

"What do you do?"

"Run."

"How far?"

"Six, seven miles."

"Where do you run?"

"Around the city. I tend to loop around the Mall, down to the Lincoln Memorial. Sometimes the Tidal Basin too. Check on Abe."

"Oh my God. Did you just make a Lincoln joke?"

"It wasn't a joke. I just mentioned the guy."

"Coming from you, it was a joke. I'd given up on your sense of humor."

I want to smile but I don't.

"Can I come with you?"

I glance over, surprised. Trying to gauge if she's serious. She looks it. "Why?"

"To *run*, obviously."

Again, "Why?"

Georgie rolls her eyes. "Whatever. Forget it."

She looks away, out at the lights of the office buildings that line the street. Ending the conversation. I should embrace it. Accept it, at the very least.

Instead, I say, "If you're ready at six thirty, you can come."

For some unknown reason, that's my response. *Actually* unknown, not like what people say when they know *exactly* why they're doing something and say they don't, so they don't have to face any consequences. I truly have no clue what compels me to agree to spend *more* time with Georgie—to add on some of the limited time not already required I be in her presence. Not to mention, I hate running with other people.

And still, I folded like a clumsy house of cards. For what? I don't care if Georgie likes me. If I hurt her feelings or prop up her ego. My actions need to be independent from hers. No matter what she says or does, my role remains the same.

Yeah, fine, I find her attractive. I'll acknowledge there's more to Georgie than the annoyed glimpse in the Oval. But it shouldn't matter. It can't. Our roles are clearly defined and carefully separated. Who we are as separate people is completely overshadowed by my responsibilities.

My *responsibility*, really. There's just the solitary, main one now. *Her*.

I'm opening my mouth to take it back, to come up with some excuse when she speaks first.

"Thank you for driving me home."

I tighten my hands around the steering wheel. Shift around uncomfortably, as much as I can while sitting and driving.

I'm not sure what to say in response. *You're welcome? No problem? Of course?* If I were on duty right now, this would be far simpler. I didn't need to stay at Founding Fathers, and I should have had the two agents who are actually on duty drive her back to the White House. I should have ignored the strange compulsion to make sure she not only left the bar safely but also that I saw her enter the residence with my own two eyes.

Georgie isn't expecting an answer. She relaxes back against the leather seat, a small smile on her face as she listens to Paul McCartney croon.

And I realize this might be a difficult assignment—for reasons I never considered, up until this exact moment.

CHAPTER SIX

GEORGIE

ETHAN IS WAITING at the bottom of the stairs when I descend them, two minutes early. I flash him my phone screen—displaying 6:28—and a proud smile.

He looks shocked. Either he didn't think I would show up at all, or he thought I'd be late, if I did.

I'm *not* surprised to see him. I knew he'd be here, and it doesn't have anything to do with the fact he's a Secret Service agent and I'm the president's daughter.

Ethan just seems like the sort of guy who shows up. Who's solid and reliable.

The few guys I've dated have all been "bad boys." Partly to piss off my father, to test out the tight boundaries his decisions have placed around me. But mostly because I found the edge—their disregard for things like timeliness—to be thrilling. It was an escape from the many parts of my life I have no control over. I don't really find owning a motor-cycle or skipping class to be appealing traits to look for in a guy.

It's occurring to me in the moment—annoyingly, because I

know why the realization is choosing this second to appear—that I might find dependability a more appealing characteristic.

Especially when it's attached to messy blond hair and startlingly bright blue eyes.

Ethan is dressed casually today. It reiterates the realization he's not on duty right now. That he's choosing to spend his limited free time with me. If we weren't about to go exercise, I'd say it feels a little like a date. A real one, not pizza with friends before hitting up a party, which is the only sort I've ever been on.

He looks me over as I approach. Not in an appreciative way—not checking me out—but rather a quick assessment, like he'd scan a room for a threat. In this instance, I think he's making sure I dressed appropriately.

I appreciate it. Not the clinical appraisal or the implied uncertainty about whether I'm capable of dressing myself. I appreciate the fact it's a much-needed reminder of our respective roles. Of the fact that the world is painted in shades of gray, and Ethan sees everything as black or white.

I cross my arms when I reach him, uncaring about the way I know it draws attention to my cleavage.

Highs are supposed to brush the nineties today. I'm wearing running shorts, a tank top, and sneakers. It's not a provocative outfit. But I suddenly feel exposed, under his scrutinizing gaze. Physically and emotionally vulnerable. Somehow, in the extremely limited time we've spent together, Ethan has managed to finagle his way onto the short list of people whose opinions I care about. Become someone I might try to impress, even.

"Ready?" Ethan's tone is brusque. He may not be on duty, but he's all business. And I guess he technically *will* be on duty, once we leave the grounds.

I haven't made peace, exactly, with the lack of freedom living in the White House allows. But I've grown accustomed, to a degree, with the lack of allowances. For some reason it hits me right now, how I can't even go for a run on my own.

The walk outside and down the driveway is spent in silence. Yesterday, I was content to simmer in it. Today it feels different.

"Guess you're not a morning person?" I ask. "In addition to not being an afternoon or night guy either, of course."

I catch a glimmer of a smile. It feels like a victory meriting a medal. The equivalent of a belly laugh coming from anyone else.

It emboldens me to continue. "Good morning, Georgie. How are you? How did you sleep? What did you have for breakfast? How far do you usually run? Do you usually listen to music? Or podcasts? I know this great one where—"

"I don't listen to podcasts."

"Of course not. Better to sit with your own thoughts, right? Brainstorm a few ideas for world peace?"

"You think you know a lot about me, huh?"

"Do I *need* to?"

I would be lying if I said I haven't been waiting for a chance to throw that back in his face.

Ethan sighs. "I just meant—"

"I know what you meant."

The memory of him telling me he needs to know *nothing* about me reignites anger. I thought we came to a truce last night. It felt like we were...not friends, but friendly. Non-combative, at least.

Maybe that was the tequila talking. I wasn't nearly as tipsy as I'd acted, but there was definitely some alcohol driving decisions last night. It's the reason we're walking next to each other. The reason I voiced a request I was certain he'd turn down. "You know what? This was a bad idea. I'll just—"

"Wait."

Usually, when people make statements that sound more like

demands, there's nothing I love less than to follow them. But something in Ethan's voice freezes me in place. Makes me comply before I've consciously decided to.

He has the sort of voice you listen to. Deep and commanding and confident. It slides over me like sinful seduction. Turns me on like nothing I've ever experienced before. And the worst part is, I'm pretty sure he talks to *everyone* like this.

I'm nothing special. Nothing important. He's here for the same reason a straight-A student signs up for the extra credit offered by the teacher.

Responsibility is the best way to describe it. He considers himself responsible for what happens to me. And he'll go above and beyond to make certain nothing bad does.

I should appreciate it. And I do. I know my dad's job makes me a target. Know the guns and the patrols around me aren't for show, that they could serve a very real purpose.

With Ethan, it feels different. I'm not sure if I could describe how. There's no distant transaction when it comes to him guarding me. Proactiveness and preparedness for a possibility we all hope won't become a reality. More than anything, it feels personal. His insults and his insistence on following every rule to the letter are all tangled.

"I'm sorry," he continues. "I shouldn't have said that."

His apology floors me. Not only because I'm used to being around people—politicians and teenagers, mostly—who appear incapable of acknowledging when they're wrong, but because he was *right*.

He *doesn't* need to know anything about me. I'm an assignment, a job.

And if anything, Ethan apologizing makes this outing seem like an even worse idea. It feels like pity.

Pity feels different from sympathy. You feel pity toward

someone you see as helpless. Sympathy is saved for those we admire or respect.

Ethan doesn't admire or respect me, and it's not until right now, as I'm absorbing his pity, that I realize how badly I want him to. How, in a matter of days, I've gone from resolved to making this assignment a living hell for him to hoping he likes it.

I'm not sure how or why or when the shift occurred.

But here I am, hopeful.

"Don't apologize."

"Why not?" he counters.

"You don't mean it."

"I don't?"

He sounds amused, and I'm annoyed by it. "No, I don't think you do," I reply.

"Makes sense. Obviously, you would know my intention better than *I* do."

I roll my eyes, then register my surroundings. I've been following Ethan blindly, more focused on our conversation than anything else.

We're rapidly approaching the side entrance, with no cars in sight.

"We're not driving?"

Ethan casts me a side look. "We're going *running*, remember?"

"Yeah, I remember," I tell him, instead of what I'm really thinking. The truth is, I've *never* left the White House grounds in anything besides an armored vehicle. I didn't even know it was possible to.

I almost say so. But I opt to say nothing, because expressing concern about his choice of exit suggests I care about following the rules and am worried about my safety. I've gotten good at acting like I don't, and it's absolutely information Ethan will use against me later, when he's trying to get me to follow his direction.

Also, I trust him. I don't think Ethan would ever put me in harm's way, and I'm certain enough that I'm willing to follow him without hesitation or asking questions.

He grabs my elbow and pulls me to a halt. "What's wrong?"

"Nothing." I try to twist out of his grip, but his hand remains, hot and authoritative. It's a reflex, not to capitulate. But it's also distracting. Confusing. His touch sears into my flesh like a brand. I imagine that possessive touch on me elsewhere—everywhere— and a flush that has nothing to do with the summer heat works its way across my skin.

"Georgie."

That's all he says, my name. And it works.

"I've only ever left the grounds in a car before," I grit out. "I was surprised we weren't taking one. That's all."

"Are you worried you won't be safe?"

"I know tax dollars aren't paying your salary just to make sure I get home safe from a bar, Ethan," I snap. "I'm not an idiot."

It's the closest I'll get to telling him he's a good agent. That his attentiveness, while annoying, has imbued me with a confidence I've never had in any of my other agents. Sure, I know they're trained. I know they take their jobs seriously. But I've never felt like any of them cared about *me*.

And I'm probably projecting what I want to see, thinking Ethan might.

"I don't think you're an idiot," he responds.

The bar is so low it must be touching the ground, yet my stupid heart flips like he just paid me the highest of compliments.

"Flattery will get you nowhere with me," I inform him. Lie, basically.

"That wasn't flattery," he replies. "That was the truth. Now, do you *want* to take a car, or are you good on foot?"

"This is fine."

He's still holding my arm. Still staring at me. "I take my job seriously, you know. I'll do everything in my power to make sure you getting home safe from a bar is all you have to worry about."

"Yeah, I know." Begrudgingly, I admit, "I trust you."

Something in his expression shifts, just for a moment, before he drops my arm and does a strange combination of a nod and a headshake. Like he's acknowledging something he's not sure he believes. Me trusting him appears to qualify. "Well, that's good to know."

The rest of the walk, from the grounds to the guarded gate house, is silent. When we reach the gate, Ethan has a brief conversation with two of the guards in the small building. The gate slides open, just a few feet, and Ethan gestures for me to walk through first.

DC is quiet at this hour. No tourists are out, snapping photos. It's a Sunday, so there aren't any commuters walking to office buildings or hurrying toward Metro stops. One middle-aged woman jogs past, not sparing a single glance in my direction, much less a double take.

Silently, Ethan starts jogging to the right, toward the proud point of the Washington Monument. Its sharp tip is a straight slash in the skyline.

The only sound is the slap of our sneakers against pavement. Ethan's breathing is rhythmic. I try to match my inhales and exhales to his. I'm in shape, thanks to tennis, but Ethan's physique suggests he'd be capable of running a marathon right now.

We reach the edge of the National Mall. Without consulting me, Ethan takes another right, heading toward the Lincoln Memorial. Sweat trickles down my spine as the sun beams down, casting a hazy glow across the city.

The silence is comfortable. Easy.

It makes me *un*easy.

I tend to be the loudest voice in the room. I'm naturally outgoing; making friends has always come easily to me. And I guess I inherited some of my father's charm, the easygoing political persona where you can make conversation with just about anyone.

Silence is rare for me, especially around someone I don't know all that well. I like to think offense is the best defense. I give people something to talk about besides my father: me.

With Ethan, I don't feel that pressure. He already thinks poorly of me. I also have a feeling he'd see through any act. Maybe that's just wishful thinking, because I feel like I see through his a little. Last night, I caught a few glimpses of the Ethan Salisbury who misses his dad and attended frat parties. Not just the stoic rule-follower.

I've never considered any of my agents outside of their jobs. I know they all have lives and families. Favorite colors and inside jokes. I just…didn't care.

When it comes to the guy running beside me, I'm rapidly realizing I care way too much. He fascinates me—*intrigues* me. Most people are easy to figure out. Ethan is like a puzzle with pieces missing. The few I've managed to put together don't show the full picture. And there are lots I don't have. I should accept that, not be wondering how to discover them.

We pass the World War II Memorial, then continue toward the columns of the Lincoln Memorial. A group of ducks float past in the Reflecting Pool. The path along here is shaded, which offers some relief from the burn of the sun. I can feel the drops of sweat rolling down my face in small streams.

We've run at least a mile and have yet to exchange a single word.

I take a stab at neutral conversation. "Do you like living in DC?"

A grunt is Ethan's only response. It could be interpreted as a yes, a no, or a *stop talking*.

"I liked living in Boston better than here," I tell his impassive expression. "Although it probably had more to do with the fact I could walk around alone there."

"Didn't you visit when your dad was in the Senate?"

"No," I reply, purely because he responded this time. "I didn't."

He says nothing to that. I lift my arms and pull the elastic out of my hair, letting the strands fall and then scooping them back up again, including the sweaty ones that were sticking to my neck. The motion messes with my pace, and I don't miss how Ethan slows his strides, giving me a chance to readjust. Despite his lack of ebullience, he's far from oblivious.

I decide to stop with the small talk and ask something I really want to know the answer to. "Would you have become an agent, if your father had done something else?"

"I don't know," he answers.

Hardly a verbose answer, but it sounds like an honest one. He asks me a question in return, which I'm not expecting.

"Are you close with your dad?"

"You saw us together." I can't shrug while running, which is the response I'd otherwise give him.

"Yeah, I did. And I'm still asking."

I sigh. "We have our moments. Happy and ugly. He's not a bad dad. Just…busy. Busy with *important* stuff, I know. Stuff he—He makes it *feel* more important than me. I think I resent that the most."

"What about your mom?"

"Uh, we're different, I guess? Like we talked about where I should go to college until we were both blue in the face. Went on campus tours and made pro con lists. But I wouldn't tell her if I had a crush on a guy. We're not friends, and we've never tried to be. She's not the touch-feely sort. Before my dad got elected, she was a college professor. Most of the time, she treats me like her favorite student."

"Interesting."

"Are you close with your mom?" I ask.

Ethan's response is immediate. "Yes."

I figured he would be, since his father is gone. "Is she happy, that you're here? That you're honoring your dad?"

"I've never asked her."

"Because you think she wouldn't be?"

He shoots me a look I'm relieved to see appears amused, not annoyed. "You ask a lot of questions."

"I'm curious about you."

He looks away. "You shouldn't be. I'm not that interesting."

I laugh, a dry, short sound that comes out as more of a wheeze. We must have run three miles by now. I don't want to slow him down, which means I'm pushing myself faster than usual.

"Are you good to keep going?" he asks.

In answer, I pick up my pace. My calves scream in protest, but I'm nothing if not committed. I'm more likely to throw up or pass out than I am to admit I'm tired.

Ethan lets out a breathy huff of a laugh that tells me he's realized the same.

We keep running in silence, reaching the Jefferson Memorial and then passing it.

"I don't usually run this fast," he tells me, as we pass the swan boats and head back toward the Mall.

"Bullshit."

When I look over, he's grinning. I'm so focused on memorizing the sight—the perfect angle of his profile, the light layer of stubble on his jaw, the dimple in his left cheek—that I almost stumble. I right myself just in time as he chuckles softly. Hopefully in response to what I said, not that I almost just faceplanted while ogling him.

It's not until we reach the White House gates again that I realize I was smiling back, the whole time.

CHAPTER SEVEN

ETHAN

THE WALL I'm leaning against is literally vibrating in time with the rhythmic thrum of the bass's beat.

Logan's place is everything Colby and mine's is not: expensive, decorated, and crowded. I take a sip of water and rest more weight against the plaster, allowing the vibration to continue pounding.

Logan is lucky he has his own townhouse in Georgetown. If a rager like this was thrown in my apartment complex, Metro PD would have been called a while ago. I think most of Logan's neighbors are here already.

Colby ambles his way over to me, taking up residence on the wall beside me. He's holding a beer and sporting an easy expression that suggests it isn't his first of the night.

"Way to be the life of the party, Salisbury."

I sip some more water. "Early morning."

"It was your day off, dude."

It's too loud in here to hear my phone ring, but I feel it vibrate against my hip. I pull it out, glance at the screen, then look at Colby. "I gotta take this."

He tips his beer in a silent *cheers* as I shove my way into the quietest corner I can find. It turns out to be Logan's pantry. "Hello?" I answer.

"Hey, Ethan." Myles sounds apologetic, and the tone immediately puts me on edge. "Sorry to bother you."

"No problem. What's up?" Someone's shouting outside the door, so I turn away, facing a row of peanut butter. A *row*. Seriously, it feels like I'm staring at the Jif aisle of Harris Teeter. I store the sight away for future teasing material.

"I'm wondering…well, honestly? I'm not sure what to do. It's just me and Kevin on duty tonight. This was supposed to be a small thing. What did she call it?"

"A pizza party," I hear Kevin grumble, faintly.

"Anyway, there's close to five hundred kids here. She's supposed to text every hour, and it's been an hour and a half. The place is packed, and I'm not sure if I should just barge in or…"

"Georgie's at a party?"

I sound more interested in that fact than I should be, but Myles doesn't seem to notice. He sighs. "Yeah."

"And you don't know *where she is*?" Anxiety sharpens the words.

"She's inside, for sure. There are other kids here with security. No one is getting out past all of us. I hate to ask you, I really do. But you can slip in, and no one will give you a second glance. Plus, Georgie seems to like you. Last time one of us walked in on…well, anyway, I think it's best if you handle it."

I want to claim the exact opposite. Whatever has happened between us, the last few times we've been alone together…

I don't like her. But I don't dislike her. Not at *all*, and certainly not as confidently as I was once sure I always would. I don't want to "walk in" on *anything*.

But I can't say that. Not when her safety is my responsibility, and definitely not when a senior agent is asking me for assistance on my assignment.

"Send me the address. I'm leaving now."

"Okay." The relief in his voice is palpable. "It's in Silver Springs."

It takes me five minutes to find Colby after I leave the pantry. He's chatting up a curvy redhead. Her friend, a petite blonde, perks up when I approach. Then quickly deflates when I tell Colby I'm leaving.

"You're the DD!" he tells me.

"Take an Uber," I tell him.

"You guys live together?" the blonde asks, regaining interest.

I have a sudden vision of returning from Silver Springs to find this random girl in my room while Colby and her redheaded friend get it on across the hall. I wish I could say I'm being paranoid, but it's happened before. Colby seems to be a magnet for women with no boundaries—probably because he possesses none himself—and is also a *more the merrier* type. Entering our apartment to find a strange woman—or three—in the living room isn't unheard of. If I were home any more than I am, which is basically never, I'd probably have found my own place by now.

"Nope," I lie. Then raise a brow I hope conveys *Don't be an idiot* to Colby, before heading for the hallway. I don't have time to find Logan in this mass, so I'll have to text him.

I'm almost to the front door when I hear my name called. Logan is winding his way through the crowd toward me, a brunette I've never seen before right behind him.

"Ethan! I've been looking for you all over. This is Megan," he introduces. "She works with me at the State Department."

I force a smile. "Nice to meet you, Megan."

Megan smiles back. "You too, Ethan."

She's pretty, with long, dark hair and minimal make-up. More casually dressed than most of the girls here, in jean shorts and a fluttery top.

Logan is mouthing something at me that looks a lot like *Last you out*. But I'm guessing he's really saying *Ask her out*. Ever since Stella and I split a few months ago, he's accused me of not putting myself out there enough.

In reality, my reluctance has been mostly because Stella told me I led her on when we broke up, and I'm not entirely convinced I didn't. I'm not in a place to commit to a serious relationship right now, and that was *before* I learned I was going to be on another coast come late August. Something I still need to tell my friends. None of them seem to have realized on their own that being part of Georgie's detail doesn't have a set expiration date for me. I know exactly why I didn't mention it before—I wasn't sure that I wouldn't try to find some way to remain in DC. It was a long shot to start with. And now…now I'm not sure if it's the choice I would make, even if I had the option to.

"I'm sorry," I say. "I've got to run. I just got an urgent work call."

"A work call late on a Saturday night?" Megan raises one eyebrow. "You must do something important."

I guess you could consider keeping the president's daughter from getting alcohol poisoning important, but I'm not exactly single-handedly saving our democracy.

"Ethan works for the Secret Service," Logan supplies.

"Oh. Wow," Megan says. "Impressive."

It's the standard, wide-eyed reaction I receive from most women. I'm pretty sure they all picture me as some James Bond-type badass, carrying out covert missions and thwarting terrorist attacks. Not rescuing a teenager from questionable decisions.

I smile. "Really nice to meet you, Megan. Logan, I'll talk to you later."

"Yeah, sounds good," Logan replies. "Thanks for coming."

When I step outside, there are a couple of guys smoking on the front porch. The scent of cigarettes saturates the humid night air as I hurry down the front walk toward my parked car. I keep waiting for my phone to buzz again, for Myles to tell me there's no need for me to come after all.

Part of me wonders if this is some form of hazing. If they're testing me out to see if I have what it takes to handle this sort of assignment. Or payback, for last night at the bar. A little *You think you can do better than us? Prove it.* kind of welcome.

Regardless of the reasoning, I'll have to handle the consequences. It's telling—and concerning—that I'm not entirely focused on the effect they might have on my career and reputation. No matter the circumstances, getting pulled off an assignment like this will be a black mark on my record. Guarding the president or a member of his immediate family is the highest honor an agent can receive.

I didn't make it this far to fail.

But it would also bother me, no longer being part of Georgie's detail. Somehow, this has gone from the last assignment I wanted, to the only one I do. Returning to my prior routine and remaining in DC when she leaves for college? Neither holds much appeal anymore.

I don't fixate on *why* that might be the case. Just speed toward the address Myles sent. It takes me twenty minutes.

The house I pull up outside is massive. Large and imposing and screams *Wealth*. A gatehouse guards the perimeter of the property, the first clue that someone important lives here, not just rich. The overweight man inside gives my badge an impatient glance, then waves me up the drive lined with luxury cars. My Explorer is only six years old, but it stands out.

Flashy sport cars transition to black SUVs, the closer I draw to the house. Georgie isn't the only one here with security, like Myles said, which isn't that shocking. I know she just graduated from Hamilton Academy, which is the typical choice for the children of DC's elite. Her classmates would have had lobbyists and diplomats and members of Congress for parents, not just your standard law firm partner or corporate executive like at most hoity-toity private schools. Power players.

I feel a flash of sympathy toward Georgie, wondering what that must have been like. Her father is, arguably, the most powerful man in the world. That would complicate high school for anyone.

I park in front of another car and climb out, pulling my phone from my pocket to call Myles. Even from out here, I can hear the heavy pulse of loud music, reminiscent of the scene I just came from. Aside from the fact it makes Logan's party look like a housewarming get-together, complete with cheese and a ten p.m. departure.

I went to some wild parties in high school. There wasn't a whole lot else to do on the weekend in my small hometown.

And I attended plenty at Dartmouth as well.

But this? This makes those parties look tame. It's the sort of scene you see in a teen comedy and think *That's so unrealistic. No party I've ever gone to was like that.*

Turns out they take place.

Before I can call Myles, I hear my name called. I glance around until I see him leaning against one of the black SUVs, Kevin in the passenger seat beside him. "You made good time."

"I came from Georgetown."

Myles winces, the apology I heard in his voice clear in his expression. I mentioned I live in NoMa when we first met each other a few days ago, so he knows I wasn't home, twiddling my thumbs. He's a nice guy. I'm guessing his grimace would be more pronounced if he knew I spent my morning guarding Georgie too. "Sorry to ruin your night."

"You didn't. Still nothing from Georgie?"

His expression changes, tenses and tightens. "Nothing."

"You've gone into these parties before?" I ask.

My training focused on evasive driving and hostage procedures. Physical endurance and proper handling of a firearm.

Not high school parties. There's no rulebook at play here.

"Once," Myles replies. "Similar situation. She wasn't answering, we got concerned. I didn't go in; it was another agent."

"What happened?"

Myles shrugs. "She and Harris got into it. He was gone within the week."

Reassuring.

"Great." I draw the word out and let a little sarcasm seep into my voice. I catch a ghost of a smile on Kevin's profile, half-turned in the passenger seat.

"You'll be fine, kid," Myles tells me.

The *kid* grates. But Myles and Kevin were trained agents back when I was in high school, so I guess it's not entirely unwarranted. Deciding there's nothing helpful they'll have to tell me; I nod and turn toward the stone path that leads to the front door.

"This is Justice Randall's place, by the way," Myles calls.

I turn back around. "The Supreme Court justice?"

"Yep. She's out of town this week."

I say nothing to that because I'm not sure what to. Never, not once, in the past ten years that I settled on this career path, did I think it would include walking into the house of a Supreme Court justice to confront the president's daughter. It doesn't just sound like the start of a bad joke—it just sounds *bad.*

I wonder, not for the first time, what my father would think of this. Whether he'd be proud of the choices I've made or wished I'd stop making them based on what I think he would decide.

The inside of the house is exactly what the outside suggests—loud, noisy, and packed with tipsy teenagers. The house itself looks like it could be featured in a magazine, clearly professionally decorated. Most of the furniture has been shoved to the periphery of the rooms, clearing the path for the dancing taking place. The air conditioning swirls with the scent of sweet liquor and expensive cologne.

The first floor has an open layout, with the exception of the central staircase people are traipsing up and down. I cringe as I watch them, knowing I'll be forced to look upstairs if I can't find Georgie on the first floor.

I walk deeper into the house, toward the kitchen. The backyard of the house is even larger than the front, visible through the stretch of French doors on the far wall, past the granite countertops. There's a pool, which is packed to capacity.

I swallow a groan, sorely tempted to turn around and march right out of here. This feels like a fool's errand, from start to finish. Even once I find Georgie, I already have a good idea of how that conversation will go. She'll be pissed I'm here, checking up on her like a child.

Rightfully so, maybe. She's an adult, and this is the furthest thing from a rave in a sketchy area. This house is easily worth eight figures, and the line of liquor bottles on the counter are all top-shelf brands. No Bud Light in sight, which was all the high school parties *I* attended had. No trouble she could get into here would be because of her father. Just typical teenage behavior.

And, as far as I can tell, no one else has security combing the premises for them. But none of them are my responsibility. Georgie is. It feels like there's more of an age gap between us than there really is. I just turned twenty-three. There's only a little over four years between us. Meaning I remember how bad decisions can sound like good ideas.

"Hey."

I'm startled by the sound of the female voice, wrapped up in my own head and absorbing the unfamiliar surroundings. I look to my left, and there's a tall blonde wearing a short dress, smiling at me. It's hard to miss the blatant interest in her expression. She has the build and the face of a model, waifish curves and sharp features.

"Hi." I give her a polite smile, then return to scanning the room.

"You in college? I know you didn't go to Hamilton. I'd remember you." She pairs the comment with a sly smirk, but that's not what gets my attention. It's the revelation she *did* go to Hamilton Academy.

I half-turn, giving her more of my attention. She misreads the interest, straightening her casual posture and tossing her long hair over one shoulder. "No, I'm not. I'm here looking for Georgie Adams. Have you seen her?"

As soon as I say Georgie's name, the blonde's demeanor shifts, turning cold and closed-off. "Of course." She scoffs. "Luke must have put that she'd be here on the fucking invitation. Good luck getting *those* legs to spread."

I feel my jaw tighten as tension spreads through my whole body. "Have you seen her?" I repeat.

"Last I saw, she was out by the pool," she tells me, then walks away, leaving me silently seething about her demeaning comment and her parting direction. The pool is pretty much the last place I want to look for Georgie, with the single exception of upstairs.

The crowds thin as I draw close to the kitchen island, with most of the people crowding around the pool and patio. There's a group of girls playing Flip Cup on the corner table of the kitchen in a small breakfast nook.

None of them are Georgie.

I resign myself to heading out to the pool next, turning toward the French doors. Then, I spot her.

For a few seconds, I forget everything. What I'm doing here. Why I'm standing in a Supreme Court justice's kitchen, looking around like a lost idiot in a sea of strangers.

All I can see—focus on—is her.

Georgie's wearing a bikini. That's it, nothing else. It shouldn't be as surprising as it is, considering her wet hair and the pool behind her. Several of the girls playing Flip Cup are wearing swimsuits as well.

I saw her in shorts and a tank top this morning. This shouldn't be that different. But it is. Droplets of water slide down her bare arms and stomach. Between her breasts, before I catch myself and veer my gaze upward.

She's holding a towel, but she's not using it to cover her body. I watch as she wraps it around her hair, then slings it over one shoulder.

She hasn't seen me yet. And now I feel especially uncomfortable, being here.

If leaving were an option, I would be long gone by now.

Georgie—finally—wraps the towel around her torso, covering up. It's a relief. The way she looks up, spots me, and scowls? Not so much.

It's expected though, so I school my expression of any emotion, especially any lust, and hold my ground as she approaches.

Rather than say anything, she grabs my wrist and drags me into what turns out to be, rather ironically, another pantry. I'm surprised enough to let her.

Georgie slides the pocket door shut and rounds on me. The light in here is already on, and there's only one reason I can think of why that might be the case. I'm careful not to lean against anything. "What are you doing here? You're off duty tonight."

"You missed a check-in. Myles said it'd been almost two hours since he heard from you."

She crosses her arms, and her towel slips down a half-inch. Hazy heat traverses through my bloodstream. I blame it on the lack of air conditioning in here. "I was swimming. They thought I'd have my phone with me?"

"Apparently, they thought this would be a smaller gathering. A pizza party, Kevin said."

Georgie snorts. Then says, "You didn't answer my question. What are *you* doing here?"

It's in everyone's interest for us to all get along, and admitting her other agents called me because they essentially didn't want to deal with her isn't conducive to that goal. I don't want to tell her the truth, but I'm not going to lie to her. Not when I'm expecting honesty from her. Not after she told me she trusts me. And honestly, I think she already knows.

"They called me."

There's no surprise on her face. "And you came. No questions asked?"

"I mean, I asked for the address."

She lets out a short laugh. Another half-inch slips. The straps of her bathing suit are on full display. They're emerald green, and I know I'll never be able to look at the color again without remembering how Georgie Adams looks in a bikini. It gives *inconvenient* a whole new meaning.

"Ri-ght," she drawls.

I sigh, annoyed and relieved at the same time. I came here for nothing. She's fine. Not even tipsy, it appears. "Next time, check in when you're supposed to. I was in the middle of…"

"In the middle of what?"

Georgie crosses her arms. I'm not sure if the move is intentional or not, but it pushes her tits up past the hem of the terrycloth, and it's distracting as fuck.

"Nothing. As long as you're good, I'll go."

"Wait." She reaches out and grabs my arm, like she's worried I won't listen to what she's saying and needs to ensure I don't move.

I glance down, at her pink-tipped fingers wrapped around my bicep. Feel the warmth of her skin seep into mine. "What?"

"You came all this way."

"It's a twenty-minute drive."

"The pool is nice."

"Oddly enough, I didn't stop and grab a pair of swim trunks on my way here."

"Hasn't stopped anyone else."

I'm not sure if she's actually suggesting she was just in a pool with a bunch of naked guys, but I'm certainly not going to ask her to clarify.

"Don't do anything stupid, Georgie. I'll see you tomorrow."

I mean the words as a parting, as a farewell. But she's still holding on to my arm, so I can't move away all that far. And I'm not actually trying to.

"Georgie." I say her name again. As a warning, this time.

"Were you at a party?"

I know I shouldn't indulge this line of questioning. Shouldn't answer. But I do. "Yes."

"And you left."

It's a statement, but I answer it like a question. "Yes."

"Were you with someone?"

Her hand tightens on my arm, like she's worried I'll escape without answering. We're veering far past *None of your business* and heading toward *Inappropriate*.

"You ask all your agents these kind of questions?" I ask.

Partly as a reminder, of the fact I *am* her agent, and partly because I actually want to know the answer.

"No," Georgie tells me, without a hint of shame or duplicity. "I don't."

"I wasn't with anyone."

I wish I could swallow the words as soon as I say them. Isn't that often how you feel about telling the truth? Uncertain? Lies are often more palatable. And in this instance, the truth is dangerous. It gives Georgie ammunition. Hope I wasn't sure I could give her, until I saw relief flare. It thrills and terrifies me in equal measure, because it tells me it was the answer she wanted to hear.

"Want to dance?"

I snort, like it's a preposterous suggestion. In reality, I'm picturing it. All those lush curves I saw barely contained by scraps of emerald, grinding against me. My dick twitches. "No."

She's undeterred by my rejection, moving closer, instead of further away. The shelves around us feel like they're collapsing. "Why not?"

"My job is to protect you, Georgie. That's it. Nothing is *ever* going to happen between us."

The reminder isn't just for her.

Once again, she appears unbothered. I wish I didn't find it so attractive. Wish she'd act more like the petulant child she did in her father's office instead of a confident woman. It would make treating her like a reckless teenager easier.

"If your job is to protect my body, wouldn't it be easier to do it…up close?"

She says *that*, then takes another step forward. Shrinks the gap between us by another foot. There's still a significant amount of air between us. We're hardly pressed up against each other, breathing each other's exhales.

I know she's attractive. Knew the first time I saw her, even when it was accompanied by annoyance about how she was acting. When she came down the stairs in a white tennis dress and when I saw her at Founding Fathers last night.

Every time I've seen her, I've known it.

Lust, I can handle. But there's more to Georgie than that. The banter and the precise questions and the times she's acted older than eighteen, not younger.

It shouldn't matter. It *can't*.

But in this tiny pantry, I admit the truth to myself: I want it to. I wish I'd felt a tiny fraction of this pull toward Stella. If I had, we'd still be together.

"It won't ever happen, Georgie," I repeat.

My voice sounds confident, and I'm relieved about that, at least.

"We'll see, Ethan."

"Text when you're supposed to." I finally recall the real reason I'm here.

"Yeah, yeah." Georgie walks toward the sliding door. Opens it. Then saunters away, toward the congregation of gyrating bodies in the living room.

I wish I were drunk.

I wish I could walk after her and take the dance she offered.

I wish lines were something you could redraw...after they've already been crossed.

I lean back against the wall for a minute. Close my eyes for a brief moment. Pull my phone out of my pocket and text Logan.

Ethan: *Can you send me Megan's number?*

Then I walk out of the pantry and head for the front door.

CHAPTER EIGHT

GEORGIE

SIX DAYS until I leave for Stanford.

I'm excited. It's a change in routine. A fresh start. A new beginning.

I'll still be Georgie Adams. But I'm hoping that will mean less, mean something different, in California than it does in the nation's capital. If that's naïve, I'm not ready to know so.

There's one snag in my excitement, and his name is Ethan Salisbury. Since Luke's pool party—six weeks ago—he's barely acknowledged me. He guards me, per his job description. Ethan and another agent, typically Myles or Kevin, are always with me whenever I leave the grounds. For practice with my coach or for brunch or for parties. They're silent, judgmental shadows.

I haven't missed a single check-in since Luke's party. And I always text Ethan first, no matter who else is on duty. Even the nights he isn't on duty. It's probably petty and partly childish.

And it's also the highlight of my night, sending those texts. Most of the hour between them is spent deciding what I'll say in the next one.

Ethan never replies. Never acknowledges them, and that's part of the thrill.

Because he *should*.

Because if all he truly cared about was his job, about protecting my body, he would respond to them.

He's done neither—until now.

I watch the dots indicating he's typing appear and disappear twice before he sends a text back, adding a blip of gray to the long line of blue messages.

Ethan: *Myles and Kevin are the ones on duty tonight.*

Over a month of conversation responded to like a brick wall, and he sends me that. Maybe it wouldn't bother me all that much, if I thought Ethan was just another suit collecting a paycheck. If I hadn't watched him fight to keep his gaze fixated above my collarbone in that pantry. If I didn't know why he pursued this career path and his brothers' names.

"Can you stop at 2584 Massachusetts Ave?" I ask Myles, who's driving.

He and Kevin exchange a glance. "Friend's place?"

I decide to be honest since they'll find out the truth soon enough. "It's Ethan's apartment. I need to talk to him about the meeting earlier."

This morning was the final in a series of meetings about the arrangements regarding my safety while I'm at Stanford. Today's was the only meeting Ethan didn't attend. That, coupled with his *not on duty* text, has made me realize he won't be the one dissipating any of the awkward tension between us.

"Agent Salisbury is on duty tomorrow," Kevin says. "You could talk to him then."

"I need to talk to him tonight." I'm putting Myles and Kevin in an awkward situation, and not for the first time, if I'm being honest. If it doesn't threaten my safety, they're not in the habit of telling me no. But I'm asking to visit an agent, while he's not my agent. "It's important," I add.

It's also a total excuse, from start to finish. I just want to see him, and this feels like a chance to do so when I'll catch him off guard and be able to talk to him without worrying who's listening around a corner.

Since he showed up at Luke's party, Ethan has kept things glaringly professional between us. No more runs together. No personal topics. He replies to my questions with *Yes* or *No*, nothing more, until I give up asking.

I know what he's doing. We inched toward a boundary, and he's tracing it over and over again with permanent marker, lest I try to pass it again.

He interpreted our conversation in the pantry as a come on, which it wasn't. Do I think he's attractive? Yes. Have I indulged in the occasional fantasy about what those muscles would look like without any clothes covering them? Also yes.

But I resent everything involving the presidency. The last thing I have any interest in is hooking up with a guy who reveres it, even if he were interested, which Ethan's immediate dismissal and near-ignoring since has made it clear he's not.

I don't know if dating the president's daughter is an explicit no-no in the Secret Service handbook, but I'm willing to bet that at the very least, it would be severely frowned upon.

And if there's *one* thing I know about Ethan Salisbury, it's that he values his reputation.

Like he said, nothing can ever happen between us. But his utter disregard toward me—his refusal to look my way or indulge in so much as a *two-word* response—annoys me.

If I'd never gotten a glimpse past the stoicism, maybe I wouldn't care. But I did, and I do.

I *like* Ethan. Like his dry humor and his awareness of the

world around him. I respect his dedication to his job, and his choice to follow in his father's footsteps. His new and perennial stubbornness when it comes to so much as being friendly toward me? Not a fan. It's like an itch just out of reach. A constant annoyance, growing increasingly unpleasant the longer it lasts and the more I think about it.

We pull up outside of Ethan's building a few minutes later. It's a large complex that looks identical to the two next door and the one across the street.

I'm glad neither Kevin nor Myles asked how I knew where Ethan lives. I'm not sure if I would have admitted to memorizing the address when I perused his file, and I doubt there's another legal explanation.

Kevin remains in the driver's seat while Myles escorts me into the empty lobby and inside an elevator.

"Security seems lax," I tell Myles, as we whizz up toward the eighth floor. "Guess Ethan thinks he can take care of himself."

Myles doesn't appear to appreciate my attempt at humor. And...it doesn't bother me. I could care less if he laughed or stayed stoic. I wonder if Ethan would have smiled before the pantry.

The elevator doors open, and we walk down a hallway that smells faintly of mildew until we reach 826. I knock—twice.

The door opens, revealing a guy who's...not Ethan.

"Oh. Hi."

Ethan's friend from Founding Fathers smiles, maybe at my inability to mask my disappointment. "Expecting someone else?"

I clear my throat. "Actually, yes. Is Ethan home?"

"Nope. He should be back soon though. Want to come in?" Ethan's friend holds the door open wider. A clear invitation.

I could leave, very easily. I *should* leave, since I don't even have a good excuse for showing up in the first place.

But instead, I tell Myles I'll be right back and walk inside.

If every definition in the dictionary had an accompanying photo, this would be the shot they'd choose for *bachelor pad*.

"I'm Colby," he reminds me.

"Georgie."

Colby smiles. "Yeah, I know who you are."

For some reason, I don't think it's a reference to my father. It makes me wonder what Ethan has said about me. *If* he's said anything about me.

I glance around the sparse apartment. "Nice place." My eyes linger on the bare walls and the mismatched stools along the island.

Colby snorts, obviously reading the subtext. "We both work a lot. And…" He sinks down on the couch in the center of the living room, assuming a pose it looks like he was in before I knocked on the door. "We're both single."

I figured Ethan was. He said he wasn't with anyone at that party he'd left and based on the fact he appears willing to pack up and move to California for the foreseeable future, that's still the case. But the confirmation isn't entirely unwelcome.

"What does that have to do with interior decorating?" I ask.

Colby chuckles. "Okay. If I asked you what to do in this space —" He spreads his right arm out, gesturing toward the entire living room. "What would you change?"

"Uh…" I survey the messy, empty space. "Everything?"

He smirks. "Specifically…"

"Curtains, paintings, lamps, rugs, pillows." I glance at the two cardboard boxes that look to be serving as a coffee table. "I'd get rid of those."

When I look back at Colby, his smirk has grown. "See, if you'd asked me what I'd change, I would have suggested swapping this—" He gestures toward the huge television taking up most of the far wall. "For a bigger one. That's why the place looks like this."

"Got it."

Colby leans forward, opens the flap of one of the cardboard boxes, and pulls out two Wii controllers. "Wanna play?" he asks, holding one out to me.

I've never played a video game in my life, but for some reason I agree without hesitation. "Sure."

Colby walks me through the basics, telling me which character to select, followed by the features of each vehicle option. He chooses a racetrack surrounded by waterfalls, and I'm so distracted taking in the colorful scenery I'm barely focused on the game. He beats me easily. Since I'm competitive, I tell him to start another round.

I've lost count of how many tracks we've raced on when the doorbell rings. I eye the door uneasily. This is Ethan's place, so I can't picture him ringing the bell. I'm guessing it's Myles, wondering what the hell is going on.

But when Colby opens the door, it's to a group of guys I've never seen before. One of them is carrying a tall stack of pizza boxes, while another is carrying a six-pack. They're too focused on unloading everything to pay attention to me, or even register there's anyone else here.

Colby seems to have forgotten about me as well. He's busy slapping backs and joking with the new arrivals. The doorbell rings again a minute later. This time, the crowd that spills in includes a few girls. It appears that Colby is throwing a party, and I wish he'd mentioned it when he invited me in. Myles is probably glowering out in the hall.

I stand, smoothing the front of my cotton dress out. The other girls here are dressed casually, in jean shorts and faded t-shirts and flip-flops. I feel young and out-of-place.

"Can I use your restroom, before I head out?" I direct the question toward Colby, but it captures the attention of everyone in the apartment. The lack of furnishings makes it feel bigger, but it's not that large of a place. Critical eyes scrutinize me, but I can't figure out if it's because they think I was here for Colby or because they recognize me.

Colby clears his throat. "Yeah, of course. Down the hall on the right."

I nod and follow his directions. The hallway is narrow and slanting, dimly lit by the single bulb in the ceiling. The bathroom is small but clean. Just a tub, a toilet, and a sink. There's a tube of Crest on the counter next to the sink, but no other toiletries in sight. I resist the urge to peek in the cabinet above the sink or the drawers below it. But I stare at the tub for a few seconds longer than I would any other, realizing it's where Ethan showers. Naked.

I pee quickly and wash my hands, suddenly eager to get out of here. I did have to go to the bathroom, but I mostly came in here so it didn't look like I'd been scared off. Stupid, considering they're all strangers and I shouldn't care what Ethan thinks about anything.

He's not even here.

He *wasn't* here.

I hear his voice as soon as I open the bathroom door. It's a low, commanding hum, annoyed and authoritative.

"—you think you're doing?"

"She showed up here, Ethan! What did you want me to do? Not open the door?" Even if I didn't recognize Colby's voice, I'd know it was him talking, based on the context.

"You should have called me," Ethan answers.

"I texted you. You're the one who took your time getting home."

"How was I supposed to know—"

Ethan stops talking when I appear in the doorway. He and Colby are standing on the far side of the living room, right next to the opening that leads to the hallway, as far away from the crowd in the attached kitchen as possible. The same crowd that's now looking over here with growing interest.

He looks good, I admit to myself. Begrudgingly. Casual, the way I haven't seen him since that night at Luke's party. Since then, it's been suit after suit.

A pair of navy shorts show off his tan calves and a white t-shirt hugs his broad chest. Covers the stacks of muscle his damp shirt clung to when we went running together.

For a few seconds, it feels like he's giving me a similar appraisal. But those end quickly, and then he's stalking forward, spinning me around, and marching me toward one of the closed doors lining the hallway. His hand doesn't actually touch me, but I can feel it hovering inches from my back.

Ethan opens the door and gestures for me to walk inside. I figure this must be his bedroom, and I'm right.

It's as minimalistic as the rest of the place. A bed and a dresser. The comforter is haphazard and there's a stick of deodorant on top of the wooden dresser, but that's about all there is to look at. It smells like him in here.

I speak first, while still looking around, pretending like there are details to absorb. Avoiding his gaze. "Myles is still out in the hall?"

"Yes."

I chew my bottom lip. I should have gone back out into the hallway and told Myles I was staying here for longer. It's probably been close to an hour by now. But if I'd done that, I would have had to justify why I was staying put, without any good reason to.

"What are you doing here, Georgie?" Ethan asks.

"Where were you?" I counter, like I have a right to ask. "Colby said you'd be home a while ago."

"I'm off duty. What I do is none of your business."

He's right, but my annoyance spills out more questions I'm not entitled to ask. It feels like we're never on the level playing field I want us to be. "Was it a big date? Or just a random hook up?"

"None of your business," Ethan reiterates. But he doesn't deny he was with a woman, which bothers me for some strange, inexplicable reason. He's a hot guy with decent conversation skills—when he chooses to use them, that is—and a badass sounding job. Of course he can get laid when he wants to.

I bury any discomfort in a teasing tone. "No happy ending? You still seem awfully tense."

Ethan crosses his arms, emphasizing my point. "What are you doing here, Georgie?"

"You weren't at the meeting this morning."

His forehead wrinkles for a second before it smooths. "I had today off."

"If you took this seriously, you would have been there."

Ethan appears torn between amusement and disbelief. "You think I don't take my job seriously?"

There's an underlying warning to the question, a reminder to tread carefully with what I'm suggesting. "You tell me."

"Showing up at that meeting, on my *one* day off a week, would have been an insult to the rest of the agents on your team. It's not how it's done, and I'm not the most senior member, as you love to remind me."

"Why wasn't the meeting held when you were on duty, then? Aren't you going to be the head of my security once we leave?"

"It's still being decided."

"What do you mean, *it's still being decided*?"

"Exactly that. I can't discuss any details, it's classified."

"It's *classified*? This is *my* safety we're talking about."

"Oh, so now you're concerned about it? Maybe if you didn't make guarding you so difficult, decisions would be easier to make."

I cross *my* arms, mirroring his defensive posture. "So we're back to Luke's party. I didn't drink. I didn't do drugs. I didn't leave his house. I missed one check-in, and—"

"That's all it takes!" Ethan snaps. "There are people out there who want to hurt you, Georgie. Who want to *kill* you. One check-in, one hour, might not feel like long to you, but it feels a hell of a lot longer when you're standing outside keeping guard. And it would make a huge difference if there was a threat."

"You think I don't know that? I do. I'm trying to protect just a *tiny* bit of normal in my life."

"You can do that *and* follow directions."

"You're not mad about me missing the check-in. You're pissed off about what happened after, when you showed up. Well, newsflash, I wasn't even trying to fuck you! All I wanted was for you to lighten up a little bit, since it's awfully unpleasant being around you when you're the human equivalent of a raincloud."

My chest heaves as we study each other.

"I'm not requesting a reassignment."

"I'm not asking you to—"

"I'm not requesting a reassignment," he repeats, as if I didn't say anything. "Which means you're going to need to get it through your pretty little head that there is a certain way security needs to be handled. I don't know what allowances you're used to, and I don't care. We'll be doing things my way, here in DC and once you're at Stanford."

"All I got from that is that you think I'm pretty."

The flash of annoyance on Ethan's face brings me great joy. "It's a saying."

"I have never heard anyone else say *You're going to need to get it through your pretty little head that there is a certain way security needs to be handled*."

He exhales, long and exasperated. "*Pretty little head* is a saying."

"Or a slip of the tongue."

Ethan's expression is saying *I'd rather stab myself than compliment you*. I don't think he did mean to, but he's fun to tease.

And...there's a tiny part of me that wonders if he meant it.

"Admit it. You think I'm pretty."

He doesn't. "That's why you came here? To ask why I missed the meeting?"

"No. I came here because I like you." His expression morphs into a look of shock. "Not like that. I just..." I fiddle with the hem of my dress, inexplicably nervous. Probably because I *do* like him like that, a little. "I want things to go back to what they were like before, between us. I'm sorry I said anything, at Luke's party. I was drunk."

I let the edge of my dress fall and study him, weighing his reaction. I might be gambling with any ounce of his respect I gained. The truth is I hadn't drunk a drop of alcohol when he showed up. But I'd rather he thinks I was wasted than believe I'm harboring a crush on him, if that's what has caused these weeks of awkwardness.

"I'm not—"

I don't even let him finish the sentence before I say, "Bullshit."

He closes his mouth and tightens his jaw before looking away. "Showing up here wasn't very professional, Georgie."

"Neither is acting like I have the plague."

"I haven't been—" Ethan exhales. "You're exaggerating."

"I'm not. And acting professional and ignoring me are two different things."

"What do you want me to do?"

"I don't know, act like you did before!" He's making me feel ridiculous for coming here. For asking him to be a decent person, essentially. Most people don't show up to work with a perennial scowl. "If you really can't stand me, try to make it a little less obvious."

"I didn't take you for this much of an egoist."

The statement hits me with the force of a sledgehammer. Maybe I read this all wrong. He hasn't been avoiding me because of what happened in Luke's pantry. I probably imagined the way he opened up to me before then, too. He allowed an attempt to get to know him and then decided it wasn't worth the effort, I guess.

I search for the glib comment or snappy retort I'm usually able to conjure on command. Right now, there's nothing. Just blank space and disappointment. I don't even want to tell him goodbye, because I'm worried he'll hear what I'm not saying in my voice.

I came here to ask him for something. And I'm not the type of person who asks for *anything*. I hate doing so, actually. Debt is a high price to pay.

So I turn away from the bed and head toward the door. Before I can take more than a step, a warm hand closes around my elbow, in what has become a move I associate with him.

"I—fuck—I'm sorry. I wasn't expecting you to..." He pinches the bridge of his nose with his free hand. "It's been a tough day."

That could mean lots of things. But something possesses me to jump to the conclusion of, "Your dad?" and not be surprised when he nods. "And your friend threw a *party*?"

There's a flash of amusement on his face, like he finds my disapproval entertaining. "It's a going-away, of sorts. They didn't know what today is."

"Because you didn't tell them."

Ethan nods. "Because I didn't tell them."

I blow out a long breath. "Coming here had nothing to do with my ego, Ethan."

"It shouldn't matter, what I think. About you, or about anything."

"It matters to me," I tell him.

He studies me, for a minute. Long enough that I want to shift under the appraisal. "That's part of the problem."

His words aren't harsh, they're soft.

The same electricity from the pantry reappears, wrapping around us in ropes of awareness. He's still holding my arm, and it feels like pulses of heat are spreading out from his touch, sinking into my skin, and swimming through my bloodstream. For one wild, thrilling second, I think there's a chance he'll kiss me.

Ethan's hand drops and he steps away. "I'll walk you out."

I'm not going to argue—to beg. So I nod and walk through the door he opens, down the hall, and back into the open space that serves as the living room slash kitchen.

The crowd has grown. I'd estimate there are close to thirty people packed in the small apartment. Ethan navigates through it with ease, mostly ignoring the many people trying to get his attention.

We're almost to the door when it opens, revealing a guy I recognize and a pretty brunette. The blond man was with Ethan at Founding Fathers. Chris? Or maybe Caleb?

He shuts the door behind them and then halts when he spots me and Ethan, his eyebrows whizzing upward before he catches himself and adopts a neutral expression. He greets Ethan with a hand slap and then glances at me. "Hi, Georgie."

"Hey, um…" I fumble for his name, feeling like a fuckboy encountering his one-night stand in the morning.

"Logan." He supplies his name with a smile, holding a hand out.

I feel my cheeks warm. Okay, so I was way off on the C name. "Right. Logan."

I glance at the woman with him, waiting for her to introduce herself as well. But she's not paying attention to me. She's focused on Ethan, who looks decidedly uncomfortable.

"Hey, Ethan," she says.

"Megan. Nice to see you," he responds.

Despite the polite greetings, there's awkwardness hovering between them, the sort that suggests Megan isn't Logan's girlfriend, which is what I'd assumed. And now she's watching me glance between the two of them, doing the same from me to Ethan.

"Are you two…"

"No! Not together! Ethan is my sponsor," I tell her. "He never lets me miss a meeting. But my old dealer is having a party tonight, and he invited me, and I shouldn't go. I know I shouldn't. But I really want to, you know?"

Megan looks confused; Logan appears amused.

Ethan is most definitely annoyed. He places a hand on the small of my back—touching, not hovering this time—and guides me toward the door. If this is my punishment for pissing him off, he's not exactly making it an unattractive option.

He stops guiding me forward when we reach the door, standing out of earshot from everyone else. "What was that?" Ethan hisses.

"Just trying to cover for you, with your girlfriend."

"She's not my girlfriend."

"She wants to be."

He doesn't dispute it. "Next time, stick to the truth."

"That you're assigned to protect me and act like it's the equivalent of receiving the death penalty?"

"I don't act like—"

"I'd rather you ignore me than lie to me."

"Georgie..."

"Bye."

I grab the door handle. He grabs my arm. "It's easier this way."

I freeze, letting those words wash over me. I think this is the closest I'll ever get to hearing Ethan admit he harbors anything besides contempt toward me. The bittersweet satisfaction gets buried.

"Easier for democracy?" I question. "For duty? For putting someone else first?"

Ethan's jaw tenses more with each question, telling me he recognizes the list he told me I didn't care about. "Easier for me."

I look down, at my fingers holding the door handle. I tighten my grip until my knuckles whiten. "I shouldn't have asked if your dad was proud you followed in his footsteps. I should have told you I'm sure he is."

I don't look at his face. Don't give him a chance to respond. I open the door and walk into the hall, past a waiting Myles.

The words are sincere. I may have resented Ethan's coldness these past weeks, but I don't think it detracted from his job performance.

Those aren't the parting words I intended to say, though. I'm vacillating between annoyance and apologetic, along with a whole bunch of other emotions. Confused by a whole lot more than just the conversation that took place between us.

Myles says nothing as we walk into the elevator and the doors close. But I can tell he wants to. Can feel his eyes on me as the elevator starts to sink with a groan that makes me a little worried we should have taken the stairs. Fortunately, we make it to the ground floor without incident.

Coming here was silly. Agents must talk, and I'm sure Ethan doesn't want anyone discussing the dynamic between us. If there was any way I could have managed to come here on my own, I would have. But I know the only way my appearance would have pissed Ethan off even more was if I'd showed up *without* agents.

It's easier this way plays on repeat in my head as we cross the lobby.

Easy and *easier* are two different things.

CHAPTER NINE

ETHAN

STANFORD'S CAMPUS looks nothing like the neat grid of downtown DC. Or the brick buildings and barren trees at Dartmouth. Anywhere I look, it's impossible to forget where I am. Forget why I'm here.

The sun is shining, tempering the first hint of fall in the air. Students are taking full advantage of the slightly cooler weather, breaking out the long sleeves and boots that it's been too warm to wear until now. If I had a suit on, I'd be broiling. Thankfully, we're supposed to be blending in on campus, not standing out. I'm wearing jeans and a t-shirt, as casually dressed as the students milling about.

A class just let out of Ferdinand Hall, a massive academic building that looms over the art gallery and the career planning center located to its left and right. A group of girls approach, all wearing lightweight jackets. Several of them stare at me. I wink at one of them, a petite blonde, and pink stains her cheeks as they continue walking past.

Myles chuckles from his post beside me, catching the brief interaction. "Ah, young love."

"I'm not that young." I'm technically the head of Georgie's security detail, but I'm well aware of where I fall in the group pecking order, which follows seniority, not titles.

He grins. "They weren't batting their eyes at me, Salisbury."

I roll my eyes, even though I know he's right. I blend in on campus, which is exactly the point of me being here. Most days, I'm confused for a student several times. It should be amusing— flattering, I guess—but I find it mostly annoying. I may look like I could be a student, but I'm *not*.

I'm here for a job. I have responsibilities on campus far more serious than writing a paper or preparing for an exam. I went through it all once already, to get here. Or a version of here that I didn't expect to look like this.

I'm here because I have no choice but to be, and I think that's enough to feed resentment in even the most loyal of men, which I consider myself to be.

"You've got tomorrow night off. Line up a hot date, kid."

I follow Myles's gaze to the stream of students still leaving Ferdinand Hall. Around half of them are female, and more than a few give me lingering stares. "I'm good."

Myles makes a small, disbelieving sound in the back of his throat, but he doesn't press the point.

There are four agents at Stanford in total: me, Myles, Kevin, and Joey. With the exception of myself, they all were assigned to Georgie's detail before this move. Aside from my age, it's the other main way I'm an outlier amongst them. Myles is the next youngest, and he's in his late twenties.

We rotate our schedule based on hers, considering where she'll be and what the potential threat level is. I spend the most time as her close guard because I draw the least attention. The least gawking, at least. The other guys—especially Myles— would say I draw plenty of attention of the female variety.

They also say Georgie listens to me more than them, which I think is a convenient excuse to keep me on duty.

It's an easy job, for the most part. Georgie possesses the same charisma that got her father elected. She's constantly busy, at class or at tennis practice or out to eat with friends or at a party. It's one never-ending blur of activity, one that I have to stand and watch flash past. Always on guard, always alert.

We've been on campus for a month. I should feel settled, have fully adapted a new routine. Instead, I grow more uncomfortable every day. I know why—it's beyond the point where there's another explanation.

It's her.

For the past month, I've watched Georgie's every move. Watched her settle. Watched her thrive.

I know her tells during tennis—can predict her serve before she tosses the ball. I know she eats Cheerios on weekdays and frozen waffles on the weekends. I know her class schedule and the way she color codes her binders.

It should be plenty. It shouldn't make me want to know things I can't learn by observing, I shouldn't *still* be intrigued by her.

Ferdinand Hall is located in the heart of Stanford's campus, close to the main dining hall and the center green. Palm trees line the pathway that connects sandstone buildings decorated with covered arcades, half-circle arches, and columns. It may look nothing like the nation's capital or New Hampshire, but it's still beautiful.

Just not as captivating as the girl laughing by the fountain.

And that's the real problem with this assignment: Georgie. I can claim it's being the youngest, most inexperienced member of the team. Having to relive higher education after having just graduated myself. But mostly, it's her.

This awareness was supposed to fade and fizzle. After she

showed up at my apartment, Georgie accepted the distance I'd carved out between us. Space I forced too late, as evidenced by her parting words.

I shouldn't have asked if your dad was proud you followed in his footsteps. I should have told you I'm sure he is.

Words that still echo in my head.

I don't talk about my dad much. Not with friends, and definitely not with women. It's a painful part of my life that the finality of death ensured will never be fully healed.

I told her, though, for reasons I'm worried have a lot to do with the fact that everything about Georgie captures me in a way not one of the coeds passing by accomplishes.

She's with a group of her friends, dressed in her favorite Nantucket sweatshirt and a pair of jean shorts. Nothing about her appears tense or uneasy, the way she often would seem when we'd drive out the White House gates or she'd attend an event with her parents. I was more removed from her, back in DC. There was a veritable army standing between her and harm. After that night in my apartment, we were never alone together again.

My phone buzzes in my pocket. I pull it out to see Colby's name displayed on the screen. Myles adjusts his posture. "Take it."

"It's fine. Just a friend."

"Only thing to keep an eye on is this blond guy. I can handle it."

I glance at the blond in question, not for the first time. He's in Georgie's sociology class. Jordan, I think his name is. They usually walk out together, while I trail behind like a lost puppy. Annoyingly, he seems like a nice guy. Which means my unfounded irritation toward him is likely rooted in emotions I'm steadfastly ignoring in the hopes they'll decide to disappear.

"Fine," I agree, seizing the opportunity to turn and walk away for a minute. Which is exactly what I do, answering the phone with a casual "Hey."

"What?" Colby gasps, dramatically. "He answered? Owen, he answered!"

"Want me to hang up?" I grumble.

Colby laughs. "Salisbury! What the fuck is up? You never pick up."

"I've been busy. You know how it is."

"Uh, no, I don't. That would require you telling me how it is."

I blow out a breath as I lean a shoulder against the rough bark of a palm. "It's fine—good, for the most part." I scuff a hole in the mulch covering the tree's roots, recalling exactly why I haven't been answering the phone lately—I don't know what to say.

I can't tell my friends—Colby especially, a fellow agent—that I'm having trouble adjusting because one look at Georgie scrambles my brain. She's a job, an assignment, an obligation. Maybe I'm making myself miserable to prove that point to myself. I haven't taken advantage of my rare days off. I work, sleep, work out, repeat.

Not all that different from my routine in DC, and that's depressing in its own way. I know plenty of other agents—Colby included—who don't let the job consume them the way I do. I told myself I'd ease off after finishing training. Then I got this assignment.

"Is it weird, being back in California?"

"A little," I respond.

"Have you gone to see your mom?"

"I haven't had more than one day off at a time," I answer.

True. But I also know if I asked, I could easily adjust my schedule long enough to make the six-hour trip to the small town in Southern California where I grew up. What's really holding me back is the argument I got in with my mom and brothers the last time I was home. They accused me of focusing too much on the job, telling me it isn't what my father would have wanted. That *he* was able to make the distinctions between life and work I appear incapable of. Coming off months of rigorous, exhausting training, it was the last thing I needed to hear. Now, it's mired in second-guessing. Wondering if this *is* what I should be doing, and where I should be doing it.

"Maybe they could come see you." Colby is close with his parents. My off-kilter family dynamic makes no sense, in his mind.

"Yeah. Maybe."

"You told them you're out there, right?"

"Of course." The lie slips off my tongue, easily and convincingly. "How are things there?"

"Oh, you know. Same old, same old."

"You still on the same fraud case?"

"Yeah, me and this guy Evan. You'd like him. We should all get a beer when you get back."

"Yeah, that sounds good."

I glance over one shoulder. Georgie is no longer near the fountain. She's standing next to Myles, watching me.

"I've got to go, Colby," I say, turning back toward the bench Myles and I were leaning against before Colby called.

"For real, or I've reached the limit of stories you'll listen to?"

I smile. I miss him. "Both."

"Whatever, dick. Pick up next time, okay? Or better yet, *you* call *me*. I miss you telling me to set my alarm and drink stuff besides beer."

"Common sense, you mean?"

"Not sure it's actually all that common."

I snort a laugh. "I miss you too. I'll call soon, okay?"

"Okay."

I hang up and walk back toward the reason I'm here.

"Ready to go?" I ask Georgie, while looking at Myles.

He's distracted, typing something on his phone. My internal thoughts might be a mess, but my external demeanor is put together. I'm good at maintaining a nonplussed exterior no matter what. I've also become excellent at interacting with Georgie without really engaging with her. Even now, as I wait for her to respond and Myles to get off his phone, I'm scanning the immediate vicinity with a trained eye, looking for anything or anyone that appears out of place.

"Yeah," she answers, and I allow myself a quick glance over. It's a mistake. We hold eye contact for too long, the din of commotion around us temporarily fading away and into the background.

"Kevin and Joey are back at Tremont," Myles tells me, slipping his phone back into his pocket.

Tremont is the apartment building where we all live. Located on Tremont Street, less than five minutes from Stanford's campus, it was selected months before I joined the team. Aside from its convenient location, it also has an underground garage and security codes on all the entrances. Each floor has five units, so we have a floor to ourselves. From a security standpoint, it's about the best you can do on a college campus. Much better than a dorm.

"Okay, let's go." I start walking right away. Georgie falls into step beside me, while Myles trails behind.

My stomach grumbles, rather loudly.

"We'll pass Chipotle," Georgie says.

"I'm fine." Georgie and her friends got Mexican food from the chain for lunch and ate it outside by the fountain while Myles and I watched. I haven't eaten since the bowl of cereal I wolfed down before her first class this morning.

"Whatever," she mutters.

We're about a hundred feet from the parking lot when she stops and looks around.

"What?" I ask, immediately tensing as I scan the vicinity as well.

"My sneaker is untied. I just need a bench or something to put my foot on…"

Her voice trails off as I bend down and untangle the laces. My thumb brushes her ankle, and I don't miss how goosebumps bloom across her skin. My mind jumps straight into the gutter. If she reacts like that to me tying her shoe, what would she do if I…

"Georgie?"

I finish knotting the shoelace and glance up—past a *long* stretch of tan leg—at the unfamiliar voice.

"Hey," Georgie replies.

"Aaron, remember? We have Psych together."

"Oh, right," Georgie responds, although I'd bet money she had no clue what this guy's name was before he told her just now. I size him up silently. Shaggy brown hair, cocky smile, tight shirt to make his muscles look bigger.

"Wanna head to the student center? I'll buy you a coffee."

I add *ballsy as fuck* to the mental list I already compiled about this guy. I'm standing right here. Georgie may know I'm her bodyguard and I'm certainly aware of it, but he has no clue.

"I'm headed home, but thanks. Maybe some other time."

I'm annoyed by her answer, but it's nothing in comparison to the irritation that flares when Aaron pushes. "Come on, gorgeous. It's just a coffee. I want to get to know you better."

"She said no," I snap, despite knowing I should stay out of it. He's not a physical threat.

Aaron looks at me for the first time, a sneer twisting what I guess most girls would consider handsome features. "Are you jealous, man? Word on campus is she's single."

"Are you deaf?" I retort. "She. Said. No."

Aaron looks at Georgie. "Sure you don't want to ditch this dick?"

My teeth grind as I glance at Georgie. She's not paying any attention to Aaron. She's staring at me, her mouth slightly agape.

Aaron takes her lack of response as wavering. He steps forward, closer to Georgie. My reflexes act before my brain can catch up. There's still a few feet of space between them. Enough for me to step into and act as a physical barrier.

"What the fuck?" Aaron growls. "Are you being serious right now?"

I blast him with my harshest glare. "Walk away, or you'll find out exactly how serious I am," I tell him.

He huffs but heeds my advice, turning and sauntering in the direction of the student center.

"Everything good?" Myles asks.

"Yeah. Fine."

He nods approvingly at me. "You handled that well."

"Thanks." I try to act like I reacted out of obligation, not raging jealousy.

Simultaneously, I'm waiting for Georgie's reaction, which I doubt will be grateful. Her voice is sugary sweet, when she speaks. "Don't sound surprised, Myles. Ethan is *excellent* at his job."

Myles raises one brow at me as Georgie keeps walking toward the parking lot. "Better you than me," he says, punching me in the shoulder before hurrying after her.

I know he's right. Georgie would have been harsher on Myles if he'd been the one cock-blocking. It's part of the silent agreement we somehow came to, where we interact with the other as little as possible. It's a lot of passive aggression and talking to other people while discussing each other.

I watch her walk away for a few seconds before I follow.

She's right; I *am* excellent at my job.

It doesn't include caring what she thinks or about what she wants.

My only job?

Is to *serve*.

CHAPTER TEN

GEORGIE

THE AIR OUTSIDE is cooler than the temperature was inside the lecture hall. There's a light breeze blowing across campus, tossing strands of my hair around. The purple that colored the ends all summer has fully faded. I miss it. I like who I am, most of the time. Coloring a couple inches of my hair didn't change my appearance at all, but it made me feel like a bolder version of myself. One who brushes up against boundaries but doesn't break them.

Unfortunately, I'm well aware of where the compulsion for rule-breaking is coming from. I love that I'm no longer in DC. Most of the time, I get to act like there's nothing unusual about my life at all. I go to class and attend parties and play tennis. If Agent Ethan Salisbury weren't here on campus, I'd be content.

But he is, and his presence rubs at me. Chafes like an irritation that refuses to go away. Every minute of every day when he's around—which is most of them—I have to think about what to say and how to act. Completely ignoring him isn't an option and neither is suggesting I'm trying to get his attention.

Pushing the limits is usually my best option. It's why I agreed to get a coffee with Jordan after class, despite the fact I know Ethan is waiting in the parking lot to drive me to the airport. Today was the last day of classes before the start of fall break. I'll be back in DC for five days. As excited as I am to see Lucy and the rest of my friends, I'd honestly rather stay here.

Jordan and I chat easily during the short walk from the lecture hall to the on-campus Starbucks. He's been a solid, reliable friend ever since we ended up in the same group during a class project the second week of school. And, based on some of the lingering stares I've caught and the way he's suggested we get coffee after every class since we met, I'm certain he's open to more than just friendship. He's kind and charming and handsome. But he doesn't have blond hair and blue eyes. My heart has never felt like it's beating so fast it might leap out of my chest around him.

A couple of people do double takes when I walk into the coffee shop, but that's the extent of any reaction to my entrance. There were some whispers and pointing during orientation. But most of the intrigue about my presence on campus seems to have worn off. It's a large campus and California is a long way from DC. I feel removed from the political circus here, in more ways than one. The only reminder I can't shake is the security that follows me around.

I keep waiting for my phone to buzz. Class let out a little early today as a pre-break treat, but the extra minutes are quickly ticking away. My absence will be noticed soon.

I order myself a latte, along with an iced coffee with a pump of hazelnut. Jordan opts for an Americano. Our drinks appear quickly. A hefty portion of the campus has already left for break, so the coffee shop is quieter than usual.

"Any exciting plans over break?" I ask, as we leave the coffee shop and walk along the main quad.

Jordan swallows a sip of his coffee and shrugs. "Not really.

Catch up with some high school buddies. See my dog. Sleep in a bed I'm not constantly worried I'll fall out of." I laugh. "You?"

"Nothing exciting either. I'll play tennis, hang out with friends, and answer a million questions from my parents."

"Your parents. Right." Jordan bobs his head. "The president and the first lady."

"They were my mom and dad first."

"Right. Yeah." He chuckles, a little awkwardly. It's an endearing sound, not the least bit suave or prepared. "It's just, uh,"

"I know, it's weird," I tell him. "For me too, honestly."

"Yeah, I'm sure. I always thought..."

I miss whatever Jordan has always thought. We've rounded the corner of the last building before the parking lot. I'm focused on Ethan, who I can see leaning against the side of the SUV. Arms crossed; expression thunderous. His eyes take me in with one thorough flick, gaze honing in on the two coffee cups I'm holding, evidence I didn't come straight here from class like I was explicitly told to do.

And there's something seriously wrong with me, because the sight of his angry expression sends happy thrills skittering through me. My heart races and my nerves tingle and anticipation builds.

Pissing Ethan off feels like foreplay, which is stupid for many reasons. I don't actually want to make his job more difficult. I don't want him to worry I've been abducted. I want him to show emotion though. I want to know he cares, even if it's just to the extent something happening to me will impact his pristine reputation.

Jordan notices I'm distracted. "Your bodyguard looks pissed," he says. There's a glimmer of nerves in his tone, like he's worried he might face some of Ethan's wrath.

I bite my bottom lip, hiding the grin that wants to appear in response to Jordan's spot-on observation. "He takes his job super seriously."

We reach Ethan. Jordan shifts beside me, visibly uncomfortable facing his scowl. It's understandable, yet it bothers me. I'm hoping he'll distract me from Ethan, and here he is, practically cowering.

Ethan makes other men look like boys.

"You're late."

I scoff, as my heartbeat quickens to rapid staccatos. Pull out my phone and glance at the time. "Two minutes."

"You went and got coffee." Annoyance drips from each syllable.

I don't confirm the obvious. I gulp some latte, then hold out his drink. "Here you go."

Ethan doesn't take it. He fixes me with a heavy stare, then uncrosses his arms and straightens, heading toward the driver's side. "Get in the car, Georgie."

I roll my eyes, simultaneously savoring how his commanding voice slides over me like a melting ice cube. A cold burn that lingers.

I glance at Jordan, who is watching Ethan climb into the SUV with a wide-eyed gaze. "Have a great break," I tell Jordan, giving him a quick side hug and somehow managing not to spill both coffees.

My stomach pitches and rolls as I step off the sidewalk and climb into the passenger seat. The waves of annoyance coming from the driver's seat feel familiar. The Ethan who told me he doesn't need to know anything about me is the one sitting next to me right now. He may not need to know anything about me, but he does, now. When I told him I needed a new chemistry notebook, he got the yellow without asking. Even the most dedicated of stalkers wouldn't have known my color coding system for each class.

I know him too. It's why the coffee I'm setting in the cupholder between us is one I know he'll end up drinking.

"Hurry up," Ethan says, tapping his fingers against the steering wheel impatiently as I set my coffee next to his and then reach for my seatbelt. "There's a storm warning from South Carolina to New Jersey. Airlines are delaying flights."

"Don't care," I mutter, buckling my seatbelt.

"You don't want to go home?"

"No."

"Because of that guy?" Ethan glances at Jordan, who's crossing the walkway that leads to the west parking lot.

There's an annoyed edge to his voice.

"Is that why you're mad? Not that I was *two minutes* late, but that I was with him?"

Ethan laughs. That's *it*; he just laughs.

And I bite down on my tongue—hard—so that I don't say something stupid. Don't admit I want him to care.

I'm starting to wonder if I misunderstood—imagined—the moment in his apartment, when he told me distance was easier. The physical distance between us isn't anything we can change. He can't guard me, miles away. But maybe I misinterpreted what he meant about emotional distance.

Since we've been at Stanford, Ethan has been distant and disciplined. I spend more time in close proximity with him than with any of the other agents here because he's younger and doesn't attract as much attention trailing behind me. Doesn't attract *questionable* attention, at least. No one is wondering if he's a Secret Service agent. They're too busy drooling over the golden skin and the muscles and the messy blond hair. None of which *I've* noticed, obviously.

We're halfway to the airport when Ethan reaches over and grabs the coffee cup out of the center console. I watch, out of the corner of my eye, as he lifts it to his mouth and sips. I quickly glance away, as his brows rise in surprise.

"This tastes like hazelnut."

"Weird," I reply, keeping my gaze focused on the highway median. Grass and trash. *Fascinating.*

"You got me hazelnut coffee?"

"Just to cover up the anthrax."

Ethan chuckles. I feel the vibrations tumble around in my chest. "You're trying to kill me?"

"I'd have to care, to try to kill you."

He says nothing to that. But I catch a flash of white, as his knuckles tighten on the wheel, before the rest of the drive is spent in silence.

The departures terminal is crowded. Ethan manages to smoothly slide between a taxi and a minivan to pull up alongside the curb. I unbuckle my seatbelt and climb out of the car without glancing over at Ethan. He reaches the trunk of the car at the same time I do, glancing back at the minivan that's close enough there's a chance the trunk will hit it.

"I'll hold it," I say.

His eyes cut to me, appearing surprised we're thinking the same thing. "Okay."

He waits until I lift it halfway, then ducks under to pull my two suitcases out and sets them on the sidewalk. I close the trunk and kick the curb. "Okay, well have a nice vacation. Nice break. Whatever."

Ethan smiles. "I'm not an Uber driver, Georgie. Come on. I'm taking you to your flight." He grabs the handle of my suitcase and heads for the automatic doors.

I hurry after him. "You might get towed."

"I'm not worried."

I scoff at that, but I doubt arguing will get me anywhere. If he wants to escort me through security, fine.

I stay close to Ethan, once we're inside the busy airport. He weaves through the crowd easily, passing currency exchanges and check-in stations without a second glance.

Then, suddenly, he stops.

"Fuck."

"What?" I ask, but Ethan isn't focused on me.

I glance over his shoulder, at the blinking *Arrivals* and *Departures* boards displayed above the line for security. Scan down the Departures list to the flight to DC. Instead of *On Time*, the status reads *Cancelled*.

"They cancelled the commercial flight flight to DC," Ethan says. "Which means..." He pulls out his phone, scrolls through something, and swears. I take it to mean I won't be going anywhere. That my private flight is cancelled as well.

"Bummer," I drone. "Let's go."

Ethan's annoyed expression turns my way. "*Let's go*? Go where?"

"Take me back to the apartment. Or better yet, I'll just take a cab."

"Georgie." Ethan almost sounds like he's going to laugh. "You seriously think I'm going to let you take a cab back to the apartment, and spend the next few days there, totally alone?"

"What do you mean, totally alone? Aren't the rest of the guys there?"

"They all flew to DC this morning. They should be landing..." He glances at one of the big clocks above the check-in counter. "Any minute."

"They're gone? It's just us?"

"Yeah. It's just us."

For some reason, it almost feels like that realization affects him as much as it's affecting me.

"And you're not staying here?" I ask. All I was told about the trip was the time of my private flight. Not who would be traveling with me. I figured Ethan was just dropping me off.

"No. I was going to go home."

"Oh."

Most logistical decisions are made without my input. I've ceded control because I've had no choice but to. Where I go and how I get there is rarely entirely up to me. I knew the planning for my fall break was extensive. Heard tidbits of conversations. But I had no idea Myles, Kevin, and Joey were leaving before me. No idea Ethan wasn't planning to leave California at all. Thanks to my snooping, I know he's from a small town called Glenson. I looked it up once and learned it's just south of Los Angeles. Not a long drive from here, but not a short one either.

"You can leave me at a hotel," I say, quietly. "I swear I'll stay there. I'll take a cab here in the morning, the storm will have blown over, and I can fly back to DC then."

He scoffs at the suggestion. "You don't even want to go to DC."

"I don't," I reply honestly. "But I want you to go home."

My answer surprises him. His brow creases, before his neutral expression returns. "I can't leave you here, Georgie." I open my mouth, to argue. Ethan continues before I can say a word. "I know you can take care of yourself. But you're *my* responsibility. If anything happened to you, I'd never forgive myself."

"Take me with you, then."

Again, I've surprised him. "Take you with me?" Ethan scoffs. "That's not in my fucking job description."

I stiffen. "Fine. I'm going to ask where the nearest hotel is."

"You're *not* staying here by yourself."

"What are you going to do, Ethan?" I taunt. "It's just you and me. Are you going to stop me if I walk away? In front of all these people? They'll think you're abducting me."

"Georgie, I swear to God—"

"You swear *what*?" I ask, stepping closer to him. "What are you going to do, Ethan?"

We hold eye contact, his blues bearing into mine with an intensity and a determination that floods my body with adrenaline. His eyes on me make me feel alive. I love playing tennis. Laughing until I cry. Hot coffee on a cold day. Falling asleep to the sound of rain.

But my absolute favorite thing in this world?

Pissing Ethan Salisbury off. Watching his stoicism falter and his gaze burn.

There's a lot of commotion around us. The storm must be affecting other flights because the customer service line is growing faster than the security one. People are bustling and shouting and hustling and lugging.

Ethan and I are standing and staring.

He looks away first, which is unexpected, reaching down and grabbing the bags he dropped when he saw the board's display. "Let's go."

I don't argue. Despite my posturing, we both know I'll end up doing whatever he decides.

He leads the way through the busy airport and back out to the curb. The black SUV is still there but the minivan behind it is gone. Ethan returns my suitcases to the trunk, then gestures for me to climb into the car.

I do, watching as he pulls his phone out of his pocket and raises it to his ear. As he talks and listens, occasionally running a hand through his hair.

After a couple of minutes, he hangs up and climbs into the driver's seat. "Put your seatbelt on."

"We live in a democracy, you know? You can't just order me around."

"Our democracy requires passengers wear a seatbelt in a moving vehicle. So put your fucking seatbelt on, Georgie."

"Who was on the phone?" I ask, as I click it into place.

After glancing over to confirm my seatbelt is on, Ethan pulls away from the curb. "My boss."

"I thought my dad was your boss."

"The president has a say in who protects himself and his family. He's not my boss."

"Fine. What did your *actual* boss say?"

Ethan doesn't answer my question. He asks, "You want to come?"

I assume he's talking about me traveling back home with him, so I don't clarify.

Because wherever he's going, that's where I want to be.

"Yes."

He holds my gaze, and we have another one of those breath-stealing, heart-pounding stareoffs. Ethan looks away first, again. Then he shifts the car into drive and pulls away from the curb.

"You're oh for two today," I tell him, focusing my gaze outside on the parking lots we're passing.

Ethan doesn't answer. He doesn't ask what I mean, either, telling me he knows exactly what I'm referring to.

"How long is the drive?" I ask, once we're on the highway.

"About six hours."

"Shit." I knew California was big, but I had no idea it was *that* big. You could drive through five states on the east coast in that same stretch of time.

"Second thoughts?" He glances at me, his expression giving no indication of whether he wants me to have them or not.

"No." I shake my head in case the word wasn't enough.

I'm worried he'll change his mind. He's spent months—ever since that night in Luke's pantry—acting cold and distant. Encouraging distance between us to every extent possible. Taking me to visit his hometown—and meet his family, I'm realizing—isn't going to allow for much, if any, of that space.

A prospect I'm excited by but I doubt Ethan is.

But he doesn't take the exit toward campus. He keeps driving, and I realize: this is really happening.

━━━

We hit bad traffic an hour into the trip. Usually, crawling along the highway at a slow speed would irritate me. But I'm content to lean back against the soft leather and look out the window. Glance into the windows of passing cars and come up with stories about the passengers.

Ethan can't say the same. He alternates between drumming impatiently on the steering wheel and rerouting the GPS, as if some new road without any slowdowns will magically appear.

By the time we pass the accident that caused the delay, we've traveled about five miles in ninety minutes.

"We're going to have to stop for the night soon," Ethan states, as he cruises off at an exit advertising gas. "I'll fill up the tank here, and that should get us the rest of the way in the morning."

I'm surprised. I figured Ethan would push through the night. It's almost ten—according to the navigation we'd arrive at our destination a little past two a.m. Not normal but not unreasonable. "I can drive, if you want."

"We're stopping for the night," he says.

I shrug, since I'm not opposed to the idea. The exact opposite actually. Me and Ethan in a hotel? I'm pretty sure he'll request one room, for security reasons. "And dinner?"

"Yeah, fine. And dinner."

He pulls up to a pump and climbs out. I watch in the mirror as he swipes a card and selects the fuel grade. Once the nozzle is inserted, he takes his phone out of his pocket.

A few seconds later, I hear his conversation, starting with "Hey, Mom."

There's a pause, while his mother must be talking, before Ethan speaks again. I only catch snippets interrupted by long breaks on his end. "Stop for the night." "Sometime tomorrow." "Bad traffic."

I'm hardly listening anymore. Not until I hear him say, "I'm not coming alone." The pause following that sentence is longer than all the others combined. When Ethan finally speaks again, he says, "No, Mom. It has nothing to do with Stella. I told you I'm not seeing anyone. I've been here on assignment. It—I—it's work, okay?"

The silence is short this time. So is Ethan's tone when he snaps "Yes, you made that clear. I didn't have a choice, okay? Her flight was cancelled."

Ethan sighs. "You don't have to—Yeah. Okay. Fine. You too." He hangs up and finishes filling up the tank. I pull my own phone out, scrolling mindlessly through social media as I wait for him to climb back into the car.

He opens my door, not his, startling me. "If you want food, come on inside."

CHAPTER ELEVEN

ETHAN

THERE'S a good chance I've set a new record for stupidity today.

In the span of a few hours, the next several days have gone from clear and unconcerning to complete and utter chaos. The storm currently barraging the eastern coast of the United States has also done a number on the state of my sanity.

Myles, Kevin, and Joe boarded a flight back to DC this morning. I was supposed to wait for Georgie to finish her last class, get her safely on a flight headed east where an army of agents would be waiting when she landed in Reagan, and have the better part of a week with no responsibilities. Sleep in my own bed, see the friends who still live in Glenson, and fix the front door hinge my mom has been complaining about.

Instead, I'm perusing the snack food aisle of a 7-Eleven, trying to scrounge up something with nutritional value that could double as dinner.

"What do you think?" I glance to the right. Georgie is holding up a *California Dreamin'* t-shirt that's about three sizes too large for her. "I need pajamas," she adds, as if that's a complete explanation.

"You didn't pack pajamas?"

"No. I have plenty at home," Georgie replies.

Probably true. But there's a pink tint to her cheeks that makes me think she *did* pack pajamas, they just aren't the sort she wants to wear in front of me. And fuck if that doesn't make focusing on junk food difficult.

"There aren't many options." I nod toward the hanging snacks.

"I said I would drive. We can keep going to a different town, at least."

I shake my head. I don't trust myself to drive at this hour. Last night was spent tossing and turning. I'm dreading this trip, as much as I'm looking forward to it. There's no way I'll let her drive, while I nap. "We'll leave first thing."

"Fine." Georgie exhales. "I want these."

She reaches past me and grabs a bag of Cool Ranch Doritos off the rack. "That's it?" I ask.

"No. Give me a minute to peruse the nutritional, filling options." Georgie stares at the limited selection with an exaggerated look of concentration. "Oh, wait…"

I roll my eyes. "Fine. We can go to a McDonald's or something."

"Really?" She perks up immediately.

"Yep. Give me your shirt."

"I can buy it."

"I have a job. You don't. Give me the shirt, Georgie."

"Well, as you like to remind me, that job has a specific description that doesn't include shit like this." She waves a hand around, gesturing at the fluorescent lighting and the dirty linoleum. But I think she's talking about us. About how it kind of feels like we're a couple, whenever it's just the two of us.

"Give me the shirt, or we're leaving, and you'll be stuck wearing whatever you brought."

She sighs but holds it out. I grab it and head for the register.

Whatever small town we've ended up in only has one option for lodgings. After devouring two McDonalds cheeseburgers—Georgie had two as well, which I was impressed by—we ended up here.

I park in the lot and turn the engine off. "I'll go get a room. You stay here, got it?"

The last thing this trip needs is word getting out the president's daughter is staying at the Laughing Oak Motel. This absolutely seems like the sort of town that has a phone tree.

"Just one room?" she asks. Her tone is neutral, not giving me any indication of how she feels about it.

Hell, I don't know how I feel about it. But… "I can't risk it, Georgie. If—"

"It's fine, Ethan." She crosses her arms and leans her head against the window. "I'll stay here."

I hesitate, because it feels like there's something else I should say here. And that's exactly what propels me out of the car and into the tiny office tucked in one corner of the motel. I pay for a room with two queen beds and then head back outside.

Georgie climbs out of the car when she sees me approaching. She pulled her hair up into a messy knot, but loose strands are already falling, framing her face. It's all brown again, no trace of purple remaining.

Streetlamps cast a golden glow over the lot that's close to empty. No cars are whizzing by. The only sound is the hum of electricity and the buzz of insects swarming the lights above.

I grab our bags from the trunk and lock the car before heading for the stairs. Silently, Georgie follows. The night breeze is cool and refreshing. No recycled air or greasy food. A light gust of wind ruffles my hair as I reach the second floor and walk past the first few doors. Our room is about halfway down.

I'm trying not to focus on the *our*. But it becomes a reality, as the door swings open and Georgie steps inside. Even more when it slams shut behind me, closing us in.

The room is neat and tidy, smelling faintly of chemical cleaner. Both beds are made with light green bedspreads. There's a small table with two chairs in one corner, facing the television. A half-open door leads to the bathroom. I can just make out the outline of a sink through the small opening.

I set our bags on the table and stretch. My back and shoulders ache from keeping the same position for hours, hunched over the steering wheel.

"I'm going to shower," Georgie says, then disappears into the bathroom with her bag.

I take the opportunity to sift through mine, pulling out a change of clothes. I lay out a pair of sweatpants on the bed, then decide to put on a pair of basketball shorts and a t-shirt instead. We're still a few hours from the southern part of the state, but the shift in climate is already noticeable. Even this late in the day, the air is warmer here than it's been at Stanford.

Once I've changed, I take a seat in one of the chairs and turn on the television. The local news is featuring a depressing special on forest fires.

I pretend it's the most interesting thing I've ever watched when Georgie walks out of the bathroom with a cloud of steam close behind.

Whatever she packed for pajamas, they must be bad, if she opted for this instead. Because the shirt she's wearing isn't hiding much of anything. It skims the top of her thighs, high enough I can see the shadow of her ass.

Fuck my life. Seriously.

Georgie strolls over to the bed where she left her bag. She rifles through it for a minute, extracting her phone and scrolling lazily while I pretend to still be watching the boring-ass documentary.

After a few minutes, she sighs. Loudly enough it's obvious I'm meant to react to the sound. I glance over, eyebrow arched. Trying not to focus on any part of her appearance at all.

"My dad wants me to call him," she tells me.

I scan the room, trying to come up with a secure solution that will allow her some privacy. Options are limited.

Surprising me, Georgie says, "Don't worry about it," then taps something on her phone. A few seconds later I hear her say, "Hi, Dad."

I try to focus on the documentary, eventually flipping channels in an attempt to find something more engaging to watch. But I don't turn the volume up, not wanting to interrupt Georgie's call, so it's difficult to get absorbed in anything.

Georgie doesn't say much. President Adams seems to be the one doing most of the talking. She calls me Agent Salisbury instead of Ethan, saying things are fine and it was a long flight home for less than a week, anyway.

The conversation ends abruptly. Georgie tosses her phone on the bed. Pulls her hair up in a ponytail. Stands and says, "I want to go outside."

I don't really think before saying "Okay." Not until she heads for the door. "You can't go out, like that."

I'm expecting—hoping—she'll pull the jeans she was wearing earlier back on. Instead, she grabs the pair of sweatpants I decided would be too warm and strides out the door before I can say another word.

I follow her because I don't know what else to do. Because I can't enforce any of the distance between us when it's just me and her out in the middle of nowhere.

She's sitting on the top of the stairs that lead from the parking lot to the second level of rooms, her chin propped on her knees. I sink down beside her, staring at the bugs swarming around the nearest streetlight and letting her pretend I'm not even here.

We sit in silence for a couple of minutes before she speaks. "He's running again." Georgie sighs. "He said he was leaning against it. That it took a lot out of him before and he wasn't sure if he wanted to put himself—put us—through it again. But he is. And he'll have the incumbent advantage this time. Meaning he'll probably win again, and I'll be pulled along on this circus for another four fucking years."

She sits up, then slouches. Runs a hand across her face and through her hair. Plays with the hem of her teal t-shirt.

"I know how selfish that sounds. How important his job is and all the special opportunities it gives me that other people would love to have. But I'm sick of it. All of it. I never asked for it. I never had a say. And for the rest of my life, it's all people will associate with me."

"You're wrong," I tell her.

She lets out another sigh, laced with an edge of annoyance. "Yeah. You can spare me the *For the people, holier than thou* speech, thanks. I've heard it all before."

"I know you have. That's not what I'm trying to say."

Georgie rests her elbows on her knees, turning her head so she's looking at me instead of the parking lot. Most of her hair has fallen out of the messy ponytail, the strands backlit by the yellow glow of the parking lot lights.

It feels like I'm seeing her for the first time. There's a surreal collision of knowing too much and too little, all at once.

"What are you trying to say?"

"You've gotten this far. You're tough. You can handle it."

She rolls her eyes. "Great pep talk, Ethan. I'll try to get that through my *pretty little head*, along with the fact it's your way or nothing."

"You're not pretty." The words are out before I've thought them through. Before I've considered how they'll sound.

"Way to kick a girl when she's down, Ethan." Georgie scoffs.

I can't leave things like that, so I continue. "You're more than pretty. Like sunshine. It hurts to look at you."

I'm not sure if she grasps what I'm really saying. That it hurts *me* to look at her. That she makes me want things I shouldn't— desires that jeopardize what I've worked hard to achieve.

"Because I called you a cloud?"

Without meaning to, my mouth tips up into a smile. I'd forgotten about her *human raincloud* comment. "Not exactly." I'm definitely not trying to tell her we belong together. In the sky, or anywhere else. I clear my throat. "It, uh, it might be a little awkward with my family."

"Why? Were they John Jackson supporters?"

I laugh. John Jackson was her father's opponent in the last presidential election. "No. Nothing related to politics. I just... Last time I was home, I didn't leave on the best of terms."

"Meaning what?"

"I had an argument with my mom, my brothers. We've talked since, but it's still touchy."

"Is that why you didn't tell them you've been at Stanford?"

I raise a brow. She shrugs. "I eavesdropped earlier."

I blow out a breath that turns into a laugh. "Yeah, I figured."

"Who's Stella?"

"My ex."

She nods, obviously expecting that answer. "Were you together for very long?"

"Eh...we were an on and off thing. We got together toward the end of high school. Broke up before college. Reconnected. Split up. I got sick of it. We wanted different things. So... I ended it."

"*You* ended it?" Georgie sounds surprised.

"Yeah, why?"

"It doesn't seem like you. You seem so loyal."

"Loyalty has its limits," I reply.

"Does it? You signed up for a job that requires an immense amount of sacrifice. Putting yourself in harm's way to protect a stranger. If that's not loyalty, what is it?"

"Patriotism, I guess. I'm guarding an institution, not a person."

"Is that how you see me?"

"No. I see you as a person. That's most of the problem."

Georgie sucks in a long, deep breath. "I lie a lot."

"To me?"

"Not necessarily. Just in general."

"Uh, okay." I'm struggling to see where this is going. Although, I should probably just be glad she didn't ask what problem I was referring to. Seeing as it starts with agreeing to this trip and ends with how I like seeing her wearing my clothes way too much.

"I like you."

I blink at her. "Uh, thanks? Considering where we started, that seems like a positive trend."

Georgie rolls her eyes. "I find you annoying and overbearing, most of the time. But I also *like* you." Her voice lowers, to a deeper whisper that sounds more meaningful. A tone reserved for secrets. "I lied before, after you showed up at that party. I *do* want to fuck you."

This is the one moment where I can honestly say all my training was for nothing. If some emergency took place right now, I'm not sure I'd react. I'm stunned silent and frozen. I've never been caught off guard more than I am this exact minute.

It's not so much what she's saying that's shocking—it's that she's *saying it*. Georgie and I have been balanced on a knife's edge. One where looks linger and words weigh a lot. A push and pull that never pushes too far or pulls too hard.

Attraction is a complicated formula. There are logical, obvious components to it. Appearance and personality and timing.

Georgie is gorgeous—in an oversize t-shirt, men's sweatpants, with damp, tangled hair. She's smart and sassy. But there's also this *feeling* I get when I'm around her, that I can't quantify. It's dizzy and exciting and thrilling and concerning. Mostly, it's addicting. There's a pull to be around her and absorb whatever it is.

"It's never going to happen, Georgie," I tell her.

She surprises me again, with a simple "I know." Then laughs at whatever expression I'm wearing. I've cycled through so many emotions this conversation, who knows. "Because of duty and patriotism and democracy and service and all the other lofty ideals you love to wax poetic about."

"I don't—"

"You *chose* this, Ethan. I didn't. That's all I'm trying to say."

"That's not *all* you said, though."

"I was being honest."

"Yeah." And that's the kicker. Georgie likes the shock factor. I wouldn't put it past her to say something outlandish, just to catch me off guard and see how I react. But she didn't say *I want to fuck you* like a taunt or a game. She said it matter of fact, like a statement you make that's so obvious it didn't really need to be said.

I know there's attraction between us. I felt it in that tiny pantry, and I've felt it many times since. I expected it to disappear, as she settled in at Stanford and could experience more freedom.

But it hasn't.

Awareness pulses between us like a live presence, persistent and impossible to ignore. Amplified by her proximity, by the shared room just down the hall, by the fact we're completely alone.

"You should be flattered."

I smile. It's such a Georgie thing to say. And I *would be* flattered, if it was some innocent, schoolgirl crush. If there were a wider age gap between us, one that would label a romantic relationship impossible. If *I* didn't want to fuck *her*.

That's what it comes down to really.

I like Georgie Adams.

And despite what I just told her—that she's more than just the president's daughter, that her life won't be defined by his legacy —when it comes to me, that's the only consideration. I see her as her own person. That doesn't change the fact the only reason I'm sitting next to her, the only reason I ever met her, is because she's currently first daughter of the United States.

That's a boundary I can't blur. A line I can't cross. Not only would it risk my career and my reputation, but it would go against everything I admire and respect about this position. The duty toward and the respect for the country I swore to protect. To preserve. To serve.

Making conversation is one thing. We spend a lot of time together. It's not all awkward silences and forced small talk.

But an inside joke or a shared laugh is very different from the sort of things I've imagined involving Georgie. Naked, sweaty things.

A door slams downstairs. An owl hoots in the distance. And I watch Georgie stare out at the parking lot, trying to guess what she's thinking. If I should respond to her comment or let the subject drop.

She looks over, lips twisting wryly when she catches me staring at her. "Are you mad?"

"No."

"Don't worry. I'll get over it."

"I'm not worried."

I am. I'm realizing I'll have a front-row seat to her *getting over it—over* me. And fuck if it isn't a prospect that pisses me off to a concerning degree.

"Okay. Good. I'm going to bed." She gifts me a rare, genuine smile, then stands, so all I can see are long legs wearing my sweatpants. "Night."

"Night," I echo.

As soon as I hear her footsteps fade away I lean back on my palms and stare up at the sky, glaring at the stars like they've personally wronged me.

I lied before, after you showed up at that party. I do *want to fuck you.* Those words, in a sweet, innocent voice, are a direct juxtaposition to the images they conjure. I can picture it so clearly, pretend we're a possibility.

I try to figure out how I got here, staring up at a sky full of stars with the girl I can't get out of my head staying in a room I'll share with her. The tropical storm named Berta is to blame for the lack of physical distance. But I can't pinpoint a moment when things changed between us. When I stopped seeing her as spoiled and started seeing her as special.

Usually, in relationships, there's a moment. I recall the

conversation during training when I realized Colby and I would become good friends. Stella asked me to junior prom, and then we started dating.

With Georgie, it's like I tripped without realizing. Was already in motion before I saw where I was headed. I can deny it to myself—more importantly, to *her*—but it doesn't change my emotions.

It feels like no matter how hard I try to push her away, we end up closer than ever.

And that scares the shit out of me.

Because not only am I about to spend several days with no option for distance, it's getting harder and harder to convince myself that's what I really want.

CHAPTER TWELVE

GEORGIE

THE BEATLES HAVE their own radio station.

"Hey Jude" was playing when we left the motel. I thought it was a coincidence, until it was followed by "Here Comes the Sun." Then, "Yellow Submarine" began to play.

Ethan put on a Beatles station. And I'd be lying if I said that didn't mess with my head, after last night. I'm not entirely sure what compelled me to tell him he's my favorite fantasy in fewer words.

Yes, he's hot. And yes, he's completely off-limits. The guy tasked with ensuring no one abducts you isn't usually the happy-ever-after one. He's prime fantasy material, and I spent a while telling myself that's *all* he is. But I'm sick of lying to myself— and Ethan, apparently—about the truth.

Last night, after talking with my dad, I needed a distraction. My dad called me in the middle of the night because it's the only time he could spare. Another four years in office won't just affect me; they'll affect my relationship with him. And at some point, I added Ethan to the list of resentments I have, the ways the presidency has constricted me.

Maybe the reasons I said something don't matter. The truth is, I'm insanely attracted to the guy, and not just because of his looks. I know Ethan's moral epicenter won't stray from proper agent etiquette, which definitely won't include fucking him out of my system. So that left telling him I *want to* and hoping his disregard will be enough to get him out of my head. Because truthfully, every guy I've met at Stanford has been compared to Ethan. It's easy to do when he's usually standing a few feet away. And when you compare two people, there's always a winner.

Ethan has yet to lose.

As humiliating as it would have been, part of me was hoping he'd laugh in my face last night. Do *something* that would solve the perennial problem where he's involved.

He said nothing would happen, sure. But he said it like he was imagining *something* happening, and the visual wasn't unpleasant.

And now we're listening to "Strawberry Fields Forever" because he remembered details from a conversation we had nearly three months ago.

So, yeah, problem *not solved*.

The drive is scenic, so I focus on that. Despite the turmoil in my head, it doesn't feel like there's any tension between us. There's an ease between me and Ethan, even when there's a lot left unsaid.

Nothing *is* said, until Ethan turns off the highway, telling me we're close without glancing at the navigational display.

He sighs. "Okay, let's get this out of the way, before we arrive."

I readjust, crossing my legs and looking away from the window, so I'm facing him instead. "Get what out of the way?"

"Well, to start off, you should know that I've never brought a girl home. Now I've told my mom and the rest of my family this is *work*, but they'll inevitably try to make a *thing* about it."

"Could you elaborate what you mean by *thing*?" I ask, innocently.

Ethan gives me his patented look. The *no way* expression I'm quite familiar with. "No."

"Then I'm not sure I'll know what to expect."

It's difficult to tell, since he's keeping his gaze on the road like the responsible guy that he is, but I think Ethan rolls his eyes.

"It's not that big of a house," he tells me. Almost abruptly. But it's the trace of embarrassment—of self-consciousness—that makes me realize what he's trying to say with that statement.

"*Wow*. You really don't think much of me, huh?"

"I just know what you're used to."

"The one-bedroom apartment next to yours?"

"You know what I mean."

I do, and it brings back memories of him telling me he thinks I'm spoiled. "Will we have to share a bed?" I ask.

"No." Ethan mutters something else beneath his breath before flicking on a blinker and taking a left.

The street we turned down is tree-lined and residential. Modest, two-story homes are on both sides of the road. Ethan pulls into the driveway next to a blue house with a yellow front door.

I study the neatly trimmed lawn and the marigolds planted by the front door. Gasp. "This is where we're staying? Quick, let me call up the closest Four Seasons."

He rolls his eyes as he turns off the car. "I get it. You were expecting my house to be small."

"I didn't *expect* it to be anything, Ethan. You should try it sometime." I look at the house again. "It actually reminds me of the house I grew up in."

"In Boston?"

"Just outside of it, but yeah."

He nods. "Come on."

Ethan opens his door and climbs outside the car. Warm air rushes in, tinged with a hint of salt. The Pacific was visible for part of the drive this morning. I focused on the sparkling, turquoise water for most of the trip, rather the silence inside the car. Unfortunately, the color just reminded me of Ethan's eyes.

The fact that's all I could focus on is proof my emotions are still all over the place. I'm disappointed my father is running again—I thought there was a good chance he wouldn't. I didn't expect for my parents to base their decisions on me. I know it's selfish, to think my father shouldn't run because of how it will affect me.

My disappointment last night also stemmed from the realization the announcement is why my father wanted me to come home. Originally, I'd asked to stay on campus for fall break. My father requested I return to DC, and now I know the real reason why—because he's gearing up to announce he's running for reelection. His campaign manager wanted me there to talk strategy. Plan appearances.

It's ironic, how I turned to a part of the problem for comfort. Ethan was there—he was the only one there. And the only reason he *was* there is because my father is the president. But what's concerning is knowing that even if I'd been surrounded by friends after that call, I still would have looked to him.

I climb out of the SUV, stretching after the long car ride. The trip here from the motel took four hours.

Ethan already has the trunk open. He's sifting through the bags piled in the back. Through *my* bags, specifically.

"You need *all these*?" he asks.

"I can carry my own stuff," I say, stepping forward. "And there's *two*. Stop making it sound like I packed ten."

He blocks me from reaching the back. "That's not what I asked."

"I packed for DC. I'll have to go through it, to figure out what I'll need here."

A sigh, followed by, "Fine."

Ethan starts pulling everything out of the trunk, stacking the suitcases neatly on the pavement.

"I'll do it." I step closer, trying to reach past him.

"Just leave it, Georgie." He turns, and just like that, we're pressed together, with hardly any space between us.

I suck in a sharp breath in response to the proximity. Ethan stills.

We're frozen, staring at each other.

"I wish you'd lied," he tells me. Abrupt and sudden, like a thing you can't help but say.

Maybe I'm projecting, since that's exactly what *I* did, last night.

"So, we're *not* pretending last night didn't happen?"

He shakes his head, annoyed like I'm being glib. In reality, I'm really asking. Because I thought we were—pretending.

"You're here!"

Ethan steps away as soon as the exclamation reaches us, grabbing the last bag and shutting the trunk with a slam. A middle-aged woman is descending the porch steps, her smile as bright and sunny as the happy marigolds dancing in the breeze.

"Hi, Mom," Ethan says.

He gives her a hug that lingers. When Ethan tries to pull away, his mother's arms just tighten. She doesn't let go for a solid minute. Once she does, it's to look him up and down. "You look tired."

Ethan rolls his eyes. "I'm fine, Mom."

"You should get more sleep, honey."

"Yeah, yeah, I'll work on it." He glances at me. "Mom, this is Georgie. Georgie, this is my mom, Laura."

Laura runs both hands down the front of her pink blouse, smoothing the cotton material. "It's very nice to meet you, Georgie."

She tucks her hair behind one ear. There's no sign of the relief she greeted her son with. Just nerves. It's obvious she has no idea what to make of me, and I don't blame her. It also makes me feel extra guilty, for asking Ethan to bring me here and essentially crashing his family reunion.

Her nerves are contagious. I'm combating anxiety I've never experienced before, meeting someone's parents. Meeting world leaders or celebrities. "It's really nice to meet you, Mrs. Salisbury."

I'm not sure what else to say.

Ethan's mother smiles. "Call me Laura, please. Come on inside."

I follow her hesitantly, up the stairs and onto the porch. Ethan follows, carrying the luggage like it weighs nothing. The welcome mat is a cheery blue color with sunflowers on it. There's a swing to the left and a stack of firewood to the right.

Laura notices me looking at the logs. "We have a fire pit, out back."

"Oh. Nice."

She smiles before opening the front door and gesturing for me to walk inside. I step into a tiled entryway. A cool rush of air greets me as I pass a row of cubbies and glance around. The floor plan is open. I can see straight out to the backyard, which includes the first pit and a swing set. A long row of built-in bookshelves covers the wall to my right. There's a television set up across from the couch. The kitchen is furthest from me, including a large center island and lots of cabinets. A staircase leads upstairs.

But more than any of the details I absorb—the fluffy rug in the living room, the bowl of lemons on the kitchen counter, the pile of shoes by the door—I note how the house feels like a home. How it holds the unmistakable atmosphere of a place where you relax. Where you find comfort.

I don't feel that way about the White House.

Maybe I harp on too much about what I've lost and what my father's choices have cost. Maybe if I'd been younger—or older —when he was elected, I'd be able to focus on the opportunities instead of the limitations.

Instead, it feels like I'm losing independence at a time when I should be gaining it. I can't even wait for a delayed flight on my own. It's not Ethan's fault—he's following orders. But that bothers me too, now. That I have no idea how much—if any—of the time we've spent together is his choice. In some ways, he's even more constrained than I am. Being the First Daughter isn't my job.

"Want to show Georgie upstairs?" Laura asks Ethan. "I have a showing at one, unfortunately."

I glance at my phone. It's a quarter to already.

"I'm sorry to run off right away," Laura tells me, apologetically. "Ethan knows where everything is. I set some towels out in the guest room. It shouldn't be more than an hour; the property is only a few minutes away."

"It's no problem," I reply. "I've got...I've got some class reading to catch up on."

Laura makes a face. "I used to hate when professors assigned work over breaks."

I smile. "Where did you go to school?"

"George Washington. It's where I met Eric."

"Oh," I say. Eric must be Ethan's father. Based on the one time Ethan mentioned his dad, I figured it might be a sensitive topic—one I definitely wasn't planning to bring up. But Laura's smile hasn't faltered.

"All right, I should get going." Laura grabs car keys from a bowl by the door. "See you two later."

"Bye," I say.

The front door opens and shuts. I glance at Ethan, who's piling our bags at the bottom of the stairs. "Your mom is a real estate agent?"

"Yep." He stacks the last one and straightens. "You seriously planning to spend your break catching up on reading?"

"If I'd gone to DC, I'd be meeting with Dad's campaign manager. Reading is an improvement over *that*, at least."

"You didn't go to DC though."

I give him a *duh* look. "Did you have something else in mind?"

"We could play."

"Tennis?" I can't think of anything else he'd be referring to.

Excitement flares when he nods. Ever since his friend mentioned Ethan turned down a tennis scholarship, I've been curious about him and the sport.

The last time I played tennis with or against a guy was probably back when I was in elementary school. Private lessons turned into tournaments. Tennis was a pursuit of curiosity, more than anything else. I wanted to see how far I could go with it. Now it just feels like part of my life.

"Yeah. Okay." I think my voice betrays my level of excitement at the prospect, but I don't really care. I mean, I told him I wanted to have sex with him last night, in cruder terms. It's not like I've played it cool on this trip so far. No need to start now.

"You sure? If you'd rather *read*, then…"

I shove his arm as I pass, and Ethan laughs. The sound—rich and deep—draws an involuntary smile on my lips. I grab my biggest suitcase and begin climbing the stairs. "Let me just change."

Steps sound behind me as Ethan follows me with the rest of the luggage. I hesitate when I reach the top of the stairs, glancing around. The hallway is lined with framed photos and kids' draw-ings, only interrupted by doorways. A striped rug runs the length of the hall.

"My mom's room is at the end. Bathroom. Your room. Mine." Ethan points to each door as he talks. My room is to the left, his is to the right.

"Okay. I'll meet you downstairs."

"Yeah. Sounds good."

"Nice Batman costume, by the way." I tap on the framed photograph of three kids dressed up for Halloween that's hanging right next to the doorframe. Ethan is unmistakable in it.

I catch his eye roll before I shut the door and survey the room where I'll be staying. It's simple—a four-poster bed takes up most of the floor space. There's also a dresser and two side tables on either side of the bed.

I unzip the suitcase and change out of the jeans and t-shirt I'm wearing, pulling on one of my cuter tennis outfits. After pulling my hair up into a ponytail, I open the door. My other bag is neatly stacked by the door. I drag it into my room and open it, since it's where I packed all my tennis equipment. Officially, the college season isn't until the spring. But I've had a few team meetings and scrimmages already. And I figured I'd make at least one trip to Hillside when I was back in DC, which required bringing my favorite racquet and other equipment with me.

All my equipment gets gathered up, and then I head downstairs. Ethan is in the kitchen, filling two water bottles. He's changed too, into a pair of mesh shorts and a Dri-fit shirt that puts his impressive musculature on full display. I watch him move around for a minute.

"How long has it been since you were last home?"

He doesn't startle at the sound of my voice, just continues pouring water. "I came back for a bit in the spring. So a little while." Ethan caps the bottles. "Ready?"

"Yeah." I tuck my racquet under one arm and take the water he offers me. "Thanks."

He grabs another racquet out of one of the cubbies and we head outside. Ethan pauses to lock the front door, and then we're walking down the street we drove down earlier.

Most of the houses look the same as his mom's. Not in a cookie-cutter development way, they're just all similar in size, shape, and appearance. Modest with large lots. Pops of person-ality come through in other ways. One house has three cherry-red Mini Coopers parked in front. Another hosts a collection of lawn jockeys. The last one before we reach the end of the block has a Slip 'N Slide on the front lawn.

"So, this is where you grew up?"

Ethan glances over at me. He hesitates before answering, and I'm not sure why. "Yeah."

"You didn't like it?"

"I liked it fine."

"But you left. Dartmouth, DC…"

He shrugs. "I wanted something different. Are you planning to move to DC, after you graduate?"

I shudder. "Definitely not. And that's *because* I don't like it. I'll always associate it with, well, you know."

"You don't always act like you hate it. You seemed to enjoy yourself at that pool party."

A light breeze blows, pulling some of my hair out of its ponytail. I don't bother to fix it. "We're discussing that too now, huh?"

"You're the one who wanted to be honest."

"You're the one who told me you wished I'd *lied*."

He exhales. "I don't know what the hell I'm doing, Georgie. This—" He half-laughs. "This wasn't covered in training."

"You *do know* what you're doing, Ethan. You said nothing would happen, and you were right."

I see the tennis courts up ahead, located next to a playground and a brick building that must be a school. We walk in silence toward the chain link that surrounds the two courts. They're relatively new, with sturdy netting and no cracks on the surface.

"Wanna rock, paper, scissors for first serve?" I ask when we reach the entrance. "Unless you have a coin."

Ethan looks at me—really looks at me—for the first time since we started walking. He reaches out and tucks a piece of loose hair behind my ear. My heart stutters. Skips. Stops. His touch disappears as quickly as it appeared, and his hand falls back to his side. But it lingers in other ways, warming my skin and heating my blood. "It's not because I don't want to, Georgie." He replies, ignoring my question.

He holds my gaze, letting me drown in those blue depths. Letting his meaning soak in.

It does, and then it *sinks*. Resting in my stomach like a lead anchor. It sits like a stalemate. Because no matter how he feels— no matter how I feel—it doesn't change anything else.

"I wish you'd lied," I tell him.

Ethan gives me a small, wry smile. "Yeah." He opens the gate and gestures for me to walk through. "You can serve first. I'll beat you anyway."

"*You* serve first," I retort. "That way when *I* win, you can't claim I had an unfair advantage."

He rolls his eyes before holding out a hand. "Fine. Rock, paper, scissors it is."

"Fine," I agree. "Ready?" Ethan nods, so I chant, "One, two, three."

We both form fists.

"Redo." Ethan is competitive. I knew he would be. He's not the sit-back-and-take-it-easy sort of guy when it comes to anything. But I think I underestimated just how competitive he really is. We're not even playing tennis yet, just a silly game of pure luck, and he's wearing a serious expression and tense shoulders.

Rather than shirk away from the intensity, I feel my own competitiveness flare.

Ethan counts this time. We both form scissors on "Three!"

He swears. I laugh.

"Okay. Again."

On the third try, Ethan forms another rock. I gamble with a flat hand, covering his fist once I see his choice.

"I could punch a hole through paper with a rock," he informs me.

"Those aren't the rules."

"I thought you weren't much of a rule-follower."

"Well, we both know *you* are," I reply.

He shakes his head with a small smile, before leaning down and grabbing several tennis balls from the basket. "People don't steal them?" I ask.

"It's a small town, Georgie. Come on."

I follow him out onto the court, staying in the closer end while he walks to the opposite side of the net.

His strides are confident. His expression focused.

I'm used to feeling unstoppable on the tennis court. I've benefitted from private lessons and professional training, but my advantage on the court has always been my drive. It's my place to channel any frustrations or anxiety.

Looking at Ethan's posture, I wonder if my usual intensity will be enough. He's seen me play before, and he still looks confident. I've never seen him on a court before. That's enough to make my confidence waver. I keep my expression neutral though, not letting him see any inner turmoil.

There's no umpire. No spectators. No ball boys or girls. Just me and him.

I stop behind the baseline, sticking one ball in my pocket and rolling the other in the palm of my hand as I prepare to serve. I scan the familiar layout of the court, the straight lines forming right angles, trying to decide exactly where to aim in the service box.

I bend my knees and roll my neck, hoping the stalling tactics might work as intimidation.

Ethan's grin is visible from here. "Serve or I will!" he calls out.

In addition to being competitive, he's also impatient. I release a deep breath, rise on my toes, toss a ball in the air, and then send it over the net with a strong flick of my wrist.

I'm expecting Ethan to return it. I'm not expecting the return to be a powerful backhand I have to sprint to reach. I send it back over the net. We continue to volley, until Ethan manages a hit just inside the baseline that nets him the first point of the game.

Ethan says nothing. There's no celebration. We're a ways off from the final point. From "game, set, match." Tennis is a grueling sport. A marathon, not a sprint.

I recite the rules I know by heart. Four points with at least a two-point advantage to win a game. A minimum of six games with at least a two-game advantage to win a set. A minimum of two sets in order to win the match.

We've barely begun. I have plenty of time to gain an advantage.

I never let opponents get in my head.

Unfortunately, Ethan is already there.

CHAPTER THIRTEEN

ETHAN

I TAP on Georgie's door.

Silence.

Another tap.

"Yeah?"

I smile at the sound of her groggy voice. I figured she fell asleep, when she never emerged from her room after heading up to shower following our tennis match. She got about as much sleep last night as I did—not much. I could hear her tossing and turning while I lay awake. Possibly thinking about the same things I was.

The door opens a few seconds later. Georgie stares at me for a minute, rubbing her eyes. "Shit. I fell asleep."

"Yeah, I figured that's what happened. You're too proud to hide away like a sore loser."

Georgie rolls her eyes. "Wow. A whole thirty seconds until you brought it up, huh?"

I smile. Honestly, I knew there was a good chance she'd beat me earlier. We tied at six sets apiece and had to play a tiebreak to determine a winner—me—meaning we stayed at the courts for close to three hours.

"Dinner's ready," I tell her.

Georgie runs a hand through her hair. She must have fallen asleep with it wet because it's falling in a myriad of different directions. "Should I change?"

I glance down at her tight yoga pants and loose Stanford t-shirt. "No. You look good." Immediately, I backtrack. "I mean, fine. You're fine. It's…dinner is casual." I mirror her motion, running a hand through my hair and praying I don't say anything else stupid.

This awkwardness, but mostly this awareness, is thanks to me. Because I had to open my mouth and tell Georgie I want to fuck her, too. And that's not all I want from her, if I'm being honest. But I didn't delve into specifics, and there's no way I'm going to. I simply wanted her to know that I…that things between us aren't one-sided. That the reasons I've kept my distance have nothing to do with her and everything to do with the situation.

I'm not convinced I shouldn't have kept my mouth shut. Telling her didn't change a thing, except for the energy between us. It crackles and sparks. It feels like possibilities. Ones I can't help but consider despite knowing I shouldn't entertain them.

"Okay," Georgie says, stepping into the hallway.

"My brother and his family are coming over," I tell her.

"Hudson or Parker?"

I'm mildly stunned she remembers my brothers' names. I mentioned them once, in passing, several months ago. "Hudson."

"He's older than you?"

"Yeah."

"And he has kids?"

"Twin boys. Babies, I guess. They're not even a year old."

We reach the bottom of the stairs. Hudson and his wife,

Celeste, have arrived. They're standing next to the kitchen island, talking to my mom. All three of them give me inquisitive, knowing expressions as we appear. I know my mom thinks there's something between me and Georgie. It was obvious in her expression when we returned earlier, sweaty and smiling. And it looks like she's passed her opinion on to my brother and sister-in-law.

"Hey, E." Hudson greets me with a wide smile, walking over to give me a hug and a slap on the back. "Good to see you, man."

"Yeah, you too."

Hudson releases me and I move on to give Celeste a hug as well. She and Hudson started dating in middle school. They went to their eighth-grade formal together and got married eight years later. She felt like part of the family long before my brother proposed.

Once I step back, I glance at Georgie, who's accepting a glass of wine from my mother. She raises her brows in a silent dare as she catches my eye, waiting to see how I'll react to the alcohol. I'm too busy deciding how to introduce her to Hudson and Celeste. It's obvious neither of them knows who she is, that my mother excluded some key details when she told them I hadn't returned alone. They both think she's here *with me*, and it's a dangerous misconception to let lie, after our conversations earlier and last night.

Mostly because it would be easy, way too easy, to slip out of roles and into a simpler acquaintance.

"You must be Georgie," Celeste says, following the direction of my gaze. "I'm Celeste. It's so nice to meet you."

"Nice to meet you—"

The front door slams. "Hello! I'm here!"

My younger brother Parker appears in the same way he does everything else—boisterous and frenzied.

"Shut up," Hudson scolds. "The boys are sleeping."

145

I was wondering where his kids were. It's not like they're old enough to be left at home yet. Hudson lives about thirty minutes away.

"Sorry," Parker replies, in a mock whisper. "I'm still their favorite uncle though, yeah? *Way* cooler than absent Ethan."

I roll my eyes. "Great to see you too, Parker."

"Aw, c'mon, I'm kidding. It's just—" He spots Georgie. "Holy. Shit."

"What?" Hudson glances around the kitchen, like a leak might have sprung or an animal may have snuck in.

"Holy shit," Parker repeats. "This is just, wow. How could you not have said anything?" He looks to our mother, who shrugs. She shared information selectively all around, it appears.

"Not said anything about what?" Hudson asks, exchanging a confused glance with Celeste. Parker has a flair for the dramatics, but this is extreme, even for him. His gaze lands on Georgie, and realization dawns. "Oh. C'mon, Parker. Don't make Georgie uncomfortable by teasing Ethan. Not after I had to sit through Christian's nephew's Christmas recital."

Parker flips Hudson off. "This has nothing to do with the Christmas concert."

"What does this have to do with, then?" Hudson still looks perplexed.

If I'd known Parker was coming, I would have prepared for this somehow. His boyfriend, Christian, works in politics. I could have predicted Parker would recognize Georgie as more than just the girl I brought home.

"Great question, Hud," Parker replies. "I'll give you two clues. One, our brother works for the Secret Service. Two, our current president has an eighteen-year-old daughter named *Georgette*. Any bells ringing yet?"

Hudson glances at Georgie, who I'm relieved to see looks

more amused than anything at my brother's antics. "Oh. Wow, okay."

Parker addresses Georgie for the first time, waving around the bouquet of flowers he brought as he talks. "Sorry. That was so rude of me. I just—You—Here. Wow. I'm just the biggest fan of your father's. The healthcare bill? And the gun legislation? I can't believe..." He laughs, awkwardly, and it's a rare moment when I see my younger brother embarrassed. "Sorry. You probably get so sick of people telling you that. It's just—you're about the last person I expected to see in my mom's kitchen."

"Her flight back to DC got cancelled," I explain, walking over to the fridge and grabbing a bottle of beer.

"Right. So, obviously, she's here in the kitchen."

I roll my eyes and look at Georgie, who's sipping wine through a wide smile. "Technically, I'm the head of her security detail." I say *technically* because most of the time Myles, Kevin, and Joey make it clear I'm the most junior agent. "So abandoning her at the terminal wasn't an option."

"Jesus fuck, Ethan. This is the sort of shit you could clue us in on. I tell all my friends you're the guy getting coffee for the guys who gets coffee for the president."

I snort as I twist the top off the beer. "Talk to Mom and Hudson. They're the one who opted out of updates."

"Ethan. That's not what we said," my mother chides. "I just thought—"

"We don't need to rehash things." I interrupt, because it's not a topic I feel like discussing—especially in front of Georgie. "Mom, you said there are burgers to grill, right?"

"Yes. They're in the fridge," she replies.

I nod, walking over and rooting through the contents.

"I feel silly for not recognizing you," I hear Celeste say to Georgie. "I actually follow politics pretty closely."

"Don't feel silly," Georgie replies. "It's actually kind of nice, when people don't recognize me."

"I'm sure." Celeste's tone is sympathetic. "It must be difficult, to be known for something you have no control over."

"It has its ups and downs," Georgie replies, diplomatically. Despite her disdain for politics, she's a natural at it.

"I just assumed you were here with Ethan. He isn't, well he's never brought a girl home."

Celeste's tone is conspiratorial. She's trying to put Georgie at ease by gossiping about me, apparently. Normally, I'd be annoyed. But since my level of professionalism appears to slip a little more every day, I listen closely to Georgie's response instead. "I definitely don't qualify. I'm just here because Ethan is dedicated to his job."

For some reason, her answer grates. She's wrong—that's not why she's here. She's here because I want her to be. Because I decided to force some proximity between us, to test myself and prove I'm under complete control. So far, I'm failing spec-tacularly.

My mom ushers everyone out onto the back patio, where she's already set out a salad and fries on the long, farmhouse-style table. My mom and Celeste ask Georgie about Stanford, while Hudson and I argue over the grill in what is a regular disagree-ment about burger distribution and heat settings. Parker is sitting and listening in silence—a rare occurrence—still looking shocked by Georgie's presence.

Parker regains the ability to speak as we all sit down to eat the overdone burgers. I make an elaborate crunching noise as I bite into mine, and Hudson flips me off when our mother isn't look-ing. He won on the heat settings, and the meat suffered.

"How's work going, honey?" my mom asks my younger brother.

"Must be slow, if he had time to drive all the way down here," I mutter. Parker lives in LA, which is an hour drive, sometimes more, if there's bad traffic.

Someone—probably Mom—kicks me under the table.

"It's great," Parker replies. "*Super* busy." He looks at me pointedly.

"And how's Christian?"

"He's good. Bummed he couldn't come, but work has been even more hectic for him. He's working on Rita Gonzales's campaign now."

Parker looks at Georgie, waiting for her to react. Georgie looks lost, telling me she has no idea who that is. "She's running for mayor, in LA," I say.

"Oh. That's cool," Georgie replies, making a valiant effort to appear interested.

"It's no big deal, compared to the national stage, obviously, but Christian is excited," Parker states.

"He's a campaign manager?"

"Sort of," Parker responds. "It's mostly an all hands on deck situation, based on what Christian has told me."

Georgie nods. "Well, kudos to him. Campaigns are the worst. I can't stand my dad's."

"Robert Alderman is known for being intense."

I'm surprised Parker knows President Adams's campaign manager by name. It must be Christian's influence.

Georgie smiles. "Yeah, he is."

"Do you spend much time with him?"

"It depends. I did when my dad was considering running. My mom and I went through media training with him. How to walk, when to smile, what to say. Now that my dad is running again, I'll probably see more of him." She glances at me. "Ethan has met him."

149

"You have?" Parker's eyes widen as they meet mine.

I nod. "Yeah."

"Jeez, Ethan. Next time we talk you could spend a little less time talking about the Capitals' season and a little more on all the important people you meet."

Georgie doesn't even attempt to muffle her laugh. "The hockey season just started," I reply. "And I haven't mentioned the Capitals once the past few times we talked."

"You didn't mention lots of things, it turns out."

Georgie shifts beside me. At first, I think she's hearing the same edge to Parker's voice—hurt—that I am. Then, I see her pull out her phone and that *Dad* is flashing across the screen. "He keeps calling," she whispers to me.

"Take it."

She stands, flashing an apologetic smile. "Sorry, everyone. I'll be right back."

I watch as she walks away, toward the old playset in the far corner of the yard. I expected my mom to get rid of it after Parker started high school. But it stayed and will probably still be intact when Hudson's kids are old enough to play on it.

As soon as Georgie is out of earshot, I look to Parker. "Can you cool it with the political talk, man? Georgie didn't run for office. She's a college student."

"Sorry if I was a little shell-shocked to find the fucking *First Daughter of the United States* in our fucking *kitchen*, Ethan."

"I had no idea you were coming," I tell him. "If I had, I would have said something."

"You should have said something no matter what. How long have you been the head of her security detail?"

"A couple of months," I admit.

Parker whistles. "Wow. It's a big deal, right? I mean, she's his daughter. His only kid."

"It's mostly scaring off horny frat boys," I say. "Nothing all that exciting."

"Well, there are probably lots to scare off. I don't even swing that way, but damn."

My gay brother admiring Georgie's looks pisses me off. "Watch it," I tell him.

Parker rolls his eyes. "Man, you take your job *way* too seriously."

I open my mouth to reply, although I'm not sure what to say. Truthfully, it's for the best that's the conclusion he came to. Before I can say a word, I hear Georgie.

"Ethan?" I glance over, to see her approaching the table, arm outstretched. "He, uh, he wants to talk to you."

Nerves swarm my stomach. I haven't talked to President Adams since we left DC. He attended most of the meetings planning Georgie's college detail, but the only time we've spoken one-on-one was the first meeting in his office, when he asked me to join Georgie's security. Kevin is the one who turns in regular reports on Georgie's safety.

I went through all the proper channels to approve the change of plans this week. Georgie is an adult. But he can't be happy about the fact she's not in DC right now, and I'm worried I'm about to hear that firsthand.

I stand because I have no other option but to take the call. Without looking at any of my family members—I'm guessing Parker is close to losing his shit—I walk over and take the phone from Georgie. Clear my throat before I talk.

"Agent Salisbury speaking."

"Agent Salisbury, it's Joseph Adams." He doesn't sound mad, but he's a powerful politician. Acting must be second nature to him. "How are you doing?"

"I'm good, sir. Yourself?"

"Fine, fine. Georgie tells me everything is going smoothly there?"

"Um, yes. Yes it is. Sir." I clear my throat again.

"I really appreciate you changing your own plans like this. You're truly going above and beyond, and it won't be forgotten."

"It's not a problem, sir."

There's muffled commotion on the other end of the line. "I'm afraid I'll have to cut this call short, Agent Salisbury. But thank you again, for everything that you've done for Georgie."

"Of course."

"All right. Have a good night."

"You too."

The call disconnects, and I stand in disbelief for a minute. Feeling shocked—and a little guilty. I doubt President Adams would be thanking me as heartily if he knew some of my motivations for spending time with Georgie.

Everyone looks over when I return to the table, not even trying to be subtle about their curiosity.

"Good chat?" Hudson asks as I sit down. His tone a combination of sarcastic and intrigued.

"Yep." I keep my response short, as I hand Georgie back her phone.

"So it wasn't like the call when Principal Michaels was worried you were being objectified in the girls' bathroom?" Parker asks, slyly. He's clearly gotten over any shyness in Georgie's presence. "Because Kathy Bishop papered the wall with your yearbook photo?"

"Oh, I forgot about that!" Hudson laughs. "Remember when Josie, Hannah, and Stella's moms all called Mom, asking about prom corsages. Because someone forgot he already had a date, *twice*?"

This is what my brothers and I do. We rib each other and

bicker. But it bothers me in a whole new way tonight, and I know why. I care what Georgie thinks of me. Her opinion matters, and yeah, admittedly, both of those things happened. I'm not coming out of this discussion looking great. There's the obvious moral of all these stories: I was a cocky little shit back in high school. Based on Georgie's silence, she's no more thrilled to be hearing the stories than I am.

"Did you ever think your middle troublemaker would leave the dinner table to talk to the president?" Parker asks Mom.

"I had my doubts about all you boys," she replies. "Principal Michaels had our home phone number memorized, no doubt."

Conversation moves on to reminiscing, not just teasing me. We finish dinner and my mom serves the chocolate cake that Celeste made. The twins wake up halfway through dessert, wailing through the baby monitor set out on the table.

I end up holding Max, the older twin by two minutes, as Hudson and Celeste rush around, getting all their stuff together so they can head home.

"Oh, by the way, be on book club lookout tonight," Hudson tells me as he takes his kid and straps him into the carrier. Not before he drools all over my shirt, though.

"What the hell does that mean?" I ask.

"Mom has her book club tonight."

"I know. She mentioned it earlier." It was a relief to hear actually. Despite my brothers both living nearby, I worry about her. She never moved on from my dad—never even attempted to. I'm glad her social life is thriving in other ways.

"Well, they tend to get pretty rowdy. I had to drive down and pick her up one month. Just saying."

"Seriously?"

"Yeah. They come up with themed cocktails for each book."

"Jesus." I laugh. "Okay."

"It was good to see you, man. I'm glad everything is going well for you. Mom worries, you know."

"I know."

"All right. Talk to you later."

He gives me a hug and heads over to Celeste, who's strapping the other twin in and talking to Georgie.

I watch them interact, trying to figure out why I like the sight of it.

Trying to figure out why it feels right, having her here.

CHAPTER FOURTEEN

GEORGIE

DINNER ENDS with the same flurry of activity it started with. Parker leaves to meet up with friends. Celeste and Hudson depart with their screaming kids. Ethan and Laura are outside, cleaning up from dinner.

I'm standing at the kitchen island, eating leftover chocolate cake.

The door to the patio opens and closes. I know without looking it's him.

"Have fun?" Ethan asks.

I shrug without looking up. "It wasn't the worst time, listening to stories about your fuckboy days."

It's at least a partial lie. Ethan's family is warm and welcoming and entertaining. I enjoyed tonight a lot. But listening to his brothers share anecdotes about a younger Ethan told me two things. One, they'd completely ruled out the possibility of a *me and Ethan*. They know their brother wouldn't view it as a crossable line. And two, Ethan used to have no issue shirking authority. I think I would rather have assumed he always colored inside the lines. Now I'm left wishing he was still the guy who liked to take risks. Who might have thought I was a risk worth taking, which this Ethan clearly doesn't.

"They were exaggerating," he tells me.

"They must have been. I haven't seen any signs of charm."

"Based on what you said last night, I don't need any."

He means it as a joke, I think, but my annoyed self takes it as more of a jibe. "That sounds like something a fuckboy would say." I give my cake a hearty stab with my fork.

"I didn't—"

"I'm headed out," Laura says, walking into the kitchen holding a stack of dirty plates. She sets them in the sink and washes her hands before turning around. "I'll be back in a few hours."

She mentioned earlier her book club is meeting tonight. I can't decide whether to be relieved or worried that Ethan and I will be here, all alone. At least, I assume that's what will happen. Parker indicated he'd spend the night at a friend's before heading back to LA in the morning. And I doubt Ethan is planning to go anywhere, since that would involve either leaving me here or taking me with him.

"Okay."

Ethan's voice is flat, reflecting nothing—and everything—regarding the tone of the conversation we were just having.

Laura glances between me and her son twice before drying her hands on a towel and patting her hair, smoothing invisible flyaways. "All right, then. Have a good night, you two."

Ethan smiles but says nothing as she walks back out of the kitchen. I continue mashing my cake until it's a pressed pile of crumbs.

"I was kidding, Georgie."

"Right." I drop my fork. "You're the funniest guy I know."

"Don't get smart with me."

"Don't make fun of me," I snap.

"I'm not. Georgie, I—I'm not, okay?"

"Whatever. I'm going to bed."

"It's eight thirty."

"So?"

"You napped."

"So?" I repeat.

Ethan sighs. "Don't *care*, Georgie."

"I'm *trying*, Ethan."

Another sigh. "Max spit up on me when they were leaving. I'm going to take a quick shower and change. Then we can, I don't know. Do something."

Despite my annoyance, a smile tugs at my lips. "Like I said— zero charm."

He heads toward the stairs after rolling his eyes at me.

Once he's gone, I finish my cake. Rinse off the plates and load them into the dishwasher. There's still no sign of Ethan. I head for the door, then spot a pad of paper next to the landline. I scribble a quick note, so he can't accuse me of leaving without telling him.

Going outside. If someone abducts me, I'll tell them you'll make them regret it. (After you finish showering, obviously.)

—Georgie

I add some extra flourishes to my signature. I'm acting like a schoolgirl with a crush.

I have lots of friends. But not many I'd trust truths with. I'm more myself around Ethan than I am with anyone else. And I can't pinpoint why. Maybe it's because our interactions got off to such a rocky start. Maybe it's because I know he's obligated to stick around, no matter what I say or do. Or maybe it's because certain people affect you, in a way most—none—don't.

The note gets set on the clean counter, and then I head outside. Cool air greets me, a similar temperature to the air-conditioned house. I skirt the patio where we ate dinner and head toward the playset, running a hand along the plastic edge of the slide and then settling on the swing.

If I had to guess, I'd say it's been years—a decade, probably—since I sat on a swing. It's stupid and thrilling, how quickly the nostalgia appears as I pump my legs and fly upward. I wish I were wearing a skirt, simply so I could feel the fabric flutter around my legs. I tilt my head back, letting the air rush between the strands as gravity pulls me back down toward the ground.

I'm not sure how long I've been swinging, when Ethan appears. He walks toward me with his hands in his pockets, the moonlight glinting off his wet hair. He doesn't look intense or imposing right now. Or like he could leap into action or solve important problems. He looks like a normal guy, walking toward a normal girl.

I feel normal, right now, and it's a sense I cling to.

"I left you a note," I tell him, still swinging.

"Yeah. Got it." He waves the scrap of paper toward me, then folds it before tucking it back into his pocket.

He probably just doesn't want to litter. It'll likely go through a few rounds of laundry and disintegrate into nothing. But seeing him handle it with care makes me ridiculously happy, and that's concerning.

When he takes a seat on the swing next to me, that feels meaningful too. We move back and forth like two pendulums, staring at the dark yard and the starry sky.

"I really like it here," I whisper, keeping my eyes on the dark expanse and the pinpricks of light. "It's been a long time since I've been around a family that felt *normal*. That laughs and jokes and burns dinner."

"The burgers were just well done."

I smile. "They were good."

"Good."

"Can I ask you something?"

"You just did."

"Something else," I stress.

"Yeah, sure."

"What did you mean earlier, about not giving updates?"

He sighs. "That argument I mentioned. It was about my job. About what I've chosen to do with my life, and why. So since then...I've been stingy with details, I guess. And there weren't many details. Until you."

"They didn't want you to join the Secret Service?"

"They were worried about why I did, I think. Hudson was eight, when my dad died. He has memories. Parker was only a couple months old. He doesn't. I'm stuck in the middle, where I'm not sure what I remember and what I made up. I feel closer to him, choosing his choices. But I never thought about how my mom and Hudson would see it. They want to preserve my dad as he was. Me in the Service? It muddies memories for them. And honestly?" He sighs. "I'm starting to wonder how much was me proving something to myself, and how much was me really wanting it."

"It's okay not to know," I tell him.

"Yeah." His legs slow, so he's barely moving at all. "It's ironic, how much Parker freaked out around you earlier. He's the biggest pacifist you'll ever meet. Thinks it's ridiculous our president has armed men and an ambulance following him wherever he goes. That we should live in a world where certain people *don't* attempt to assassinate an individual who's trying to create a better life for us all. Threaten his family. Make our jobs as relevant as they are."

"I'd like to live in that world," I reply.

"Yeah," Ethan says. "Me too."

"What did my dad say?" I ask. I have a good idea, but I wait to see what he'll say.

"He wanted to thank me. For, you know, looking out for you."

Exactly what I thought. "Yeah, you're one hell of a public servant."

Ethan snorts. "Thanks."

Something brushes against my leg. I reach down and slap it. "I think the mosquitos have discovered us."

"We should head in anyway."

I pump my legs faster and fly higher, savoring the rush of air and the thrum of oxygen through my lungs. Then I let go, literally soaring through the air until my feet hit the grassy lawn. Except my left foot fumbles, throwing my balance off and causing me to stumble.

Ethan is there, grabbing my arm before I fall.

"I'm fine," I tell him.

"Really?" He appears dubious, which pisses me off.

"Really." I pull my arm away and stalk toward the patio, letting myself back into the house.

Sometimes Ethan's overprotectiveness feels nice, like he's looking out for me. At other times, it feels suffocating. Like a reminder of the things I can't do. I'm not sure how to separate the two. Not sure if I should.

I pour myself a glass of water from the pitcher in the fridge, feeling flushed despite the fact that the temperature inside the house is cool. Half the glass gets chugged with one sip.

Ethan's eyes are on me. I feel them, like a physical touch. "Are you tired?" he asks, as I drain the rest of the glass and add it to the dishwasher.

I look at him, then the digital numbers displayed on the stove. "It's nine-fifteen, Ethan."

He shoves his hands into his pockets and rocks back on his heels. Despite suggesting it was too soon to get to bed earlier, he seems at a loss for what to do now. We should retreat to our rooms. I could call Lucy, who I was supposed to see in person before the storm derailed my trip. Or Jordan, who texted me earlier saying he hopes I'm having a good break.

"We could watch a movie?"

I should say no. I should go upstairs and come up with a strategy that doesn't involve becoming more entangled in feelings toward Ethan. Instead, I say, "Okay," simply because it's the answer I *want* to give.

"Okay," he repeats.

I follow him into the living room. Rather than cue up a streaming service, Ethan pulls out the drawer beneath the television, revealing it's filled with DVDs. "Ladies' choice," he tells me.

"Does that make you a gentleman?" I tease.

"It could, I guess."

"People pay more attention to devils than to angels."

"People? Or you?"

"Both," I reply, before looking down at the drawer of movies. There's a wide selection to pick from, everything from action thrillers to slasher flicks to romantic comedies.

I scan the options, stopping when I spot familiar red lettering. I pull out *Jaws* and hand it to him.

Ethan's eyebrows raise as he looks at my selection. "You want to watch *Jaws*?"

"Uh-huh." I head for the couch, trying to get comfortable before Ethan comes over and I have to take his tall frame and broad shoulders into account. He changed into a pair of joggers and a t-shirt after his second shower. But I got a good idea of what he'd look like shirtless earlier, when his Dri-fit shirt was drenched in sweat, and the mental image feels like it's burned into my brain.

"Have you seen it before?" Ethan sets up the movie, then walks over to the couch as the opening trailers start to play.

I grab a pillow and hold it against my chest, like a down-filled shield. "No. You?"

"A while ago." He starts to fast-forward. "You're sure this is what you want to watch?"

"I've always wanted to see it. It's a classic."

"Why haven't you watched it then?"

"We used to go to Nantucket in the summers," I tell him. "I was scared to."

"Shark attacks are extremely rare."

"I *know that*. I'd just rather not have the image of a leg getting chomped off and blood spraying everywhere while I'm lying on the beach."

Ethan chuckles. "Can't handle gore?"

"I can handle it."

"You sure?"

"You have no idea what I can *handle*, Ethan."

All traces of teasing disappear from his face. "Don't do that."

"Talk? Sure, I'll work on it."

His jaw flexes as he leans back beside me, careful not to let his arm brush mine. The movie starts, showing a moonlit beach. There's a couple sneaking away to kiss, which is not the sort of unromantic atmosphere I was going for with my film selection.

We both relax as the movie progresses, the unrelenting tension between the two of us easing some. Ethan laughs every time I jump, which is every time the shark appears, pretty much.

"What did you think?" Ethan asks, when it ends.

"I loved it," I tell him. What I don't say is that I think my enjoyment stemmed more from him than the acting skills. Not to mention the mechanical shark.

"Yeah. It's good."

"How long do you think your mom will be gone fore?"

Ethan rolls his eyes. "No idea, and according to Hudson, I'll probably have to go pick her up."

He makes a drinking motion, and I smile.

"I was in a book club, back in middle school. We'd meet once a month, at someone's house. It was fun. Nice. Felt normal."

"There's no such thing as normal, Georgie. Everyone's life is different."

"Yeah, maybe you're right," I reply, adjusting positions. "Want to watch something else?"

Ethan hesitates, but then stands and walks over to the television. He returns to the couch as the opening credits for *Big* start to play.

I glance over, surprised by his selection. I would have pegged him as more of a James Bond or Jason Bourne fan than Tom Hanks. "Interesting choice."

"It's good," is all he says.

I snuggle deeper into the cushions. My eyelids start to feel heavy about halfway through the film. I fight them for a while, blinking and muffling my yawns. And then I eventually just let myself doze off.

The last thing I'm aware of is the weight of a blanket getting draped over me.

CHAPTER FIFTEEN

ETHAN

A CREAK on the stairs is what wakes me. I blink, tossing a hand over my eyes to block some of the morning sunlight streaming in through the windows. Except, my room has curtains. I blink again, parting my fingers as I register my surroundings. Bookshelves instead of bare walls. No ceiling fan. I'm not in a bed, but on a couch. And, most importantly, I'm not alone.

My first thought? *This is nice.*

My second thought? *Fuck.*

Georgie's hair is barely visible under the tangled mess of the blanket I put on her last night. She fell asleep halfway through *Big*. I decided to watch the rest of the movie and wait up for my mom. But apparently, I fell asleep too.

I sit up, careful not to jostle Georgie as I slip off the couch and turn off the television. I walk into the kitchen to find my mom in a fluffy robe, rummaging through the cabinet.

She turns with a smile. "Morning. Sleep well?"

I grumble a "Yes," running my fingers through my hair to smooth some of the bedhead. Technically couchhead, I guess. "I didn't mean to fall asleep."

"I figured." She's still smiling.

"I was waiting up in case you called. Hudson mentioned you might need a ride…" I trail off, catching her annoyed expression.

"Your brother—" My mom shakes her head, as she measures grounds into the coffee maker. "Needs to learn to mind his own business. That happened *once*."

I raise my hands. "I'm staying out of it. Just, it's why I was on the couch."

"You sure about that?"

I raise a brow, silently daring her to keep talking.

"Georgie seems very sweet."

"Mom," I warn. "She's a job."

"Very pretty too."

"She's only eighteen. Way too young for me."

At that, my mom actually laughs. "Oh, Ethan."

I shove away from the counter and stand. "There's nothing to talk about. I'm going surfing. Georgie usually sleeps in; she probably won't be up for a while."

"Mm-hmm," she replies, still appearing amused.

I sigh and roll my eyes before heading upstairs to change into my swimsuit.

I laughed at Georgie last night, but the main thought in my mind, as I float on the surface of the Pacific, is an article I read about how sharks have terrible eyesight. How, when they attack humans, it's usually surfers who look like seals from the ocean's deep, dark depths.

So surfing isn't exactly clearing my head the way I'd hoped. I wait for the next wave, which I ride in toward the lone figure on the beach. It's a decent one, so I decide to end with it. Sitting out at sea is an easy way to lose track of time. I'm not sure how long I've been out here, but the sun is burning high and hot, suggesting it's been at least an hour.

It's not until I'm nearly to the shore that I realize I recognize the figure drawing patterns in the sand with her toes.

"How did you get here?" I ask.

Georgie turns, hair flying everywhere and a wide smile on her face. "I biked."

I was hoping my mom drove her, at least. It's only a little over a mile. But the thought of Georgie biking through an unfamiliar place alone bothers me. I'm annoyed with myself for allowing it to happen. "You should have stayed put," I say, gruffly. "I wouldn't have left if I'd know—"

"Relax, Ethan. Nothing happened."

"It could have."

"It didn't," she counters.

I sigh, because there's no point in continuing this conversation. She waits a minute, before speaking again.

"I didn't know you surfed."

"Yep."

Georgie rolls her eyes. I'm guessing at my lack of a verbose response. "I didn't mean to fall asleep last night."

"I know."

"Are you mad about it?"

"That you fell asleep before midnight?"

She doesn't smile. "Among other things."

"No," I tell her. "I'm not mad."

"Okay." Georgie glances at my surfboard. At least, I *think* that's what she's looking at. I'm shirtless, only wearing board shorts since the water here is much warmer than the Atlantic's in October. I know I'm in good shape. And yeah, I purposefully clench my abs as I adjust my board, knowing she's looking. "You, um, are you finished surfing?"

"Yep, I'm done."

We head for the parking lot. The black SUV is one of only two cars in the lot. We're long past peak tourist season and it's a Friday. Most people are at school or work, not the beach.

I recognize the orange bike parked between a row of palms and the edge of the lot. "Have you been here for a while?"

"Yes," Georgie replies, blunt as always.

I grimace as I load the bike and the surfboard into the car. "Sorry. I figured you'd sleep in for a while."

"Don't apologize. This is supposed to be your vacation."

"Doesn't matter. Your safety is my responsibility."

"Hardly anyone knows I'm here."

"That doesn't matter, Georgie! If anything happened, I..." My sentence trails, as I realize I can't really put into words the panic and fear that would incite.

"You can't prepare for everything, Ethan," she tells me. "I don't want to live my life constantly worried something might happen."

"I'm not asking you to, Georgie. That's my job, I'm just asking you to not make it any more difficult than it already is."

"I biked to the beach to watch you surf, Ethan, I didn't go around trying to find a strip club or a casino. And if you'd woken me up, instead of sneaking out this morning, it wouldn't have even happened."

I don't have a good response to that, so I opt for nothing. Just shut the trunk and head for the driver's seat, waiting for her to climb in the car as well.

It's not too hot yet, so I leave the windows down as we wind through the streets of my small hometown. My second one, at least. I think a part of me will always consider DC to be my true hometown, simply because of my dad.

"The house is the other direction," Georgie notes, after a few minutes.

"I know."

"If you want me to inform you of my location all the time, the least you could do is clue me in on yours."

It's a fair point, which I acknowledge by telling her, "We're getting breakfast."

"Huh."

I resist the urge for a minute, then ask "Huh *what*?"

"I was expecting you to avoid me this morning, after we slept together last night."

I look away from the road long enough to catch her smirk. "Georgie," I warn.

"Ethan." She echoes my name in the exact same tone.

She's right—about the phrasing and the planned avoidance. Both are correct. And I should have the sort of willpower where Georgie saying *We slept together last night* doesn't affect me at all, since I was there, and I know exactly what happened. What didn't happen. But still, there are R-rated versions of what could have happened during the movie last night playing through my head right now.

I force myself to focus on the road. On pulling into the parking space right in front of Tina's Café—my intended destination. Georgie looks around the small downtown section curiously before following me inside.

Tina's Café is fancier than it sounds. The interior is mostly white and minimalistic, the polar opposite of a greasy spoon diner. The chalkboard menu boasts a long array of elaborate drinks and meals.

"Huh," Georgie says, taking in the potted plants and the vintage-looking furniture that decorate the space.

I fall into the trap of saying "Huh *what*?" again. I figured this is the sort of place she'd like—chic and trendy. But Georgie has a habit of surprising me, so maybe I read it wrong.

"I just...I don't know, I figured we'd go to somewhere...older."

"Older?" I ask, bemused.

Georgie is combing her fingers through her long hair, trying to tame the wayward strands. "Like a hangover joint. Extra-strong coffee, extra hash browns sort of place. Whatever. This is nice."

"I thought you'd like this place."

"I do. It's nice. I just—I feel like I'm inconveniencing you a lot. I don't want to eat here, just because you think it's what I want."

I blink at her, startled. Georgie seems to be taking a new approach with honesty, and I'm not sure it's entirely welcome. I'd rather think she doesn't like the interior decorating than know she doesn't want to *inconvenience* me.

"You're not inconveniencing me."

Georgie rolls her eyes at me. "Don't bullshit me, Ethan. We both know I am. I basically begged you to bring me. The whole thing with your brother last night, my dad calling, the couch, and then you getting annoyed this morning."

I'm tempted to laugh, at first, because I wouldn't call Georgie telling me I had two options *begging*. But then I take in her serious expression, the earnestness that suggests she really means what she's saying, and I can't laugh. "It doesn't feel like you're inconveniencing me," I tell her, which is true. "It's nice, having you here." True, as well. I liked having her at dinner. I had fun last night. And my annoyance this morning was mostly born out of irritation with myself that both were the case.

Saying so also feels too honest. I feel like I can see the distance between us closing, even as we both stand stationary right now.

Georgie doesn't seem to linger on what my words imply. She's refocused on reading the menu. I told her the attraction was mutual yesterday, but I'm alluding to a lot more than that right now.

Our conversation changes to neutral topics—namely what we're both ordering—up until we reach the register. I smile at Tina, the owner, who's good friends with my mother.

"Ethan! It's so good to see you." She beams at me, and I return the smile. "Your mom mentioned you were back last night."

I take that to mean Tina is another member of the infamous local book club. "Yep. Just visiting for a few days."

"You picked a good time of year. The weather has been gorgeous lately."

I nod my agreement. Tina's gaze slides to Georgie. It's filled with curiosity but no hint of recognition, which is a relief. My choice of career is common knowledge around here, which amplifies the risk of someone realizing who she is. When most people think of Secret Service agents, they think of protecting the president, not the many other jobs the role can include.

"What can I get for you, sweetheart?" Tina asks Georgie.

She orders a coffee drink and a breakfast sandwich. I list off what I'd like and Tina rings us both up. Georgie pulls out a card to pay, and I shake my head at her. We have a silent argument, which Georgie acquiesces with a sigh.

My drink appears as I'm signing the bill. "Yours will come out down there," Tina tells Georgie, pointing toward the edge of the counter. She passes me a small, plastic tiger. "Someone will bring the food over to your table as soon as it's ready. Enjoy your visit home, Ethan."

"Thanks." I smile at her, before moving down the counter.

Georgie follows. "You don't have to pay for me, Ethan. We're not on a date."

"I'm well aware we aren't dating," I tell her. "I get paid to pay for you, though."

"Really?"

No. "Yes."

"Fine."

"I'm going to grab a straw. I'll be right back."

I head for the table set up in the middle of the café, covered with different creamers and sugar and extra lids, each neatly separated in small baskets. I rifle through one for a straw, glance up, and have to hide the grimace that wants to appear.

Stella and her friend Kerri are walking into the cafe from the attached deck, holding dirty plates and heading straight toward the bin for used dishes, which happens to be only a couple of feet from where I'm standing.

Stella has already spotted me. She holds my gaze as she and Kerri approach, her expression blank and her shoulders squared. She's cut her hair since the last time I saw her. It hangs just past her shoulders now, making her look older.

Kerri speaks first, breaking the awkward silence. "Hey, Ethan."

"Hey Kerri." I give her a smile and a quick hug. I've always liked Kerri. She's warm and bubbly, friends with everyone. She never took sides during mine and Stella's tumultuous relationship.

"Are you home for long?" Kerri asks.

Home. It technically is, even if it's never fully felt like it. "Just for a few days. Had a little time off work."

I glance toward Georgie. She's still standing by the espresso machine, chatting with the barista as the guy fixes drinks. An involuntary swell of annoyance appears. I tell myself it's because the more attention Georgie draws to herself, the higher the chances are that someone in here will recognize her.

She avoids the political spotlight as much as she can, but she's attended plenty of high-profile events with her parents. Even in this small town, there's a chance someone will realize who she is.

But mainly, I'm jealous.

"How have you guys been?" I ask, refocusing on the conversation in front of me. And intentionally aiming the question at both of them, because Stella hasn't said a word. We parted on poor terms, but not antagonistic ones. And since I was the one who ended it, I'm guessing she's purposefully playing it cool.

"Good!" Kerri says, cheerful as ever. "Business has been booming, lately."

"That's great," I say, meaning it. Stella and Kerri formed a floral shop after college. They cater to local weddings and other events. I know Stella was excited about it, and anxious about its longevity. Although, I suppose, I'm probably the last person she'd want to tell if it wasn't succeeding. She was perpetually annoyed by my choice of career, and especially how it required me to be in DC.

"How have you been?" Stella asks, speaking for the first time.

I focus on her. "I've been good."

She nods. "Good. That's…good."

"Guess it's true what they say about small towns. Everybody knows everybody, and all."

Georgie's voice joins the conversation. It's a welcome distraction from Stella's expression, which suggests she was hoping I'd be a little more depressed without her.

I glance to the right, watching Georgie approach. Her gaze

bounces between me and the two women. The awkward meter moves higher as she stops next to me.

Since I'm the common denominator here, I clear my throat. "This is Kerri and Stella. We all went to high school together." And middle school. And elementary school. But most of the formative drama took place as teenagers, so I leave it at that.

"It's nice to meet you guys." Georgie gives both of the women a polite smile, which they both return. Stella's is a touch tighter than Kerri's, which makes me nervous. "I'm Georgie."

She doesn't give herself a title, and I don't add one. I'm not going to announce she's closely related to one of the most powerful men in the world. We're friends, I suppose, but it doesn't feel quite right to call her one since most of my thoughts about her veer straight past friendly and right toward lust.

"Nice to meet you too," Kerri replies. "Is this your first visit to Glenson?"

"Yeah, it is," Georgie replies. "I really like it so far. Everyone is super friendly."

Her expression stays smiling, so I'm not sure if she's being earnest or is alluding to Stella's blank expression. One of Georgie's many talents is a spectacular poker face. And the acting skills she inherited from her father.

"Have you caught up with Pat or Tanner?" Kerri asks me.

I shake my head at the mention of two of my closest friends. "No. I'm not sure…this is a quick trip."

Truthfully, I planned to text them as soon as I got to my mom's to see if they were around this week. Georgie's presence complicates catching up. I can't leave her unattended, I saw how that worked out this morning. And even if I let her talk me into having her stay at my mom's, I'd be worried the whole time and unable to enjoy myself.

Bringing her with me would involve a host of potential problems as well. If they recognize her, word will spread around town and possibly jeopardize her safety. If they don't, they'll assume the same thing as Kerri and Stella undoubtedly have—that we're together.

Basically, it's a lose lose situation. I try to avoid those.

"Well, a whole bunch of us are getting together tonight down by Parson's Point. Last I heard, Pat and Tanner will both be there. You should stop by, if you can. I know they'd all love to see you."

"Yeah, you should come," Stella adds, shocking me. I figured she'd be more likely to invite me to...nothing, actually. We weren't good friends before we started dating. I figured the fractured end to our romantic relationship would run through any future interactions.

I offer a vague "Maybe" in response.

Stella hears the hesitation. She sighs. "Look, I know I said some things...I was hurt, Ethan."

I shift uncomfortably. This isn't a conversation I want to have. And if I *am* stuck having it, this wouldn't be my first choice of venue. But especially, I don't want to have it in front of Georgie. I'm more worried about her feelings than I am Stella's, which is confusing. Despite the rocky split, I don't harbor any ill will toward Stella. We wanted different things. The way I'm feeling right now is more a testament to how I feel about Georgie than any bad blood toward Stella.

"I know," is the best I can come up with.

Stella nods. Kerri jumps in. "Okay, well, enjoy your breakfast, guys. Maybe we'll see you later. Nice meeting you, Georgie."

"You too," Georgie replies.

Stella and Kerri head for the door. I head for the first open table I see, tucked along the wall overlooking the flower garden outside. Georgie follows. I've barely set down the plastic tiger on the tabletop when our food arrives. The waitress delivers the plates with a smile, and then we're alone.

I wait. For a teasing comment or a fuckboy joke. Nothing. She takes a bite of her breakfast sandwich, chews, swallows, and then glances at me. "Were you worried any sharks might think you were a seal this morning?"

Georgie has no issue being blunt. She loves to tease me. It's a game between us, without winners or losers. One I often enjoy just as much as she does, even if I won't admit it.

She's giving me a free pass. Letting me avoid something she knows I won't want to talk about. It doesn't feel like a game, it feels like support.

It feels *real*.

Something between me and Georgie suddenly feels very real.

"The thought crossed my mind," I admit. Just like that, my chest feels lighter and loose again. And I wish, so much, that this was a date. That in some small way, she could be mine.

She grins. "I knew it." Then takes another bite of her breakfast and looks out at the small garden behind the cafe.

I stare at her. Trace the features that I could probably paint from memory. The slope of her nose and the curve of her cheek. The one strand of hair that still bears a trace of lavender. The faint, half moon-shaped scar on the left side of her chin.

I stare, and I wonder.

Is this what falling in love feels like?

My mom is scooping leftover pasta salad into a glass container when I walk into the kitchen. I glance around. "Georgie hasn't come down yet?"

"No. Not yet."

"Okay." I drum my fingers against the counter. I wonder if she would tell me if she didn't want to go tonight. She knows I won't go without her.

I forgot just how small of a town Glenson is. My mother stopped into Tina's Café this afternoon for a pastry and ran into Kerri's mother. Tina "just happened to" mention my interaction with Stella and Kerri earlier. Apparently, Kerri's mother is also part of the book club that is starting to sound like more of a gossip front. Our breakfast came up at dinner, as did the invitation for tonight. Long story shortened, Georgie and I are headed to Parson's Point.

"Everything alright, Ethan?" My mom sticks the leftovers in the fridge, then turns to me with an expectant expression.

"Yeah. Fine." I sigh. "I'm just unsure about tonight. Technically, I'm working. It doesn't feel very professional to go to a party."

"Maybe you should take a long look at how you ended up here with her, honey." She gives me a meaningful look, which I ignore.

"It won't take long. The extent of it was a tropical storm and a plane cancellation."

My mom shakes her head, calling me out on the fact I had other options. "She's not just a job to you, Ethan. Admit that to yourself, at least."

And…that's the problem. Part of it, at least. I can't separate my feelings. I have no idea how much of the protectiveness I feel toward Georgie is because she's my responsibility or because she's…Georgie. I'm not sure how to determine that or if I even should.

It won't change anything.

Steps sound on the stairs. I hesitate before glancing over. If the amount of time Georgie spent getting ready is any indication, she put some effort into her appearance. Based on the fact she regularly makes my heart race with no apparent effort at all, I'm a little worried about how I'll react.

It turns out to be a valid concern.

Georgie appears, wearing a pair of dark skinny jeans that hug her long legs and curves. Paired with a coral halter-style top that bares her shoulders and hints at her cleavage, it's certainly not helping me battle my attraction.

My mother's eyes ping-pong between me and Georgie like we're a tennis match she's watching. "Ready to go?" I ask Georgie, trying to ignore my mom's rapt attention.

"Yep," she replies. "See you later, Laura."

"Have fun, kids." My mom's eyes are practically sparkling with mirth.

Based on her excitement tonight, you'd never know she used to spout safe sex and smart decisions speeches off before letting me or my brothers leave the house.

I guess she's assuming—correctly—that I'll be too focused on monitoring Georgie to get into any trouble tonight. Parson's Point is only a couple of blocks from my mom's place. We're walking, but I'm not planning on drinking. I'll be on high alert the entire evening. Even if none of my friends recognize her, they'll definitely hit on her.

I roll my eyes, telling my mom "Good night" before heading toward the door. I pause to grab a house key from the bowl next to it, then glance at Georgie, who's right behind me.

"Want a jacket?" I ask, glancing at the coats hanging in the row of cubbies.

"I'm good." There's a hint of something in Georgie's voice, a bit of a challenge, maybe, but I don't engage. My mom is pretending to wipe the kitchen counters while watching us closely.

"Okay." I open the front door and follow her outside.

"Were you trying to get me to cover up?" Georgie asks, as soon as we reach the sidewalk.

"No. Your shirt is fine."

That earns me an eye roll. "Gee, thanks."

I rarely pay attention to what a woman is wearing. I couldn't describe what Stella or Kerri had on earlier, and I doubt I'll take note of any other woman's outfit tonight. The main allure of Georgie's attire is I'm imagining it on my bedroom floor—and there's no way that I'll say that to her.

"You don't need me to compliment you, Georgie. You know you look good."

"I never said I *needed you to*. It would have been nice, though."

I sigh, then say her name in the same scolding tone I use whenever she says or does something we both know she shouldn't have. That toes the line toward inappropriate. But this time, it's not really aimed at her. It's more to chastise myself. Because I know I'll say "You look beautiful, Georgie" long before the words leave my mouth. Know I'm an equal participant in the gnarled mess that only seems to ravel further between us no matter what I do.

"It doesn't count if you don't mean it," she replies.

"Then it counts," I respond. Because I *do* mean it.

And I can't figure out why it is—how she affects me so much. Among my close friends and family—the people who know me best—I'm known for my discipline when it comes to my job and my poor track record when it comes to relationships. Firm professional attachments and flimsy personal ones, when it comes to romance.

Somehow, Georgie transcends both of those core characteristics. She makes me forget she's a job. She makes it hard to remember why I thought I wasn't cut out for a serious relationship.

I spend the short walk to Parson's Point bracing myself for a long evening. The sand here is darker and rockier than at the town beach where I surfed earlier. It means most residents and tourists go elsewhere, making it an ideal spot for late night activities.

A volleyball net is set up in the center of the beach, but no one is playing. They're all milling about, drinking to the tune of a rap song I vaguely recognize. It sounds and feels and smells like nostalgia. Like younger, simpler days.

It feels like a dangerous sensation, with Georgie right next to me. I've built our four-and-a-half-year age gap up into a brick wall. It was easier to do when we first met. She was one day out of high school. I'd graduated college.

But it's crumbled, bit by bit. Over the course of our more serious conversations. When my mom laughed, earlier. And now, since it feels like every high school party I ever attended.

Right now, four and a half years just sounds like another boundary I'm failing to enforce.

There's no dramatic halt in the music or pause in conversation when Georgie and I cross the sand to join the gathering. But I feel eyes on us. On me and on her.

I was wilder in high school than I was in college. Academically, I always did well. But I spent large chunks of high school surfing and going to beach bonfires in this exact spot, sneaking beer and engaging in the other activities my brothers were teasing me about last night. On the occasions I've returned to Glenson since graduating high school—which have been few—I've hung out with a smaller group of people I stayed in touch with. This is a much larger gathering.

A broad-shouldered, shaggy-haired guy breaks away from the

group standing next to the bonfire and heads straight toward us. "Ethan! How the heck are you, man?"

I return Pat's grin and hand slap. He's the type of person you can't help but loosen up around. Laidback and cheerful, no matter what. "It's good to see you," I say, meaning it. We went surfing the last time I was in town, but I've only exchanged a couple of messages with him since.

"You finished training, right?"

"Right."

"Man, that's awesome. You must be doing all sorts of cool shit." He notices Georgie before I have to reply. A slow smile I've seen many times before spreads across his face. "Hey. I'm Pat." He holds out a hand, grin still intact.

"Georgie." Her arm brushes the sleeve of my hoodie as she shakes it. "It is *very* nice to meet you."

She gifts him with a wide, genuine smile, and it chafes at me. Pat glances at me, trying to suss out our relationship. I give him a hard stare and a head shake. His eyebrow rises, as surprised by the response as I am. It answers the possessive or protective question I was pondering earlier. She's in no physical danger, but Pat continuing to hold her palm has me contemplating some light physical violence. Like a hard shove that would require two hands to recover from.

"Interesting," Pat says, finally letting go.

Georgie glances from him to me, trying to figure out what she missed.

"Come on, drinks are this way." Pat leads the way over to a couple of coolers propped up next to some extra driftwood for the fire. As we walk, he fills me in on his latest venture—a bait and tackle shop one town over. It's always something new with Pat, which is part of his charm.

I grab a soda when we reach the coolers. Georgie glances at

me before grabbing a Corona. And she holds my gaze, as she pops the cap and takes a long pull of the beer. I say nothing. I'm not going to embarrass her by making a scene here. And it feels hypocritical, when I did plenty of underage drinking and I know most people her age do the same.

But I still feel a kernel of guilt—of shame.

Taking Georgie to a party and letting her drink wasn't what President Adams had in mind, when he thanked me yesterday. Letting personal feelings impact professional performance wasn't the sort of agent my dad was.

I chose this career knowing full well the amount of responsibility it could entail. At the moment, I'm tasked with a shocking amount of it. If anyone tries to cause Georgie harm, I'm the sole barrier in their way.

There's a reason joining the Secret Service is such a selective process. Why the subsequent training lasts months and tests your mental endurance along with physical stamina.

I thought I was up to the challenge. Qualified. Prepared. I never considered the toughest trial might be this. Might be her. Might be an internal battle.

"Hey, Ethan. Good to see you." Chase Lawrence appears. Grabs a bottle of water from the cooler and drains most of it in one gulp.

"You too," I answer. We played tennis together, but I haven't talked to him in several years. Last I heard, he was living in Oregon.

Before I have a chance to ask if he's moved back to Glenson, he says "Trying to get a volleyball game going. Any interest?"

"I'll play," Georgie answers, before I can say a word.

"Awesome," Chase responds, looking her over appreciatively.

I grind my molars, watching them walk off together. Georgie leaves without a word to me, leaving her half-empty beer in the sand. She doesn't need my permission. And I should be glad, to have some space. To have the chance to catch up with friends and not deliberate over how to introduce her.

But I don't feel relieved.

Pat is chatting with a group of girls who came over to get drinks. I recognize a couple of them, and one is eyeing me with interest. But I'm not in the mood for chitchat, and I'm certainly not here to hook up with anyone.

"Ethan fucking Salisbury. How are you, hotshot?"

I turn to see Tanner Hoskins approaching, holding a can of cola and sporting an easy grin.

"Hey Hoskins," I reply, giving him a hug. Tanner was easily my closest friend growing up. We kept in close touch during college and since. Out of everyone here, he's who I'm most excited to see.

"Reminds you of the good old days, huh?" he asks, gesturing to the crowded stretch of beach. A salty breeze whips along the shoreline, carrying the scent of smoke and the sound of laughter.

"Yeah, it does."

"So, what gives?" Tanner punches my shoulder. "You plan a trip out here and don't tell anyone?"

"It was last minute," I tell him.

"You didn't teleport here, dude. Know how I found out you were in town? My mom called, after her book club last night."

"That fucking book club," I mutter.

Tanner laughs. "So?"

"I got a new assignment. It's kept me busy. And then this trip...got complicated."

I glance at the source. The volleyball game is underway. I watch as Georgie spikes the ball. It lands in the sand with a smack and everyone on her side of the net cheers. Apparently, Georgie's athletic prowess doesn't end at tennis.

Tanner follows my gaze. "You brought a girl home?"

"Technically."

"Technically? It's more of a yes or no answer, Ethan."

"She's—there's…" I give up on explaining. I trust Tanner. He won't say anything. "She's the president's daughter. I'm on her security detail while she's at college. There was an issue with her flight to DC for fall break, so she came back here."

Tanner's eyebrows are basically brushing his hairline. "You're serious."

I nod.

"Your new assignment is the First Daughter? And you brought her home with you?"

"Yep."

"Do you like her?"

I pretend to contemplate the question, knowing there are bounds I need to keep my honesty contained within. "I don't *dis*like her."

Tanner chuckles. "Wow."

"I'm not going to do anything about it. I *can't* do anything about it."

"Yeah. That would be tricky."

"Tricky?" I scoff.

"If anyone can handle it, it's you."

I should appreciate the vote of confidence. Instead, it makes me feel worse. Because I'm not sure I can. I change the subject, asking Tanner about work. I glance at Georgie every so often. The volleyball game ends. Rather than head this way, she ends up at the fire pit, talking with a large group of girls.

My fears about her getting recognized or awkward conversations introducing her were unfounded, it appears. She seems totally at ease each time I look over.

Tanner leaves to go stoke the fire. I catch up with a few other guys I haven't seen in a while, then end up back by the coolers, fishing out a fresh drink.

Pat reappears as I'm cracking the can of ginger ale open. "So, you dating her?"

"Who?" I ask, knowing full well who he's talking about.

He rolls his eyes, recognizing the same. "The hottie you showed up with. Georgie."

I opt for the truth. "No. But she's off-limits. Don't hit on her."

"I'm not sure if she'd notice if I did. She's into *you*, Salisbury."

"You don't know what you're talking about," I tell him.

Pat smiles. "Uh-huh, sure. We've been standing here for a couple of minutes. She's looked over here eight—nope, make that nine—times."

I resist the urge to turn around and look for the bonfire. "You don't know what you're talking about," I repeat.

Pat has no idea what the whole story is between us.

"If you say so."

He punches my arm and walks away. I look over a shoulder.

Georgie is standing a few feet away from the roaring bonfire. The orange flames backlight her the same way the lamps did in the motel's parking lot, glowing behind her like a spotlight. She catches my gaze and holds it, a small smile playing on her lips.

I look away first. I clutch the cold can of soda and skirt the makeshift volleyball court, walking down to the ocean's edge. The sea is calm, gentle waves washing across the sand and retreating in rhythmic patterns. Bubbles pop and foam fizzes with each new pass. It's a soothing soundtrack, a sound that eases some of the tension I'm carrying around.

This problem with Georgie has a simple solution: do nothing. Without a doubt, it's what I should do.

But it's not what I *want* to do, and I finally admit that to myself. My job description doesn't include making Georgie smile. Or enjoying our conversations. It definitely doesn't involve kissing her or seeing the curves I glimpsed at that party this summer again.

I don't need it to include that. But I want it to exclude it.

I'm not sure if there's an official policy preventing a romantic relationship between me and Georgie. It would be heavily frowned upon. My judgment would be considered compromised.

Problem is, I'm not sure it's not already. If, God forbid, something ever did happen to Georgie, I'm not sure how I would handle it. *If* I would be able to handle it. There's no way I'd be able to view the situation through the same logical lens I handled hypothetical hostage situations with during training.

That probably means I shouldn't be on her detail as it is. But requesting a reassignment would mean entrusting her safety to someone else. If something happened and I wasn't there—because I *asked* not to be—could I live with myself? Not to mention, I've dedicated the past five years to this goal—to becoming an agent like my dad. Changing assignments, especially after I was hand-picked for this one, would not look good in my file. Could affect my whole future.

All for a girl looking for a good time? For a fuck, like she told me last night?

I'm a novelty for Georgie. A thrill. A challenge, when she's used to guys tripping over themselves to get to her.

Some hot sex isn't worth my career.

"It got chilly." I turn to see Georgie walking toward me, rubbing her arms to chase off the bite to the breeze. The motion lifts her shirt a couple of inches, flashing a strip of stomach.

I swallow. Once. Twice. I should remind her I suggested she grab a jacket. Act the part of the elder who's in charge. Instead, I shrug out of my hoodie and hand it to her.

Usually, I wouldn't consider an oversize sweatshirt on a girl to be all that sexy. But when Georgie tugs the material over her head, I reconsider. Maybe because it's *my* oversize sweatshirt, and that sets the possessiveness she incites in me to a satisfied simmer.

"Thanks." Georgie smiles up at me, pulling her hair out from underneath the hood and letting it fan out across her shoulder.

I experience one of those moments that hit you like a head-on collision. Impossible to ignore and hard to move on from. We've come a long way from that first meeting in the Oval. I know that. Know spending time with her is no longer the chore I once considered it to be.

But *this* is different.

I realize that not only do I not mind spending time with her, but it's what I want to be doing. It's what I would choose to be doing, right now, if I had the choice.

"Did your team win at volleyball?"

"You know the answer to that. I saw you watching."

"Not sure how you managed to win, if you were watching me the whole time."

She rolls her eyes. "You came up, during the game."

"Oh, yeah?"

"Yeah. According to Amanda Aikins, you were a lot more fun in high school."

"A lot of people I went to high school with would probably say that." I shrug. "I grew up."

"Leaving a trail of broken hearts behind?"

She's kidding, I think. "Amanda said something to you?"

Georgie shrugs. "Just asked if there was an *us*." She smiles. "Don't worry. I told her I'm interested, and you're not. That you're hung up on your high school girlfriend. Or girlfriend*s*, rather. It sounds like you had quite the harem."

"Please tell me you're kidding."

"I'm kidding. Well, about the second part."

"You told her that you're into me and I'm not into you?"

"Yep. Your heartbreaker reputation is safe and intact, don't worry. If anything, I gave it a boost."

"I don't have a heartbreaker reputation."

"Some girl named Daphne would beg to differ, apparently. You two 'dated' for a whole week, sophomore year."

"Jesus." I rub a palm across my face.

Georgie laughs. "Yep. I feel like *I* went to your high school, after talking to them for an hour. Learned a lot."

She steps away, moving to head back toward the party. I stop her. "Like what?"

She holds my gaze. I can practically see her weighing what to say. "You really want to know?"

"Yeah."

"She said you *looked* interested. That you could barely keep your eyes off me." Her eyes bear into me, sharp and seeing. "Still glad you asked?"

"Honestly? No."

"Yeah, that's what I thought."

She starts past me again.

This time, I don't stop her.

I'm not sure which is more terrifying: the certainty that Georgie and I would be more than a fling or the fear that if I don't find out I'll regret it forever.

CHAPTER SIXTEEN

GEORGIE

ONE WEEK after returning to campus following the end of fall break, I leave Stanford again. I skip my Friday class and land in DC before noon. This trip came at my father's request, to attend a benefit and log a family appearance as a potential two-term president.

That's my cynical side talking, because I know my parents both miss me. Despite their busy schedules, we'd never gone more than a few days without seeing each other up until I left for college.

I'm not looking forward to the gala. But the main reason for the scowl on my face is because Ethan isn't traveling with us. He has the weekend off, because his higher-ups were so impressed by the way he handled the unexpected changes over fall break.

I'm happy for Ethan to receive recognition and praise. But his choice to accept the offered weekend off—to stay on campus—has resulted in me questioning what he'll be doing.

Who he'll be doing.

I've never seen Ethan flirt with a woman. Whenever we're together, he's automatically on duty. On guard. On alert.

He admitted he was attracted to me while we were away on fall break. Ethan also told me he'll never do anything about it—that we'll never happen. He's single, free to do whatever and whoever he wants.

I shouldn't care. But shouldn't and don't are two different things.

Seven hours have passed since I left, and the what ifs are already eating me alive. What if he hooks up with someone I know, and I have to hear about it? What if he meets another girl and they start dating? What if—

"We're here," Kevin states, jarring me out of my spiraling.

I glance outside, surprised I managed to zone out for the trip through downtown DC and through the gated entrance to the White House. We're already parked in front of the residence.

I climb out of the SUV, inhaling the cooler, crisper air. There's a stray leaf on the path, but the rest of the grounds are as impeccably manicured as always. The solitary leaf crunches underfoot as I walk through the familiar doors and into the diplomatic reception room that leads to the center hall. I head for the Yellow Oval Room, assuming that's where my mom will be. She's seated on the striped couch in the middle of the room decorated with smoky browns, golds, greens, and blues that looks straight out at the Washington Monument.

"Hi, Mom."

She looks up from the book she's reading.

"Georgie!" My mom tosses the book aside and stands, carrying the familiar scent of honeysuckle over with her as she embraces me. She pulls back and scans my appearance. I don't think I look any different than when I left DC. I dressed up somewhat, in a cotton dress and blazer, knowing I'd be photographed at the airport. "Was your flight okay? Any issues?"

"No issues," I reply, stripping off the starched blazer and tossing it on the back of the couch. "The trip was fine."

"Good. I know your father felt terrible about what happened before, for your break."

"Well, if there's one thing Dad can't control, it's the weather." My mother doesn't react to my joke. "Mom, seriously, it's fine. No one tried to abduct me."

"It's not a joking matter, Georgette. I know you have your issues with the security measures, but there's no other option."

I sigh. "I know."

"Are you hungry? I can have Henry fix you something to eat."

"No, I'm good. I'm going to go shower the airport off and change."

"All right. We've got the meeting with Robert Alderman at four. Your father said he'll be here by three-thirty. And we have the gala at eight."

"Got it." I grab my blazer and turn to head for the hallway.

"Wait a minute. How was it?"

"Huh?" I spin back around. "How was what?"

"Your fall break. How was it?"

"Oh. It was good. Fine."

"Really? Your father said the agent is one you had issues with. That you didn't want him on your detail."

I fiddle with a button on the blazer, trying to figure out why she's asking. My mom has never brought up an agent with me before.

"Yeah, well, I got over it, I guess. Like you said, I don't have another option."

My mother studies me for a minute, before nodding. I'm worried my face might give something away, so I turn quickly, and leave the room.

It's a short trip from the White House to the ritzy hotel where tonight's gala is being held. But it takes a while to travel the few miles. The presidential motorcade contains forty-six vehicles. I ride with my mother and her chief of staff in one armored limousine, while my father is in the other with his. We're flanked by SUVs filled with a counter-assault team and dozens of Secret Service agents. Behind us are cars carrying other staff members, a communications van, an ambulance, and Metro police cruisers.

Subtle, it is not.

We roll through the center of two-lane streets, stalling traffic in both directions. Flashing lights and loud sirens surround us, muffled by tinted glass and reinforced steel.

I play with the bow tied around my waist. The dress I'm wearing tonight is the color of champagne. It's made from a shimmery, silky material that refuses to wrinkle. My hair and makeup were both professionally done. I know I look good, and I hate how my first thought when I saw my reflection in the mirror was that I wish Ethan were here to see it.

My attraction toward Ethan isn't surprising. People can say they value personality and integrity over appearance all they want. The simple truth is looks matter—more than they should. Most humans fall into the trap of judgment and comparison. We judge people based on what we see and immediately draw conclusions that tend to stick. Guys who look like Ethan have a head start over the ones who aren't quite as conventionally attractive.

But the real kicker—the reason I've thought of him an embarrassing number of times since I've been back—has nothing to do with Ethan's blue eyes or abs. I wasn't supposed to like him more, as I got to know him. And it's not the comfortable sort of familiarity, the sort you establish with a coworker or a friend of a friend. It's thrilling. Goosebumps across your skin and a pounding in your chest. I feel off-kilter around him, never relaxed. It's an invigorating, addicting form of uncertainty, like constantly climbing toward a peak and not knowing what you'll discover on the other side.

I'll never find out. Ethan isn't going to ever allow himself to cross that line with me, and annoyingly, I can't even blame him. I haven't forgotten anything he told me when he first joined my detail. He considers me spoiled and childish. That may have changed some. We've shared enough moments that have felt meaningful, where I think he sees more than me lashing out against the world. Him admitting he'd hook up with me means nothing if he won't actually do it.

We pull into the hotel's attached garage. I climb out after my mother, wobbling a little in my heels. I spot both Myles and Kevin standing near the elevators. Automatically, I glance around for Ethan. Even though I've spent most of my time in DC bemoaning his absence, I'm used to seeing him standing next to them. But, of course, he's not there.

I zone out as the massive entourage moves about, talking with the hotel's staff and confirming details that have undoubtedly already been double- and triple-checked. I end up in the elevator, sandwiched between my parents.

My dad glances over, as the doors close and we start to rise. "Are you too old to watch a movie with your old man tomorrow night?"

"It depends on the movie," I reply, with a smile.

"Your choice."

"Okay."

"Okay," he repeats, giving me the warm, genuine smile that makes me feel like I'm five years old again. In a comforting way, like hot cocoa during a snowstorm. He doesn't look like an important, powerful man right now. He just looks like my dad.

Then the doors open, and we're swept into a sea of light and commotion. The organization being honored tonight is a global humanitarian fund. But you'd think this was a birthday party for my father, based on the response to his arrival. I make polite small talk with all the people who approach us, then migrate over to a tray of champagne at the first opportunity. I snag a flute before beelining toward Lucy. She breaks away from the crowd she's talking to when she spots me.

"Hey!" Lucy gives me a tight hug, then glances at my choice of drink approvingly. "Look at you, flouting authority in public. I'm proud."

I roll my eyes. "No one's paying attention to me."

It's true. To a stranger on the street, I might be a big deal. A novelty, at least. But among the crowd of DC's elite gathered here tonight, I'm a minor attraction, not the main one. My father is the big deal. I'm irrelevant, just like I wish I were in other situations. It would be nice if I was always separate from his infamy.

Lucy steers me over to an empty table in the corner. Sits and looks at me, expectantly. "Tell me everything."

So, I do. Lucy is the closest friend I made in DC. And most of my friends from Boston were too shell-shocked by the realization my father suddenly was the president to keep in close touch. Lucy and I exchanged memes and short messages since departing to our respective universities, but nothing of much substance. I fill her in on the tennis team at Stanford. On my classes. The apartment complex where I'm living.

And then she smirks. "What about guys?"

I glance down, watching bubbles rise to the top of my glass. "I met someone," I tell her, swirling my glass around to watch the fizzy contents slosh up the edges of the crystal.

"What? Seriously?" Lucy asks, lifting her chin from its spot propped on her hand and staring at me with wide eyes.

"Yeah."

"Georgie! Tell me everything! What's his name?"

I improvise, dropping the first letter of his name and swapping the last two. Ethan is a common name. But it feels too intimate, using it here. "Theo."

"Theo. He sounds hot."

"He is. But he's also...I feel different around him, you know?"

"So are you guys officially together, or..."

"No, we're not. It's complicated. He's older."

"Oooh! How old?"

I sip some champagne. "He's a senior."

Technically, not that far off from the truth.

Lucy visibly deflates. "That's not very scandalous."

"It has nothing to do with scandal. I—"

"Miss Adams?" I turn to see one of my father's staffers standing a few feet away, smiling nervously. "Your father is making his speech shortly. He'd like you to come up on stage."

I sigh. "Right." Down my champagne, enjoying how the bubbles fizz in my belly. I stand and glance at Lucy. "I'll talk to you later?"

She raises her glass in a silent cheers. "I'll be here."

I smile, before following the staffer over toward the stage. My father's speech lasts twenty minutes. When it ends, I get swept into a group discussion with the Secretary of State.

When the conversation ends, I wander over to the balcony that juts off the far side of the room. Step out and stare into the night. My elbows rest on the galvanized metal, cool to the touch now that the sun has been down for several hours.

After a minute, I slip my phone out of the clutch I've been

carrying around all night. It's after eleven here. Only eight fifteen on the west coast. I waffle and waver, trying to decide if I should text him or not. I mean, I know I shouldn't. It's more a matter of whether or not I'm going to anyway.

"Hiding out?"

I turn to see Luke walking out onto the balcony. I'm not surprised to see him here—our parents often attend the same events. "Just getting some air," I respond.

"Shouldn't you be at Stanford? You're not on break, are you?"

"Duty called."

"Right." Luke's mom is a justice on the Supreme Court. Justices' families aren't exposed to the limelight the same way politicians' are, but he still has to attend a fair number of political events. He understands the obligation to attend, to smile and act like there's nowhere else you'd rather be.

I turn toward him, propping a hip against the hard railing. "How's Georgetown?"

He shrugs. "Eh. It's fine. Feels like being back at Hamilton Academy, a lot of the time. You were smart, to get out of this town."

"All because of tennis," I tell him.

"Yeah. Sure."

My phone buzzes. For a second, I hope it's Ethan. But it's Lucy, asking where I am. I respond, telling her I'll meet her back at the table shortly. When I glance up, Luke is looking at me. Stupidly, I blurt out the first thing I think to say. "You're a guy."

Luke smirks. "Nice of you to notice."

"Okay. Hypothetically, say you know a girl likes you. And you told her you're...interested, except there are complications."

"Complications like the girl's dad is the president?" Luke asks, slyly.

"*Hypothetically*, yes. Would you want her to text you?"

195

"You met a guy, huh? Linc will be hurt."

I roll my eyes. Luke's best friend Lincoln and I had a fling at Hamilton that fizzled out a few months before we graduated. He owns a Ducati and was always late. "I'm sure he'll get over it."

Luke grins. "Yeah, sure. So this guy. Have you hooked up?"

"No."

"Kissed?"

"I don't see how that's relevant."

"I'll take that as a no. Are you *sure* he's into you?"

I flip Luke off. "Forget it."

He laughs, then turns serious. "Wow. You really like him." There's surprise in his tone.

"Whatever. I'll get over it."

"No way. That's not the Georgie Adams I know. Come on, cuddle up." He holds an arm up, gesturing for me to step closer.

I don't move. "What are you doing?"

Luke reaches out, grabs my hand, and hauls me under his right shoulder. "*Hypothetically*, if I was into a girl, I wouldn't love seeing another guy hanging over her." He grabs my phone out of my hand and swipes to activate the camera. "Smile. Actually, no. Look at me like you're dying to tear my clothes off."

I laugh. "I really don't think—"

A light flashes as Luke takes the photo. He squints at the screen. "Fuck. This is perfect." He turns the phone toward me. Before I can get a good look at the screen, he turns it away, and I realize my face just unlocked it. "What's the guy's name?"

I should say nothing. This is stupid and juvenile, and I'm certain Ethan won't be shy about telling me so. Even worse, he might not care. Maybe it will be a relief to him. Not only am I out of the state, he won't have to worry about me flirting with him when I return.

I've kept any smiles or suggestive comments to myself since

our trip together. Something about that time spent together—about meeting his family—enhanced things between us. Made them feel more real. Before, interacting with him was intriguing. A tease. A game. Now, more than anything, it hurts. Because I caught of glimpse of what it would be like, mattering to Ethan. And it's a lot harder to give something up, once you've had it.

"Ethan," I say. "His name is Ethan."

"E-t-h-a-n." Luke spells out each letter as he types. "Got it. Sent." A quiet *whoosh* confirms it.

"Shit," I realize. Then repeat. "Shit."

Things between me and Ethan are at a comfortable impasse. For the seven days we were back on campus after visiting his mom, we were cordial. We haven't spent any time alone together since returning to Stanford. Myles, Kevin, and Joey were all waiting at the apartment complex, full of apologies about how Ethan was left to guard me alone. He's a hero in their eyes. In my dad's as well. Like he worked overtime without pay, which I guess he did.

"Stop freaking out," Luke tells me.

"It wasn't *actually* a hypothetical situation, Luke. I'll have to talk to him when I get back. Explain why I sent him a photo of me with some random guy."

Luke holds out my phone. "Or, you could talk to him now."

I glance down. *Ethan* is flashing across the screen. I scramble to grab the vibrating phone. "What did you say to him?" I demand. I can't look in my messages to check, now that there's an incoming call.

"Relax. I just sent him the photo. This is good."

"*Good*? He's probably calling to tell me not to send any more photos."

Luke laughs. "Nah. He'd just ignore it if that were the case.

Trust me, Georgie. Answer it." He smiles, then walks off the balcony, leaving me alone with the ringing phone.

I take a deep breath, then answer it. "Hello?"

"What the fuck, Georgie?"

Ethan sounds angry—annoyed. And I can read his tone perfectly because the background is silent. It doesn't sound like he's out at a bar or a party, and it lightens some of the lead that I have felt piling on my chest since I left.

That, paired with the fact Luke was right—he *didn't* need to call me back—emboldens me some. "You don't sound very professional, Agent Salisbury."

"I'm off duty this weekend."

"I heard. Doing anything fun?" I keep my tone light. Upbeat.

There's a long pause before he answers. "Not really. The Capitals are getting annihilated."

"I've never seen a hockey game."

"I hadn't either, until I moved to DC. Colby is super into it. He roped me into this fantasy team thing, so now I feel like I have to follow it."

"Maybe I'll try watching a game. See what I think."

"They're better in person. It's a whole thing. You can hear the boards rattle and smell the ice."

"I want to see for myself. You offering to take me to one?"

Another long pause. "Who's the guy, Georgie?"

"He's a friend. From Hamilton. That's all."

"Why did you send it?"

"Why did you call?" I counter.

His heavy exhale echoes across the country. "Fuck if I know."

"Don't lie to me, Ethan."

"Nothing's changed, Georgie."

"You say that—but you called."

There's a long beat of silence. "How does it feel, being back?"

I rub my finger against the railing. "Fine. Weird. Good. It's like, I don't know. Familiar and strange, all at once. I remember exactly what it's like—the motorcade and the attention. But I got used to pretending like I didn't, if that makes any sense."

"It makes sense," he says, softly.

"It's strange, not seeing you." It's not an *I miss you*, but it's close.

"Myles and Kevin know what they're doing."

I sigh, annoyed by his deflection. "That's not what I'm talking about, Ethan."

He pulls back, just like I knew he would. "I should go."

"Are you going out tonight?" I scrunch my face up as soon as the words come out, pissed at myself for asking.

There's a long silence in response. But when he answers, I regret asking the question a lot less. "No."

"Good night, Ethan."

"Good night, Georgie."

He hangs up first.

I stare out at the sprawling lights of the nation's capital, a beguiling mixture of hope and heartbreak battling in my chest.

CHAPTER SEVENTEEN

ETHAN

I'VE NEVER LIKED FOOTBALL. It's filled with long delays. Too many players to keep track of. It lasts hours and the main source of entertainment is a bunch of men scrambling to hold a ball.

"They should swap out Bush for Reynolds," Joey comments, before taking a bite of his soft pretzel.

I grunt, pretending like I know who either of those players are. My ballcap and sunglasses shade my face from the late afternoon sun, hiding the fact I'm not even looking at the field. I'm fully focused on Georgie.

I guess I could call it close monitoring. I'd notice any issue before Joey, who's glancing over between bites and plays. But I can't sell that lie to myself very convincingly, anymore. Can't tell myself I'm absorbed by the fact she's an important assignment and I'm out to prove myself among more experienced agents.

It's a relief—looking at her. Knowing she's safe and smiling. Last weekend, she was back in DC. Surrounded by a veritable army of agents the entire time. And yet, I couldn't relax. Couldn't get her off my mind. Couldn't pretend I was anything close to indifferent about her absence.

I accepted the offer of a weekend off because it felt rude to refuse. Because, truthfully, it would be my first in a while, and constant vigilance is exhausting. Because, recently, spending time *with* Georgie hasn't involved enforcing any boundaries, so maybe distance would be more successful.

I called her less than twenty-four hours after she left, though, so I can confidently say the experiment was a complete and utter failure.

"Nooo! They're putting in Marks instead." Joey shakes his head.

I grunt again, too distracted to share any commentary, even if I had more interest in the sport than I do.

I'm in a fucking mess. Fighting an invisible battle. I can't get involved—more involved—with Georgie. But the thought of her with another guy, like in the damn photo she sent me, pisses me off more than anything else ever has. I've never felt this protective—possessive—over someone before.

There's no easy choice. I can't pursue her without risking my job and my reputation. But more and more, it's feeling like I can't do nothing, either. For a long time, my responsibility as an agent felt like the be all and end all. But she's starting to overshadow that focus. Ignoring my feelings and hoping they'll disappear with the last traces of fall isn't feeling like an option any longer.

I should look for a distraction. Go out on one of my nights off and find a girl who's looking for some no-strings sex. The problem is, it feels like I *have* strings. No matter how hard I try, I can't muster any interest in the song and dance of a random hookup. It sounds too predictable and meaningful.

Exactly what I used to want. What I should still want.

Finally, the football game ends. Stanford won. The streams of scarlet-clad spectators descending the stadium stairs are jubilant.

Joey stretches besides me. "Fuck, these seats are uncomfortable." I don't disagree. I lost feeling in my ass a while ago. He pulls his phone out and scans the screen. "Kevin and Myles are waiting outside."

"Okay," I say.

We're trading shifts. Joey and I are off for the evening, while Kevin and Myles will take over Georgie's security.

"I've gotta run to the bathroom. Can you let Georgie know we're shifting?"

"Yeah. Sure."

Joey disappears, leaving me to approach Georgie. She's standing with the group of friends she came here with. I watch, as she laughs at something the guy next to her says. I've seen Georgie talk to him before, and I recognize the way he's looking at her. I'm sure I've worn it before myself. She shoves his shoulder, playfully. Something tightens in my chest, to the point of physical pain.

I stand and start down the steps. This is a job, and right now it involves passing on logistical information. Nothing more.

Georgie glimpses me approaching. She says something to the guy before breaking away from the group and walking toward me. His eyes jump from her to me. I'm surprised—and a little smug—to see he's eyeing me as more of a threat than a bodyguard. He saw us earlier when Joey and I brought her to the stadium; he knows we're agents here to protect her. But still, she's walking away from him. Walking toward me.

"Good game, huh?" Georgie smiles, her ponytail swinging in time with the last few steps of her approach.

"I guess. I'm not a big football fan."

"Right. You're all about the winter sports, California boy."

"I like surfing," I remind her.

"And how many surf competitions have you gone to?"

"Zero," I admit. "But I've attended plenty of tennis matches."

"Speaking of which, I want a rematch. Soon, before things get crazy with Thanksgiving break and finals and winter break and the start of the season."

"Maybe."

"You got something better to do, Agent? Wouldn't you rather play than lean against the car and watch me practice by myself?"

"Play with Myles."

"Myles asked me how many *periods* are in a tennis *game*. I don't think he'll give me much of a workout."

I don't miss how she manages to make the last sentence sound dirty. And that's mainly why I shouldn't agree, because a large part of me wants to. Because spending more time with her—especially time when she's sweating and wearing a short skirt and it's easy to imagine her out of breath and bare-legged in other contexts—is especially problematic.

"You've got teammates. Ask one of them."

"Or...Austin was just telling me he took lessons in middle school. Maybe I'll ask him."

She's teasing me. Taunting me. And fuck if it doesn't work like a charm. "*Lessons in middle school*? He'll be lucky to win a set."

Georgie grins, either at the compliment or the obvious annoyance in my tone. I shouldn't give a shit whether she decimates some random guy on the court, and we both know it.

"Yeah, probably. I got the impression he'd prefer to do something else, anyway."

Something else and its insinuation simmers between us until I can't take it anymore.

"Are you into him?" I ask.

I sound angry. Jealous. And I can't bring myself to care. To school my reaction the way I know I should.

"Why?"

This is when I should walk away. Instead, I say, "Answer my question."

Georgie crosses her arms. "You answer mine."

"You..." I grab the back of my neck, trying to resist the urge to shake her. Or kiss her. "Don't be difficult."

"Admit *you care*. Admit why you're asking, Ethan."

"He seems like a tool."

She laughs, but it's amusement with a hard, mocking edge. "Based on..."

Nothing. He's probably a nice guy, and it pisses me off even more.

I work my jaw, letting all of the things I'd like to say marinate. I swallow them all. "Myles and Kevin are taking over for the night. They're both outside."

That's *all* this conversation was supposed to consist of—telling her about a changing of the guard. I let a college freshman completely distract me.

"You're leaving?" Her voice has changed, from defiant to disappointed.

"Yeah. My shift is up."

"You could still stay."

"And do what? Watch you flirt with him? No thanks."

"You told me we'd never happen, Ethan. You can't get mad at me for talking to a guy who actually wants me."

"*Wanting* isn't the problem, Georgie. You know exactly why I can't, why we can't—" I pinch the bridge of my nose. I need to get out of here. I exhale. "You're right. I'm sorry. Talk to whoever you want."

"I'll probably do a lot more than just *talk* to him."

I hear the challenge in the words—the bite. She doesn't *want* me to acquiesce, and that makes doing so that much harder.

"Don't do that, just to get back at me."

She scoffs. "Don't flatter yourself."

"Don't fuck him, Georgie."

Forget crossing the line; I'm so far past the line I can't even see it. But I don't backtrack. I bore my eyes into hers, letting her see how much I mean it.

It affects her. I see her swallow. Her arms cross.

"Can you give me a reason?" she asks.

Georgie's words are contrary to her expression. There's something in her eyes that looks like hope. I pull in a deep breath that tastes like regret, because we both know I can't. The last time she asked me for one, I could. That was about guarding her, about ensuring I succeeded at this assignment.

I hold her gaze for a minute. Then I shake my head, turn around, and walk away.

———

Joey and I end up at a pizza place for dinner. It's crowded and noisy, filled with plenty of college students loading up on carbs before a long night of drinking.

We end up in a corner booth, splitting two of the veggie specials. Joey's a vegetarian, it turns out, something I feel badly about not already knowing. I haven't made much of an effort to get to know any of the other agents I'm here with. We spend a lot of time together, but most of it is on constant alert, which isn't conducive to much more than exchanging small talk.

While we eat, I also learn Joey grew up in Texas and is allergic to strawberries. He planned to enlist in the army, before getting a full ride at UT Austin and applying to the Secret Service after graduating, on a lark.

When he asks me why I applied, I hesitate. There are a lot of ways I could answer that, and I'm not sure which is most accurate anymore. "My dad was an agent," I finally tell him. "It was always a thought, in the back of my mind. I fooled around a lot in high school. Did well in school, but never focused. Didn't know what to focus on. When I started college, pursuing this felt like a good goal. Something to focus on. So…" I shrug. "Here I am."

"When did it change?"

"Huh?"

"You said it *felt* like a good goal. Past tense. When did that change?"

"Oh. Uh, not sure."

It's a lie, one I think Joey catches and lets drop.

"Well, you're one hell of an agent. I've never met anyone more focused and dedicated."

It's a challenge—not to laugh. I feel like I'm the furthest thing from focused and dedicated. I'm distracted and questioning everything. The chuckle that wants to escape gets forcibly swallowed, because I know Joey is being serious. Being nice. "Thanks, man. I appreciate it."

We finish our pizza and leave the restaurant. The whole time, Joey's question echoes in my head.

When did it change?

I know the answer: when I met her.

CHAPTER EIGHTEEN

GEORGIE

MY HEART POUNDS a little faster with every floor I feel the elevator rise. Myles and Kevin are chatting easily, oblivious to my rapid pulse. Probably relieved this turned into an early night, that they only had to watch a bunch of college students dance and drink and make out until a little past midnight.

Other parties I've attended have gone much later, and I usually feel guilty about it after the fact. They chose to become agents, but they had no say in getting assigned to a college campus.

Not that I had a say in having them here.

The elevator doors open. They both wait for me to exit first, then follow me down the hall to my door. I dig my keys out of my purse and unlock it, shoving the door open and stepping to the left of the doorframe.

Myles waits in the hall with me while Kevin checks the apartment, on the off-chance anyone managed to sneak up here and break in. Most of the security measures are ones I think are silly and over the top. But the one time Joey forgot to check my apartment when I returned from class, I went room to room with the door key clenched between my fingers before relaxing.

As we stand, Myles's stomach grumbles. He gives me an apologetic look, and I smile. "Do you want a snack? I've got some stuff left over from the last grocery trip."

I eat most of my meals in the dining hall, but the kitchen of my apartment is well-stocked.

"Nah, I'm okay. Thanks. Joey and Ethan got pizza earlier. Joey said he stuck the leftovers in my fridge."

The mention of Ethan's name hits me like a splash of hot water. I'm immediately, entirely, distracted from conversation with Myles.

Don't fuck him, Georgie.

The memory of that moment—of his commanding tone and intense gaze—isn't perfect. But even the hazy recollection packs a powerful punch. My stomach muscles clench and lazy heat traverses through my veins.

Kevin reappears. "All good."

"Great. Night, guys."

I push into the apartment and shut the door before either of them say a word. I lean back against the door, letting out a long exhale. All the resolve I felt earlier—watching Ethan walk away —falters. Putting yourself out there is hard. Putting yourself out there when you know there's a high chance of rejection is masochistic.

But I can't keep balancing on a knife's edge. Teetering between *Nothing will ever happen between us* and *Don't fuck him, Georgie.* Either something will happen to snap the sexual tension that's been building between us for months or Ethan will turn me down and I'll know for certain that he's a lost cause.

I kill time for ten minutes—brushing my hair and slipping off the underwear beneath my dress, because it makes me feel like

I'm bold enough to be a seductress—until I'm sure the hallway will be empty. Then I slip out of my apartment and walk down to Ethan's door.

Two deep breaths are necessary before I knock.

The door swings open a few seconds later. Ethan's hair is wet, he must have recently showered. He's wearing nothing but a pair of sweatpants that ride low on his hips, looking casual and unbothered. Relaxed, like the conversation at the football game earlier never took place.

He says nothing. Neither do I. I force my eyes to stay on his face, not the V his waistband is clinging to.

I never realized how loud silence can be. How it can amplify and spread, filling each cavity and every crevice.

Ethan breaks it first, crossing his arms and leaning against the doorframe like me showing up at his door late at night is a normal occurrence. It's not. "Have fun at the party?"

"No."

He glances past me, at the empty hall.

"Myles and Kevin are already back," I say, realizing what he's looking for.

"I know."

"You know. So you knew…you knew I was back."

"Yes."

There's no trace of vulnerability. Of interest. I'm staring at a cold, hard exterior. The guy who smiled when I said he'd be gone in a week. He was right and I was wrong. The joke is on me —again.

I scoff. "Great. Good night."

For someone intent on leaving, I don't get very far. Ethan's quick reflexes stop me before I'm even halfway turned around. "Georgie."

"What?" I spin back around, then shove him for good

measure. "*What*, Ethan? I'm so sick of this. You're not interested? Fine. Then stop asking me if I'm into other guys when you know how I feel about you. Stop acting annoyed when I go out and stop saying nice things when we're alone. Just *stop*."

"Stop acting like I have a choice here, then. We both know I don't."

"Stop acting like you *don't*."

"Georgie."

"Ethan."

He stares at me, and I stare back. Then I shake my head, because once again, I've overplayed my hand.

"Forget it."

"Yeah, I've tried that. Doesn't seem to be doing shit."

"Can I come in?"

His jaw flexes once before he nods and holds the door open wider. I walk inside, taking in the interior of his apartment for the first time. It's the same layout as mine, just flipped in reverse. The kitchen is to the left and the bedroom is to the right.

"Want some water?"

"Um, yeah. Sure." I'm taken aback by the shift from distant to angry to accommodating.

I follow Ethan into the kitchen, leaning against the counter next to the sink as he grabs a glass from the cabinet and fills it with water from the fridge. Carries it over and holds it out to me.

I grab it, purposefully wrapping my fingers partway around his. We're close enough I can see his throat stutter as he inhales.

"Georgie," he whispers.

Ethan says my name a lot, I've noticed. Maybe he just likes the way the syllables sound. Maybe he's trying to say other things, by saying nothing else at all. But this sounds different. It hovers in the air with an aftertaste of torture, like it's physically paining him to say.

"Are you going to kiss me?" I ask. Both because it feels like he might, and because if he won't I'd rather know sooner, rather than later.

"I shouldn't."

"That wasn't what I asked," I tell him, taking the glass and setting it down on the counter. "This isn't working, Ethan." I gesture between the two of us.

He exhales some combination of a snort and a laugh. "No shit."

"So, I think we should have sex."

He looks surprised, then amused, and finally settles on incredulity. "I don't think—"

I shove away from the counter, colliding our bodies. The heat of his bare skin burns through the thin fabric of my dress, marking my skin like a brand. "We'll get it out of our system, and both move on."

Those last two words sting a little, on their way out. There was a time when I *did* think that all it would take to get over Ethan Salisbury was some time under him. That my interest would be fleeting. A passing interest that would fade once I got him to admit his. I'm much less certain of that now but not about to mention it.

"Fantasy is always better than reality," I add. "It will help."

One corner of his mouth turns up a little but other than that, he doesn't react. "You've fantasized about this?"

I don't hesitate. "Yes."

Ethan presses against me. I can feel him through his joggers. Long and thick. *Hard.* His hand lands on my waist, then slides down, teasing the hem of my dress. One finger trails up the inside of my thigh, tugging the material up with it.

My heart goes haywire. The quick thrum thunders in my ears

as blood whooshes. His hand moves higher, and my stomach dips like I'm on a roller coaster headed straight down.

"You told me not to fuck him," I whisper. "So, I didn't. I listened to you, even though we both know you like it when I don't."

"I wouldn't have liked it this time." The sentence is a growl, annoyance and lust warring in his words. Even if his erection wasn't rubbing against me, I'd know he's affected right now.

His fingers end their steady climb between my legs, and Ethan discovers I'm not wearing any underwear. I bite my bottom lip as his fingers slide through the wetness that's gathered there. I grind against his hand, trying to force his fingers to slip inside me.

Ethan groans, deep and gruff. His blue eyes meet mine, and I can see everything reflected in them. The indecision and the desperation. He wants this, but I watch him deliberate over how far he'll take it.

I say nothing. I don't touch him. It's up to him to decide how far this will go.

His hand moves, one finger sinking inside my entrance. I gasp at the unexpected intrusion. Moan at the sensation spreading.

A hungry expression spreads across Ethan's face as he watches me react. The intensity I've seen him display many times before appears, entirely focused on me. It's a heady, dizzying feeling that turns my mind blank and my bones to jelly.

He brings me to the brink of an orgasm with a few deliberate motions, then pulls his hand away and steps back. I stumble while standing in response to the loss of his touch and body heat, gripping the edge of the countertop in order to stay upright.

Ethan smirks at my lack of balance, before licking his fingers. My cooling blood warms as I watch him deftly untie the string of his sweatpants and tug them down. He isn't wearing anything underneath. His hard cock bobs out from a neatly trimmed patch of pubic hair. I got a sense of his size when he was pressed against me, but it's still intimidating to take it in, fully erect. His penis is an angry red, already leaking precum.

So far, I've barely touched him. He's that turned on, from touching *me*.

I'd immediately focused on his crotch—I'm not sure who wouldn't—but now I ghost my gaze up, over the stacked slabs of muscle that cover his stomach. I got a glimpse of him shirtless when I surprised him surfing, but that was under a very different context. I didn't feel like I could really *look*—just steal glances.

Now, I look. I've seen two guys naked, before tonight. I was attracted to both of them. But Ethan is...*more*. Everything about him is more. From the dusting of blond hair on his chest to the throbbing vein running the length of his long cock to his strong thighs. The casual confidence with which he stands, letting me check him out, is sexy as hell too.

He smirks when my eyes finally travel high enough to meet his gaze. "Take off your dress."

It's incredibly erotic, how we're standing in his kitchen. How he's completely naked and I'm fully dressed. My sex life so far has mostly been fumbled hookups in the dark, often on a strange bed at a party. I wasn't expecting sex with Ethan to be anything like that. But I'm overwhelmed, by just *how* different this feels.

By the fact that it's happening at all.

And those past encounters had one other glaring difference to this: they didn't mean anything. They were with guys I liked as people and liked looking at. But they were fueled by hormones and curiosity, sometimes alcohol. This, with Ethan, feels like nothing I've ever experienced before.

I sweep my hair over one shoulder before fumbling with the zipper at the back of my neck. My fingers aren't cooperating, jittery with a combination of nerves and anticipation and excitement. It takes me a minute to locate the very top of the zipper and tug it down. It exposes nothing from the front, the neckline of the dress just sags a little.

Ethan waits expectantly as I slide the straps off my shoulders. The material pools at my waist, then slides down until it's a puddle on the floor. I kick my shoes off as well, letting them fall in the heap of fabric. I'm wearing a bra, but it's no more than a thin layer of turquoise lace that hides nothing.

He steps forward, closing the few feet between us so I'm pressed against the counter again. I'm not sure if that means he plans to have sex in his kitchen or not. I'll follow his lead.

Usually, I hate ceding control. I like exerting power when I can, since plenty of decisions are made without my input. But right now, I want Ethan to be the driving force. It's a role he plays naturally, easily, most of the time. I like him telling me what to do, the same way he likes me pushing back.

Most of the time, I've been the aggressor between us. Ethan seizing control is the sweetest sense of victory. There's nothing more arousing than witnessing some display of how I affect him.

His warm palm cups my left breast, massaging the skin through the lacy fabric. My head falls back, some of the sparks of pleasure his fingers coaxed out before reigniting. He moves closer, so I can feel him between my legs. I gasp as his cock brushes my clit, a sharp burst of euphoria running through me.

Ethan lets me rub up against him for a minute, until I'm dangerously close to coming from the contact alone. "God, you're so wet," he rasps, letting go of my breast and sliding his right hand down my stomach. His fingers dig into my hip, keeping me from moving against him.

His left hand tilts my chin up, forcing me to look at him. "One night."

Anticipation races through me like lightning. Up until now, I was worried he would change his mind. That's how we usually work—pushing boundaries then pulling back. "One night," I repeat.

Those two words throw gasoline atop simmering flames.

We explode.

Ethan's lips hit mine at the same time his hands slip under my thighs, lifting me up and pulling me against him. I wrap my legs around his waist, as he sucks my bottom lip into his mouth.

I almost wish the kiss was underwhelming. That it felt like kissing every other guy I've ever kissed, which is more than the two I've seen naked.

My eyes are closed, so I can't even see Ethan. But there's something different about being consumed by something—or someone—you really want. At some molecular level, every cell in my body knows this is Ethan kissing and touching me. Knows how long I've wanted this to happen and how much it matters that it is.

I feel his abs clench and his back muscles shift, as he starts to walk. I tighten my grip, having no idea how he knows where he's headed but trusting him all the same.

The light around us dims, which is the main reason I'm aware we've moved to a new room. It's hard to focus on anything that isn't Ethan.

My back lands on the soft fabric of a comforter. Ethan moves to the left, and the glow of a lamp illuminates our surroundings again. I sit up on my elbows, glancing around at his bedroom. It's minimalist and neat, similar to his bedroom in DC. I've barely taken in the black dresser and the t-shirts draped over the hamper before Ethan moves between my thighs, effectively distracting me from anything except him.

"You taste like tequila," he tells me.

"I did a shot, before I left the party." I suck my bottom lip.

"You taste like me."

His hands spread my legs as his face hovers inches from their apex, cluing me in on his intention.

"No one's ever…"

Blue turns navy, as his eyes darken with possessiveness. "Good."

Then his tongue is there, licking and sucking and coaxing me toward the peak I'm already so close to. I thought I'd be embarrassed—if a guy ever did this. But this feels better than sex ever has.

I dig my heels into the comforter and lift my pelvis, trying to give him better access. Trying to chase more of the pressure that keeps building and building until I can barely breathe.

Ethan keeps pushing me toward the edge and then pulling me back right before I fall. I'm sweaty and panting and basically delirious, chanting his name like it's the chorus of my favorite song.

It feels so fucking good.

His hand returns to my breast, tugging the lace down impatiently, so he's touching bare skin. His tongue circles my clit at the same moment his fingers pinch my nipple, and I come so hard I scream. Harder than I've ever come. I'm overheated and extra sensitive.

Ethan kisses a trail up the center of my body until he reaches my ear. "You know all the times I've told you something wasn't in my job description?"

"Yes." The word is a pant, pleasure still overruling my every instinct.

"You can't fucking scream my name like that, or everyone on this floor will know I'm thinking about this—" He grinds against me. "When I'm supposed to be thinking about schedules and security threats."

I moan, aftershocks still rippling through my body as I hear the crinkle of a condom wrapper. I want to be more of an active participant. But the incoming promise of pleasure is erasing everything else. I'm lost to the lust swirling between us, so thick I could choke on it.

I force my loose limbs to cooperate, sitting up and jacking my hand up and down his hard length, feeling the smooth skin jerk beneath my touch. I lean down and suck the sensitive tip into my mouth, savoring Ethan's husky groan before I pull back and lie down, watching him roll the condom on.

He stares at me for a few seconds, sprawled on the sheets in front of him, before he crawls over me, lining up our bodies. I feel him at my center, pressing against my entrance but not pushing inside. My hands run over his shoulders and up into his hair.

"Spread those legs for me, Georgie."

I open my thighs as wide as physically possible, and I feel his chest reverberate with a laugh.

Ethan doesn't hesitate. He lifts my leg, hooking it around his hip as he starts to press inside me. I let out a moan that turns into a gasp, as he slides deeper. Ethan is big—bigger than any other guy I've been with. Knowing that is different than experiencing it. I can feel my body stretching to accommodate him.

"Fuck. You're—fuck." I writhe beneath him, trying to adjust to his size.

"You can take it," Ethan tells me, in the same bossy tone he's used to demand I text him hourly or instructed me to wait until he's surveyed a space.

And this time, I don't push back. I hook my ankles behind his back, giving him more space and allowing him to sink deeper. He does, pushing inside until he fills me completely. And I know, as I clench around him, that it will never feel this way with anyone else.

"Holy fuck, you're tight."

"You're big," I reply, smiling when he laughs.

Our mutual amusement fades fast, as he starts to move. The tightness fades with a new rush of arousal, and I just feel full. Quicker than I would have thought possible, the heat in my belly begins to build. Ethan tugs my bra up and over my head, so there's nothing between us. Just skin pressed against skin.

Ethan's apartment is completely quiet. All I can hear over the rapid beat of my heart is the sound of him thrusting inside of me. The air smells like sex. Like him. Like me. Like *us*.

He takes my hands and lifts them over my head, keeping me from touching him. It arouses me even more, not being able to touch him. Knowing he's using my body to chase his pleasure, setting a torturously slow pace that builds and builds.

Our eyes meet and hold, in a tangible connection that feels just as intimate as his penetration inside of me. His mouth hovers close to mine, but he doesn't kiss me. He just looks at me, and I look back. It's familiar and new, all at once. I know exactly what Ethan looks like. But I've never seen him like this before.

My hips arch off the bed as he grinds against me, managing to hit every pleasure point.

"You wanted me to fuck you, Georgie?"

I moan, because I lost the capacity to form complete words a while ago. His speed quickens to a punishing pace, pounding into me over and over again as his weight presses me into the mattress. His hand lets go of mine and slides down to grip my leg, his hold tightening with each roll of his hips. My hands drop too, my fingernails digging into his shoulders and sliding down his back, so I feel his muscles tense and expand. So I feel him *fucking me*.

There's nothing about it that's gentle or tentative. Ethan doesn't treat me like I'm fragile. He presses into me like there's some deeper place he hasn't managed to reach, slamming into me and stimulating with each stroke.

It's too much—all of it. The gravel in his voice as he praises me for taking him so well. The way his hot skin sears mine, making sure every inch of me feels his touch. The way he groans, every time I clench around him.

I'm reduced to the basest of instincts. I don't try to savor how good this feels or stave off my orgasm. I don't allow myself to think about how when this ends, *we* will end.

Ethan growls my name, but it's not a sound I've heard before. It makes everything inside me tighten…then release.

I'm hit twice, at once.

First, there's a realization. *I'm in love with Ethan Salisbury.* I don't think there's anything else you can call this, the need and desire and certainty. Whenever we're together but especially now, when the space between our bodies isn't large enough to slide a piece of paper between.

Second is the rush. It coats me completely, working its way through me in endless waves of heat. I don't say his name; I scream it. It's too much. Too good.

He keeps thrusting as I come, prolonging my release before I feel him jerk inside me. Ethan coming is an aphrodisiac. His eyebrows clash and his jaw strains almost like he's in pain, even though I know he's not. And it's the most powerful thrill I've ever experienced, knowing he looks that way because of me. That the pleasure he's experiencing is *because of me.*

Neither of us speak. The heat inside me spreads and slowly fades, leaving me lax and thoughtless. I'm not worried or wondering.

Ethan breathes against my neck, his exhales hot and heavy. Then, in a move I'm not expecting, he kisses me. It's soft and sweet, a gentle press that slowly deepens. I tug his bottom lip between my teeth, listening to the appreciative rumble in the back of his throat. We kiss until my lips feel swollen and it's hard to catch a breath, and then Ethan rolls away, slipping out of me and taking care of the condom.

I don't know what to do next. Whether I should stand and leave or just keep lying here. I opt for the former, because the bed is comfortable and warm and I'm not ready to leave it just yet.

Ethan lies down beside me after balling up the tissue. I could see his expression, if I turned my head. But I keep staring at the plaster ceiling instead, feeling exposed in a way that isn't uncomfortable but is certainly vulnerable.

"You good?" he asks, his voice quieter and more serious than I've ever heard it.

"Yeah," I reply.

I'm more than good. I just had sex with a guy I've wanted for months. But my reaction to the aftermath says everything I haven't fully admitted to myself—Ethan means more to me. I want this to be the first of many times we have sex, not the only time. The thought of him lying here like this, after sleeping with someone else? It feels like a serrated blade sawing through my chest.

Ethan starts humming. It's surprising enough I roll my head to the right, so I can watch him. He's staring up at the ceiling, the same as I was. And it takes me a minute, to realize why the sound is familiar. To recognize he's humming "Blackbird."

Do you keep falling, after you acknowledge you love someone? Is it a slow tumble or a fast cascade? Can love change or is it always tied to the moment you first acknowledge it?

I don't know.

But Ethan keeps humming my favorite song.

And I realize: I'm completely and totally, utterly screwed.

CHAPTER NINETEEN

ETHAN

I DON'T KNOW how I keep getting myself into these situations.

Actually, that's a total lie. I know *exactly* how. Georgie fits a mile into each inch I give her, and I let her, because I want it just as much as she does.

It's dangerous and reckless. Pointless and predictable. Secret relationships have a poor track record of staying secret, especially in political circles.

But here I am, despite knowing I should keep my distance. Kevin and I are the ones on duty tonight. I'm the near guard, despite knowing I'm far too close already. Kevin is outside the library, waiting to provide back-up if necessary, while I sit at the table two down from Georgie's study group. I should have taken Kevin up on his offer to near guard tonight. Should have done a lot of things differently.

I don't regret having sex with Georgie, even though I probably should. Unfortunately, it just reinforced the fear I already had —that there's no simple solution when it comes to her. We had sex three times that night, neither of us willing to stop until exhaustion took over.

That was five nights ago. I know exactly how she tastes, how she feels. And instead of feeling satisfied, I feel hunger.

I still want her. Still feel murderous at the thought of another man touching her.

So...suffice it to say Georgie's suggestion we fuck each other out of our systems wasn't a solid one. But that wasn't the point. It was an excuse, one I happily bought into because it involved getting something I wanted.

But now I'm stuck with the consequences. The memories of how it felt to have her writhing beneath me.

I flip the page in the thriller I'm reading, trying to ignore the quiet murmur of voices and the whisper of Georgie's laugh. We're on the top floor of the library, among the stacks few people venture along. And, based on the touches between the couples I've seen wander past, those that do come up here aren't doing so for academic reasons.

The chair at this table isn't very comfortable. It's a hard wooden one that digs into my spine. But I spread my legs out and try to relax, finally losing myself in the intrigue of an unsolved murder and a missing child.

I startle, when I sense her approach.

Georgie taps her fingers on the table, surveying me with a knowing expression that affects me more than I let on. I close the book calmly, shoving away from the table and standing so I have the height advantage.

"Ready to go?" she asks.

A glance behind her confirms that everyone else has already left, a poor showing for the fact I'm supposed to be on guard right now. I was trying so hard to act like I wasn't paying attention to her that I actually stopped doing so.

That's a problem, a major one.

I didn't buy Georgie's reasoning that sex would resolve everything between us. But I didn't consider this outcome, that it might muddy things to the point where my presence here is compromised. If I can't do my job, I shouldn't be here.

My response is measured, trying to overcompensate for the lapse. "If you are."

She nods.

I tuck the book back on the shelf where I found it, then follow her toward the elevators. At least, I *thought* we were walking toward the elevators. Georgie turns left and heads down a row of books, then takes a right. Pretty soon, we're in a spot similar to where I bet most of those couples were headed.

"Looking for a book?"

Georgie rolls her eyes. Glances left, then right. She drops her backpack on the floor and then steps closer to me. I can smell her shampoo. Feel her body heat. And it's all amplified, because now I know exactly where this could lead.

Her hand lands on my chest, sliding down my sweatshirt and then up beneath the bottom hem. I shiver as her hand coasts along my stomach, feeling my muscles tense in response to the light contact.

"Georgie," I rasp. "*Georgie.*"

"Unless you want us to get caught, you should shut up."

"We said one night." I remind her. Remind myself, though I haven't forgotten. I just want to.

Her hand slips south, palming me through my joggers. The cotton doesn't do much to muffle the sensation. More blood rushes down. "I want to touch you," she murmurs. "All night, I've thought about doing this."

"Fuck, I—fuck." Her hand slips inside my pants and down my briefs. "We can't do this here."

My voice holds no conviction. Zero authority. We both know who is control here, and it's no longer me.

Georgie ignores my half-hearted objections, sinking to her knees and tugging the material covering my erection down with her. I'm uncomfortably hard, feeling reason slip away like I'm trying to hold on to water. Her warm hand grips me as she leans forward, running the crown of my cock along the outline of her lips.

My hips jerk involuntarily, seeking more contact. I could come from this alone, paired with the visual of this. Of her, on her knees in front of me. Eager and willing.

She sucks me into the wet heat of her mouth and I groan, flexing as she tightens her grip, working me over with a rhythm that makes my skin start to prickle and my balls begin to tingle. I'm not prepared for her mouth to move to them, her tongue running circles as her hand continues to pump my cock.

My hands form fists as I lean back against the row of shelves. I should be concerned about someone walking down here and seeing this. I should be stopping this, holding firm on the promise I made to myself that this would stay contained within one night. Instead, praise spills from my lips, as I tell her how good it feels. How deep she takes me and how close I am to exploding.

Her mouth returns to my dick, sucking me deeper than before. Her tongue swirls, making it hard to think straight. I barely have the chance to warn her before I feel heat trickle down my spine.

Georgie doesn't pull away, and that's what sends me over the edge. I spill my release into her mouth, feeling her throat bob as she swallows everything I give her, which is a lot. She's a fucking fantasy, on her knees, pleasuring me. And it's more powerful because it's her. Because I know Georgie Adams doesn't kneel.

She stands as I tuck myself back into my sweatpants, surprising me when she wraps a hand around my neck and tugs my lips toward her. We make out for a minute, before she pulls away.

"I taste like you," she whispers.

"Goddamnit, Georgie." I sound mad, and I am—at myself.

I kiss her again, hard, rough, and bruising. We're locked in a battle of wills and a tangle of tongues. I grip her hip, my touch tight and possessive. Then I slip a hand between her legs, rubbing her through the leggings she's wearing. She arches into my touch, a breathy moan leaving her lips. "Did blowing me make you wet, baby?" I ask, cupping her sex possessively.

"Yes," she breathes.

I lower my face so it's tucked between her neck and her shoulder, leaving a trail of kisses that ends when I suck the skin into my mouth. It's stupid and reckless, leaving a mark on her. Evidence that she was intimate with someone. Chances are it will come up with the other agents, wondering where they were when someone had their way with her. But right now, I can't bring myself to care. It's just her I'm focused on, the breathy moans and the rocking of her hips as she seeks more pleasure. Pleasure she wants from me.

And, since I've already allowed this to go way too far—again —I push the boundaries more. I dip into the waistband of her leggings, slide beneath the lacy underwear she's wearing, and push two fingers inside of her. Her eyes flutter close and her head tips back, as I fuck her with my fingers.

My name spills from her lips, over and over again. If I thought I was possessive of Georgie before, it's nothing compared to now, as she begs me for release while my fingers move in and out of her fluttering pussy. I feel it when her inner muscles tighten, signaling she's close. And because I can't resist her, can't control myself when she's saying my name like it's her saving grace, I slide my other hand up under her shirt, until I find her breast and massage the full handful.

Georgie convulses around my fingers, fresh wetness flooding my hand as she comes.

For a few seconds, I entertain the fantasy of this going further. Of stripping the black leggings down and thrusting inside of her.

The distant ding of the elevator jars me back to reality. Slowly, I remember where we are. Who I am. Who *she* is.

"Fuck." I pack a lot into the four letters.

Anger with myself for succumbing—again. Annoyance with her for pushing the boundaries, over and over again. And acceptance, because I know what this means. I pull my hand out of her pants, wiping it against the side of mine before I jerk my head to the left. "We should go."

She looks at her for a minute, her expression blank and unreadable. "Yeah. Okay."

We weave through the maze of shelves silently. There's a petite redhead waiting for the elevator when we reach it. She gives us both a tired smile, shifting her bag to her other shoulder as we all wait for the elevator to arrive.

It eventually does, with the same quiet ding that I heard earlier. The ride down to the ground floor is only punctuated by the whir of machinery. The redheaded girl is busy on her phone. Georgie stares straight ahead. I can't get any read on what she's thinking, and it bothers me. She instigated things upstairs, though I was far from unwilling. Does she regret it? Is she second-guessing what the hell we're doing, the way I am?

I spot Myles as soon as the elevator doors open. He's leaning against the wall opposite the circulation desk, typing something on his phone. Mine vibrates in my pocket, cluing me in on who he must be messaging. He glances up and spots us approaching, slipping his phone back into his pocket.

"Hey. Long study session?"

"Yeah, it ran late," Georgie answers. Lies, rather.

"You ready to go?" Myles asks her.

"Yeah. I am."

The three of us head for the exit. I'm oblivious to the stares that follow us. Georgie's presence on campus is well-known by now. It's common knowledge on campus that the president's daughter attends school here. But that doesn't completely curb interest. I'd probably be staring too, if I were a college kid watching a classmate walk around with an armed escort.

It makes me sad for Georgie. There's no disputing parts of her life are charmed. But there's also a heavy weight no person should have to carry. Especially someone who didn't know what they were getting into. I understand why her safety is a priority, and I know Georgie does too. But that doesn't make living your life under constant surveillance any easier.

The drive back to the apartment complex is silent. I'm lost in my own thoughts and Georgie appears to be too. I notice Myles glance between the two of us, and something tightens in my gut.

As far as I know, none of the other agents have even considered the possibility there's anything going on between us. Since arriving on campus, we've always been distant in public, at least when others are in earshot. But the side look is a much-needed wake-up call.

It crystalizes what I already know—I can't justify staying here any longer. If I do, I know it will happen again. If the elevator didn't ding earlier, I have no idea how far things might have gone between us.

Myles parks in the underground garage. The elevator from the garage takes us straight up to our floor. I opt to check Georgie's apartment while Myles stands outside with her. My perusal through her bedroom lasts longer than all the other rooms. Mostly because I stare at her bed for a solid minute, wishing I could spend some time in it tonight.

Once I've finished sweeping the apartment, I step back out into the hall. "All clear," I say.

Myles nods. I avoid looking at Georgie before she heads inside the apartment, the door closing with a slam behind her.

"Night, Ethan," Myles tells me, yawning as he opens his own door down the hall.

"Night," I reply, crossing the hall and unlocking my apartment.

I turn on the lights and take a seat on the couch. Pull out my phone, and stare at the screen. It takes a long time—a lot longer than I thought it would—for me to press the name I know I need to. It feels like a loss, as soon as I do.

He answers on the second ring. "Special Agent Mark Malloy."

I clear my throat. "Hi Mark. It's Ethan—Ethan Salisbury."

"Ethan. Everything all right out there?"

Mark is too practiced to sound panicked, but I hear the subtle urgency in his tone. He's not the guy you call for social reasons. "Everything's fine," I assure him. "I'm just...well, I'm calling to request a reassignment, actually."

"A reassignment?"

It's a rare request, and the surprise in his voice reflects that. I forge ahead, before I can backtrack. "Yes."

"The president has been very impressed by your work out there. Are you sure?"

"Yeah." I exhale. "I'm sure."

There's a long pause.

"Okay. I'll get the arrangements underway. You'll be on a flight next week."

"Thank you, sir."

There's a pause. "Everything alright?"

"Just a personal matter. It has nothing to do with my current assignment."

"All right. I'll be in touch with the details."

"Sounds good. Good night, sir."

"Good night."

I let the phone drop and lean back, massaging my temples. Trying to figure out why I don't feel an ounce of relief.

CHAPTER TWENTY

GEORGIE

FOLLOWING our encounter in the library, Ethan has basically ignored me. I knew he would, and I know why he's forcing distance between us. But still, it stings.

I don't regret instigating it, not exactly. I wanted it.

I do wish it hadn't ended us up in this place, where he makes a point to ignore me, most of the time. Our conversations never extend beyond anything professional. There's a twenty-minute meeting held with my four agents to discuss travel plans for my upcoming Thanksgiving break, and he doesn't make eye contact once. Just nods along to everything Kevin suggests like a dutiful soldier.

The worst part is, I can't even blame him for the way that he's acting. He's doing exactly what he should do. Acting exactly how we agreed upon.

And even if I wanted to try to instigate another encounter between us, I couldn't. Ethan makes a point to not be alone with me. Whenever he's my near guard, there are other people around. When my study group meets the next week, Joey is the one who goes with me. I'd think it was intentional, even if Kevin hadn't let slip that Ethan altered the schedule for the week.

It seems like Kevin, Myles, and Joey are all oblivious to any change between us. Ethan has always been constantly vigilant and professional around me, and the extent of our more casual encounters has involved the occasional jibe, which the other agents find amusing more than anything.

Myles parks the SUV in the underground garage of the apartment building. We just left campus, following my last class of the day. I climb out immediately, and Ethan frowns at me.

"You're supposed to wait."

"Oops," I say, like I have no idea I'm supposed to let them clear the garage before I climb out. It's mostly empty in here, and yeah…I was trying to get him to talk to me. Small moments of disobedience are the best way to do it. I wonder if he ever considers other ways to boss me around.

Probably not. Ethan is excellent at indifference, when he's committed to it.

I follow Myles into the elevator. Ethan is right behind me.

It's a slow bit of torture, watching him stand in front of me. His shoulders tense and lift as he scans the key fob and types in the code, before hitting the button for the right floor. He rubs the back of his neck as it climbs. Shifts from foot to foot, like he can feel my eyes boring holes into his back.

Myles coughs, then shows Ethan his phone screen. "Can you believe this, about Ovechkin?" he asks.

"Yeah, I saw. Season is off to a rough start."

Myles shakes his head. "Get tickets for a game, when you're back."

I feel twin lines appear between my eyes. When Ethan is back in DC? Based on the conversation at our recent meeting, he's spending the Thanksgiving break back in Glenson. Joey is visiting his family in Texas.

Myles and Kevin are the two traveling with me back to the east coast. Maybe the Capitals are playing a California team? Maybe Ethan's plans changed? He hasn't been back to DC in a while, since he didn't come on the trip a couple of weeks ago. A small thrill of excitement unfurls in my chest, at the prospect. But I say nothing, not wanting to betray any interest.

I think Ethan is creating distance between us because he feels like he should, not because he wants to, but I don't know that for certain. It's possible a couple of hookups are all he wanted from me.

The elevator doors open. I walk down the empty hallway between the two agents, unlocking my door when we reach it. "I'll go," Ethan says to Myles, pushing the door open and walking inside my apartment.

I wish I could say the idea of leaving an artfully placed piece of lingerie out on my bed or on the couch has never occurred to me. The only reason I never have is because my agents all take turns checking my apartment when I return. I don't want anyone but Ethan seeing it.

Myles is silent as we stand in the hallway. I switch my bag to my other shoulder, restless. I've got an essay to finish and submit tonight. I also need to finalize my course schedule for the spring before I meet with the tennis team's academic advisor next week.

Training will ramp up in January, with competitions that affect rankings starting soon after. My social life will dwindle down to almost nonexistent, and my course load will lighten. Lucy has also been badgering me for more details about "Theo." I promised I'd call her tonight and am not sure what to say when I do.

If I tell her we slept together, she'll have lots of questions. Part of me wants her advice on how to interpret Ethan's actions.

But I can't tell her the whole story, can't tell her he's one of my agents. And that's highly relevant information when it comes to interpreting his behavior.

Ethan reappears. The expression on his face is unexpected. He looks...uncertain. I watch as it shifts and hardens, turning resolute. "Can I talk to you inside for a minute?"

At first, I think he's talking to Myles. I figure he found some issue in the apartment. Last week there was a problem with the thermostat. But when I look at Ethan, he's looking at me.

"Me?" I ask, glancing at Myles. I'm shocked Ethan is singling me out like this. He's *never* asked to talk to me alone. Further confusing me, Myles doesn't look the least bit surprised. He looks like he's expecting this.

Apprehension trickles down my spine. It takes me a few seconds to nod.

Ethan waits for me to walk in first. I drop my book bag on the floor next to the couch, then spin around and cross my arms. Ethan shuts the door and walks toward me, stopping a few feet away.

And...we're alone.

There's an awkward amount of space between us, which I acknowledge with an eye roll. "You don't have to stand halfway across the room."

I'm asking for a snappy retort, some mention of the fact I essentially jumped him the last time we were alone together, but it doesn't come.

"I'm leaving." Ethan speaks the announcement shortly and crisply, like it's a simple statement with no consequences.

It feels like the ground is moving beneath my feet. Maybe it's the earthquake California is overdue for. But I'm still upright. Ethan is still standing in front of me. Everything around me is stationary. The shift is invisible.

When I regain the ability to speak, I hiss one word. "Coward."

Ethan's jaw tightens in response to the insult, but he holds my gaze, disproving the accusation. He also opted to have this conversation in private. If he really was a coward, he would have told me this somewhere else. Somewhere I couldn't react the way I am right now. If he'd mentioned this at the Thanksgiving break meeting, I wouldn't have been able to say anything at all.

It's harder to hate someone you respect, but I fight to summon it anyway. Maybe I shouldn't have reacted at all. Let him stew over what *that* means, the way I overanalyze everything he does. But I'm too taken off guard…and I'm sick of pretending.

"They're sending someone out to replace me tomorrow," he tells me. "Jeremy Owens. We went through training together. He's good. A nice guy. He'll make sure you're safe."

"Is he hot?"

My mouth burns as the words leave it, the bitter aftertaste of regret settling on my tongue. Worse, Ethan doesn't react. He works his jaw a couple of times, holding my gaze. "My flight leaves tonight. I've got to go pack my stuff."

"That's…this…" Anger and shock are ebbing away, quickly being replaced by annoyance. Hurt. "That's *it*? You're just…*leaving*?"

"Yes."

Countless emotions churn through my gut, swirling so fast it's a struggle to identify each one. Irritation—that I'm only now learning about this. It's obvious this has been in the works for a little while. Myles knows, which must mean Kevin and Joey do too. They've already selected someone to replace him.

Maybe I should have seen this coming. But I didn't. I took Ethan's presence here as a guarantee, no matter what happened between us.

"You're leaving before a job is finished. Won't that look bad on your spotless record, *Agent Salisbury*?"

His shoulders tense. "It needed to happen."

Why? I want to ask.

It's obvious this change is because of me, but I can't figure out the subtext. I thought we'd settled back into a working arrangement. We agreed sex would be a one-time thing.

I've struggled with his distance since, but Ethan has acted unbothered. Is that what it was, an act? Does he care more than he's let on? Or does he want more distance for other reasons? Is he worried I'll freak out if he moves on and I see him with another girl? That I'll make it obvious something happened between us and that will damage his reputation more than this will?

Ethan turns to leave, and desperation seizes me. This is it. He's *actually leaving*. I step forward, words spilling out before I've thought them through or filtered. "It won't happen again, Ethan. Any of it. I won't flirt. I won't kiss you. I'll let you clear the fucking garage before I climb out of the car. I won't mention—"

"It's *done*, Georgie. Don't make a fool of yourself."

I flinch away from his harsh tone. "Right. Especially when you're already doing a bang-up job of making me feel like one."

He exhales loudly. "Don't do anything stupid, all right? Check in with Owens and the rest of the guys. Don't pull any of your disappearing crap."

"I don't see why you'd care," I snap. "I'm not your problem anymore."

"I care about your safety."

"Because it's part of your job description." He says nothing, and it succeeds at pissing me off further. "What about *fucking me*, Ethan? Did that come up under the list of duties?"

"So much for not mentioning it, huh?"

"You're leaving no matter what I say, right?"

"Yeah, I am," he confirms.

"Doesn't really matter then, does it?"

Ethan shakes his head. Scoffs. "Bye, Georgie."

"Would your dad have walked away from an assignment?"

I regret the question as soon as I say it. Exponentially more when I see the fury flash, transforming Ethan's handsome features into a scowl. But when he speaks, his voice is even and measured. "My dad wouldn't have gotten himself into a situation where he had to make that choice."

My heart and my pride war with each other. I don't know if there's anything I can say that might convince him to stay. My heart chases the possibility; pride staples my mouth shut.

"Stay. Please." My voice cracks between the two words, right where a lot of others want to spill out.

For a split-second, there's a flash of emotion across his face. A sign that I got through to him—more than anything else I've said did. But it disappears just as quickly, his expression shuttering back to blank, stoic certainty. "This is for the best."

"For you?"

"For both of us." He sounds sure of it, and it lends me some of his perspective. Forces me to acknowledge that sneaking around wasn't much of a feasible, long-term plan. And if nothing can happen between us again, his presence would just be a bittersweet reminder.

But it was *something*. And I wanted it. Wanted anything and everything he was willing to give.

Which is nothing, as it turns out.

He's probably right, that this is for the best. But *I* wouldn't have been able to give *him* up so easily. That's what smarts—

stings—the most. If the roles were reversed, I don't think I could have chosen to walk away from him.

I thought I meant *something* to him. Thought this would be a challenging choice to make. Ethan looks like it was the easiest decision in the world. And if *he* doesn't care, then I'm sure not going to keep acting like I do.

"Yeah. You're right. You should go." My voice is neutral, and my face feels tight—blank.

For a second, he hesitates, and I think that's what will force some emotion from him—my sudden lack of it.

"Goodbye, Georgie."

The second time sounds just as final as the first.

Ethan walks out of the apartment without a single glance back, shutting the door with a quiet thud that ricochets through my chest. I take a step back. Three. Five. Ten. My back hits the wall and I slide down slowly, not stopping until my butt hits the hardwood floor. I tilt my head back against the plaster, staring up at the ceiling and battling the telltale pinpricks of heat appearing in my eyes.

After a few minutes of fighting tears, I slide my phone out of my pocket. I take a deep breath before unlocking it and tapping on a name.

I banish all emotion from my body as it rings.

"Georgie?" Margot, my father's secretary, answers.

"Hi, Margot. Could you put me through to my father, please?"

"Sure. One moment."

Hold music starts to play. I keep staring at the ceiling, waiting for him to pick up.

I owe Ethan this.

CHAPTER TWENTY-ONE

ETHAN

DC IS COLD. I'm underdressed for early November on the east coast, wearing the shorts and t-shirt I threw on as I packed up my apartment. There wasn't much to take. The living space came furnished. All I had to do was stuff my clothes into a couple of duffels and catch a car to the airport.

Myles offered to drive me, since he was off duty tonight. But I declined. I told all the guys I'd decided to leave for personal reasons but didn't provide any additional details.

Acting overly professional around Georgie to counteract the many moments I acted anything *but* has one upside, I guess. It has left Myles, Kevin, and Joey with the impression I'd do anything for this job.

They all assumed it would take something extreme to pull my attention from this assignment and didn't ask any questions, just said they hoped everything was okay. I didn't want to give Myles the chance to ask for more details. I told him to enjoy his evening off and ordered an Uber.

There's a car waiting for me here. My steps are slow as I walk out of the terminal and toward the black SUV. I toss my bags in the trunk and climb into the passenger seat. Mark is sitting in the driver's seat. He gives me a friendly smile with the guarded edge he always has.

I like Mark a lot. He's at the very top of the chain of command I report to. His responsibilities are vast and consequential. I've always felt a kinship with him, since his father was also an agent.

It's uncomfortable to realize my choice to request a reassignment might have altered his opinion of me.

We make small talk. About my flight. About the Capitals' poor start to the season. About the unseasonably cold weather. Late autumn in DC is usually pretty mild.

We're fifteen minutes into the drive—close to downtown— when he asks. "You know what you're going to say?"

"Yes." I found out about this meeting thirty minutes ago, and I've spent most of the time since thinking about it.

"Good."

That's it for conversation until we reach the White House gates. Mark flashes his badge. I pass mine over as well and we're waved through. He takes a right, heading toward the West Wing instead of continuing straight in the direction of the residence.

"I'll be here," he says, pulling off the road and into one of the permitted spots.

"I can take the Metro or Uber back."

"I don't mind. We'll need to discuss your new duties, anyhow."

I swallow and nod, climbing out of the car and walking over toward the circular office that juts out slightly from the rest of the white building. My badge gets checked again at the door and then I'm ushered into a hallway I recognize. It leads directly to a familiar door.

It's close to ten p.m. eastern time, but there are still plenty of staffers in suits bustling about. I'm wildly underdressed for a meeting in the Oval Office, the same thing I'd judged Georgie for.

Irony is a bitter pill to swallow.

I saw the text from Mark that the president wanted to see me after I'd already landed in DC. Otherwise, I would have dressed more appropriately.

President Adams' private secretary glances up from her desk right outside the door as I approach. Her gaze lingers on me, but I don't feel like she's judging my attire. There's something like curiosity in her expression. "You can go right in," she tells me. "He's expecting you."

"Thank you," I tell her, shoving the nerves away as quickly as they spring up.

I turn the knob to enter a room I never thought I'd get to enter. I wonder how long you have to be president for before the thrill of having this as your workspace disappears. If it ever does.

The Oval Office looks as spotless and immaculate as it did the one and only other time I've been inside here. I shove the memory of that meeting far away, because it's painful in its own way.

President Adams is sitting in one of the two armchairs angled near the fireplace. The grate is clean and empty. Papers are spread across the coffee table and the couch, being shuffled by a middle-aged woman who I recognize from events as the president's chief of staff.

They both look up when I enter the room. The woman's eyebrows rise in response to my arrival. Or maybe my casual appearance.

I feel obligated to say, "I'm sorry, sir, I came straight from the airport—"

"I'm not concerned about your appearance, Agent Salisbury."

I swallow. Because he says it like there are other things he *is* concerned about. And why shouldn't there be? He asked me, personally, to join his daughter's security detail. Entrusted me with her safety. I didn't let him down in that regard, but I was far from a model agent.

"Can you give us a minute, Anne?"

The woman nods, grabbing a few papers and then leaving the room. The door closes behind her with an ominous snap.

I straighten, clasping my hands behind my back. President Adams tosses the papers he was holding onto the table and leans back in his chair, watching me closely. "I'm very appreciative of the sacrifices you and your colleagues make to keep me and my family safe, Agent Salisbury. It doesn't go unnoticed. Outside of logistics involving my own detail, I don't like to interfere in any security matters. I know you and your superiors have everyone's best interest in mind. But, with Georgie...she struggles with authority. She loves to push back. She hates the constraints my decisions have placed on her. So I reached out to Agent Malloy, knowing there would need to be changes to Georgie's detail when she left for Stanford. He recommended you. Told me if he had a daughter, you were the agent he would entrust her with."

I keep my expression impassive. But fuck if I don't feel about two inches tall right now.

"I received reports that Georgie was thriving at Stanford. Happy and well-adjusted and *safe*. You guarded her, on your own, for close to a week without a single incident. And a month later, you request to be removed from her detail and reassigned."

"It wasn't an easy request to make, sir."

"I don't doubt it. Your file is filled with glowing reviews, Agent Salisbury. Nearly every one mentions your commitment and dedication. That you're a man who takes his responsibilities seriously." He pauses, letting that sink in. A compliment and an accusation. "Was it not an exciting enough assignment for you?"

241

"No, it wasn't that at all, sir. I appreciate the fact that guarding you or your family is the highest honor an agent can receive. The confidence you and Agent Malloy placed in me was immense. I never compromised Georgie's safety, nor would I ever."

President Adams tilts his head, appearing mollified and confused by my answer. We're circling closer and closer to the heart of the matter, and I wait to see if he'll just ask it.

He does. "Why did you request a reassignment, Agent Salisbury?"

"I—I realized I wasn't the best person for the assignment."

"Your superiors would differ. They had a lot of difficulty deciding who to send in your stead."

"I have a lot of confidence in my fellow agents."

"But not in yourself?"

I swallow. "I was becoming distracted."

"Distracted?" For the first time, he sounds surprised. "Were there personal matters you weren't given sufficient time off to resolve?"

"I—" *Fuck.* How the hell do you tell the President of the United States you were distracted by his daughter's smart mouth? By her body? "No, that wasn't the issue."

"What *was* the issue then, Agent Salisbury?" He's losing patience.

"I was distracted *by* Georgie. I…I developed some feelings I shouldn't have."

His eyebrow rises a little, but that's his only facial reaction. "I see."

I wait. For him to figure out how to fire me. Freak out. Instead, he asks, "Did she?"

"Sir?"

"Did my daughter develop feelings for *you*, Agent Salisbury?"

Not what I expected him to ask, and my hesitation before

242

answering reflects that. "You would have to ask her that question."

"I'm asking you."

"I can't speak for someone else's feelings."

A hint of the anger I was expecting to appear a while ago finally does. "Don't treat me like a fool, Agent Salisbury, and I'll extend you the same courtesy." I swallow. "Did Georgie ever say or do anything to make you think she has romantic feelings toward you?"

I'm sweating. It feels like I'm a witness in a murder trial. On display and under intense pressure. "Yes," I answer.

He sighs. I can't get any more of a read on his expression. "I understand your decision to leave. But, to be clear, I'm not requiring you to take a reassignment after what you've shared. I respect honesty. If you want to return to California and resume your assignment, that's your decision. Georgie is an adult, fully capable of making her own, as well."

It's more than I expected him to offer. More than *I* would offer, if I had a daughter. But I hold steady. "I made my decision already, sir."

He nods. "Understood. I'll approve your reassignment immediately."

"Thank you, Mr. President."

I turn to walk away.

"Ethan?"

I swallow before turning back around. No matter how many times I do, my throat still feels dry. I don't miss how he used my first name this time. "Yes, sir?"

"She called me. A few hours ago."

I swallow—again. I don't need to ask who *she* is. And we certainly didn't part on the best of terms. "Did she ask you to fire me?"

There's a flicker of a smile across his face, so fast and small I almost miss it. "She hasn't asked me for anything since she was a little girl. But she did tell me to give you your first choice of reassignment, even if I had to 'rearrange things.'"

Dammit. I didn't want this confirmation she cares. I'd rather leave things angry and resolute.

I nod in acknowledgement. Then turn and walk out of the Oval Office.

⊏⊐

I'm drained, upset, and angry by the time I fit the key into the lock of the front door of my apartment and push it open. I'm not expecting the dozen or so people hanging out in the living room, who all turn to me at once with surprised expressions that almost look choreographed.

I didn't prepare an explanation for Colby on why I'm back in DC, weeks ahead of schedule. My next visit was supposed to be over Stanford's winter break. And I certainly wasn't expecting to have to answer questions from Logan or Owen or anyone else here tonight.

Usually, there's nothing I'd love less than to display emotion. I keep everything locked down with Fort Knox-level security. But for the first time in a long time, I simply don't care. I don't care about *showing* I care.

It tells me I made the right choice—leaving. That my judgment where Georgie is concerned was already significantly impaired and if I'd waited any longer it would only have gotten worse.

And it also hurts like hell.

"Ethan." Colby stands, the first one to move as I shut the door behind me and shove my keys back into my pocket. "What are you doing here?"

"Last I checked, I live here."

Colby doesn't crack a smile. "Did something happen? Is Georgie okay?"

Everything inside me tenses, when he says her name. "She's fine," I clip. "I requested a reassignment."

"You...*requested* a reassignment?"

Colby looks stunned. Giving up isn't in my nature, and he knows it. She did too, and it makes me feel like the coward she called me.

Would your dad have walked away from an assignment?

God, I hate that she asked me that. Hate that she knew me well enough to think it.

"Yep." I open the kitchen cabinet over the sink and then open the freezer, pulling out the bottle of Gray Goose in there Colby keeps around for special occasions—aka when he's trying to impress a woman by showing off the skills he acquired bartending in college.

I pour a generous amount of vodka into the glass and down it all in one big gulp, welcoming the burn, followed by a trickle of numbness. I fill and drain the glass again before sticking the icy bottle back in the freezer and rinsing the glass before placing it in the dishwasher.

I clean up my messes.

When I turn back around, Colby is staring at me like I'm a total stranger.

I hardly ever drink. When I do, it's a cold beer at a sporting event or out at a bar. I don't suck vodka down like it's water.

"I'm going to bed." I grab my duffle bags from the spot by the door where I dropped them and start toward the entrance to the hallway.

Colby grabs my bicep, pulling me to a stop before I reach it. "Ethan. What the fuck happened, man?"

"I fucked up."

And apparently, I left my filter back in California.

Or maybe a flood of vodka washed it away.

Colby's forehead wrinkles as he tries to make sense of my words. "What do you mean?"

"I don't want to talk about it."

Colby is one of my closest friends. I know if I told him about Georgie, he'd never breathe a word to anyone.

I also know I'll never say anything. Not to him, not to anyone else. I pull my arm away and keep walking down the hall. He doesn't follow me. Doesn't say anything else.

It takes me fifteen minutes to unpack everything. The commotion out in the living room is muted, everyone out there obviously attempting to be quiet and to not disturb me. No one knocks on my door or tries to get me to talk. I was convincing about not wanting to.

I don't want to talk to anyone…except her. The one person who could pull me out of this funk in my head is the one person who caused it.

I wonder what she'd say, if she could see me now. Sprawled out, scowling, with liquid fire simmering in my stomach. I wish I didn't know she'd called in a favor for me. Or tried to—rather, since the Secret Service doesn't ask you where you want to go. They send you where you're needed, and you go without question. I never, ever thought I would question.

But here I am.

Georgie wouldn't have wanted me to know she called on her behalf. I'm certain she had no idea her father would tell me she had.

Because she thinks I don't care about her and doesn't want me to know that she might care about me.

She's wrong.

If I really didn't want anything to happen between us, it wouldn't have.

I wanted her—too much.

That's why I had to walk away.

Why I hate that I did.

CHAPTER TWENTY-TWO

GEORGIE

I SLAM the tennis ball with so much force a string on my racquet snaps. I keep swinging anyway, returning another serve from the machine with just as much intensity.

Sweat trickles down my face. My muscles burn.

I should have stopped practicing a long time ago—like when all my teammates did. I've kept my feelings compartmentalized, since Ethan left. I go to class. I hang out with friends. I kissed Jordan at a frat party last weekend. He asked me to get dinner with him on Friday night, and I accepted.

I'm like a duck. From the surface, I look unbothered and serene. Floating around and enjoying life.

Underwater, I'm working hard to stay afloat.

And it's only here, on the tennis court, that I'll let that control slip. Where I'll push myself until I can't think anymore.

The machine runs out of balls to throw. Even if I wanted to keep going, I can't. Exhaustion hits me like a wave as I lower my racquet, my arms numb and tingly. My legs feel like lead as I walk over to the bench where I left my tennis bag, grabbing a towel and a bottle of water out of it.

I sink onto the warm metal, guzzle a healthy amount of the bottle, and wipe the sweat off my forehead before leaning back and letting the late afternoon sun warm my face.

Adrenaline wears off slowly, leaving me drained and on edge again. I didn't think Ethan would be easy to forget. But I thought I *would* be able to forget him.

It's not the sex or the sneaking around that I miss, as hot as they both were. It's the rapport we built, the reliability and the sense of safety when he was near. For months, we spent almost every day together. That sort of proximity forges a different sort of intimacy, a partnership that feels permanent. Or at least unshakeable in the ten days since he left.

I keep thinking of things to tell him. A guy in my Astrology class was talking about the Capitals yesterday and I wanted to remind Ethan he should take me to a game...before promptly remembering that will no longer be happening.

Loss likes to hit you in waves, I'm learning. Punish you with a sucker punch you're not expecting.

I wipe my face with the towel again before tossing all of my equipment back into my tennis bag and zipping it up. I sling the strap over one shoulder and stand, crossing the colored concrete toward the chain link fence surrounding the court.

Jeremy climbs out of the SUV as soon as he sees me approaching. Wordlessly, he takes the heavy bag from me and places it in the trunk while I climb into the backseat.

I like Jeremy. He has the same strong, silent presence as Ethan, but he lacks Ethan's edge, the snarky comments and the eye rolls that always bubbled below his stoic exterior and emerged more the longer we spent together. Jeremy is agreeable and easy-going, with warm brown eyes and messy hair. He's always pleasant.

The last few months would have been far more peaceful if

Jeremy had been my new agent all along. Anyone who's met me and Ethan would probably predict our personalities would clash. But I get why Ethan was considered the superior agent—at least on paper. He has an intensity about him that is difficult not to trust. If I was in a life or death situation, he is the person I would want by my side.

He obviously felt differently, or he wouldn't have left.

"Do you mind stopping at CVS?" I ask Myles, who's driving.

"Of course not," he answers, pulling into the parking lot a few minutes later. Jeremy climbs out to go inside with me, acting as my near guard.

I wander through the aisles in a way I hope looks aimless and casual. I put on a ball cap on the short trip here. I tug on the brim, trying to cover as much of my face as possible. A random assortment of items gets flung into the shopping basket: a box of granola bars, Crest toothpaste, a birthday card, a bag of Doritos, Band-Aids. Jeremy hangs a few feet behind me. He's good about giving me space. About only making his presence known when he needs to.

Predictably, he glances away when I start down the feminine hygiene aisle. I grab both pads and tampons before continuing down. My steps veer toward the right side in a way I hope is casual. I reach out and grab a pregnancy test, quickly dropping it in the basket and shifting the Doritos so they cover the pink box. Every muscle in my body wants to turn around and see if Jeremy noticed or if he's still avoiding eye contact. But I don't want to draw more attention to myself.

When we reach the end of the aisle, I sneak a glance at Jeremy, while pretending to survey the display at the end of the aisle. He looks as relaxed and at ease as he did when we entered the store, which makes me think he didn't notice.

I have an excuse prepared—I'm buying the test for a friend—but I don't want to use it. For one, it's not super believable. Any true friend would know the potential consequences of a photo of me buying a pregnancy test.

I grab a bottle of Gatorade and head for the check-out. Jeremy doesn't comment as I go toward the self-check-out instead of a cashier. I scan everything quickly and bag it efficiently before leaving the store.

The drive to the apartment complex from the pharmacy only lasts a few minutes, but it feels like much longer. I've staved off the fear about what the possible outcome of this could be by telling myself there's no reason to panic, until I know for sure. Now that I'm about to reach that point, it's not much of a reassurance.

I'm silent for the trip through the garage and up to my apartment, and so are Myles and Jeremy. Myles is the one who checks my apartment, and then I head inside alone with my purchases.

I walk straight into the bathroom, tugging my sweaty shirt off so that I'm left in my sports bra and leggings. I dump the bag out onto the tile floor, sorting through everything I bought until I find what I'm looking for.

I stare at the box. I don't really want to be doing this alone. But I don't have a choice. I'm not close enough with anyone here to trust they'll keep it to themselves, even if it's just an accidental slip at a party after too many shots. It could wreck my father's reelection campaign, especially if it's positive. I can't keep this baby—I don't want a baby—and that will leave a trail that could be dug up. Political careers have ended for far less. And I may not want my father to win again, but I don't want to be the reason he doesn't either.

The only other option is Ethan.

Annoyingly, I wish he were here. I also know he'd come, if I asked. I wouldn't even have to tell him my period is late. If I called him and told him I needed him to be here, he would be.

And then he'd leave all over again, with more resentment and bad blood between us.

I shake the plastic stick out of the box and pee on it, then perch on the side of the tub, waiting for the results. We were safe. The chance I'm pregnant is low. I've been stressed lately. Barely eating, hardly sleeping, and logging twice the time on the court. It's normal for my body to be responding to those extreme choices.

I know other girls who got pregnant as teenagers. Lacey Michaelson, who attended the same Catholic high school I did in Boston before my dad got elected freshman year. Her family was extremely religious, so she kept the baby. And then, according to the Hamilton Academy gossip mill, Hannah Harris had an abortion our junior year. I'm not even sure if it was true, but it's all anyone could talk about for months. Judge about. Parents, too, as if their own kids weren't having sex.

Both girls were shamed for being in that position. And I know I would be judged just as harshly—harsher—if anyone ever found out, thanks to the magnifying glass my family lives under. Thanks to the high standard and relentless pressure of being the First Family. Of being a perfect family, if such a thing exists.

The timer on my phone goes off. I glance down at the stick to see just one line. I don't need to look at the box to confirm what that means. Dizzying relief hits me so fast I feel nauseous.

I shed the rest of my clothes, turn on the shower, and step under the steamy spray. Dried perspiration washes away as my skin turns pink. I'm giddy with relief.

But there's also a small part of me that thinks, *If you had been pregnant, you would have had to talk to him.* That part of me wouldn't have hated the excuse.

I let that thought disappear down the drain with the soap suds.

CHAPTER TWENTY-THREE

ETHAN

"ARE YOU SEEING ANYONE, MAN?"

The fuck?

I look over at Logan, both brows raised. "You're not my type."

Logan flips me off, then takes another bite of pizza. We're standing in his kitchen, eating a few slices before the third period of the Capitals game starts.

"Is Megan?" he asks, once he swallows.

"Megan?"

Logan rolls his eyes. "Megan, my coworker. You've met her at least five times. She went to the going away party you and Colby threw."

"That Colby threw," I correct. Another eye roll. I search my memory, coming up with a vague recollection of a brunette Logan showed up with. "Yeah, I remember her."

"And?"

"And what?"

"She likes you, idiot. Asks about you all the time. I tried to set you guys up over the summer, and then you flew off to California. But now you're back—for good. So…are you seeing anyone?"

"I'm not looking for a relationship," I reply, which is true.

"I don't think she's expecting a marriage proposal. Just ask her out, have dinner together. See if there's something there."

Logan makes it sound simple and easy. But there's a gnarled knot in my chest at the thought of going out with some woman. Of flirting and paying attention to what she says and kissing her at the end of the night. So, I hesitate. "I don't know. I'll think about it."

"Is there someone else?"

"Why would you think that?"

"Because you've been back in DC for three weeks. We've gone out together every weekend. You haven't looked at a single girl, much less gone home with one."

"Paying a lot of attention to my sex life, huh? Yours must be crap."

"You didn't say *no, there's no one else*, Ethan."

I work my jaw, debating how much to say. "It's over."

Logan's eyebrows climb up to the middle of his forehead. "So there was someone?"

"Yeah. There was someone."

"You were exclusive?" He asks the question incredulously. Logan knows how long it took for me to commit to a relationship with Stella and how quickly it fell apart.

It's not that I have any issue being faithful to a woman. It just implies a level of seriousness I've never been interested in before.

"I guess." I didn't hook up with anyone else, while I was at Stanford. Based on the amount of time we spent together, I don't think Georgie could have been either, without me knowing.

"And you haven't been with anyone else since?"

I shake my head and take a swig from my can of Coke, hoping that will be the end of it.

"So you were really into her."

He states, rather than surmises. I shrug, sticking with nonverbal answers.

Georgie and I aren't in a relationship. We were never in a relationship. I'm not uninterested in other women out of some loyalty or obligation toward her.

The truth is worse. Georgie and I will never happen again. Once I have sex with someone else, she'll never be the last person I slept with again.

"Who was she?"

"You don't know her," I mutter, before biting into a piece of crust.

"Did it bother Georgie?"

The question is so unexpected I fail to control my reaction. I choke, cough, and wash the bit of dough down with more soda. "Why would you ask that?"

"It was obvious she was into you at the bar that night. At your going-away party. You stopped complaining about guarding her a while ago. Almost seemed like you enjoyed it, being part of her detail. Makes the fact you quit out of nowhere all the weirder."

"Game is back on!" Colby shouts from the living room.

I scoop a stray piece of pepperoni out of the pizza box and pop it into my mouth. Grab the red can off the counter. "You should introduce Megan to Silas. He's a great guy. Maybe they'll hit it off."

Logan just looks at me, the half-concerned, half-contemplative expression he's worn on his face for the entirety of this conversation still present and accounted for.

"It was her, wasn't it?" he asks in a low voice. I tense.

"Georgie wasn't jealous because…it was her. That's why you stayed. That's why you left. Holy fucking shit, Salisbury."

"Are you guys deaf?" Colby yells. "Game's back on, morons!"

Neither Logan nor I say anything, locked in a silent stare-off. "You like her," he says, sounding shocked. "You *really* like her."

"I liked her. Like I said, it's over."

"She's the fucking *First Daughter*, Ethan!"

I set the can down and grip the edge of the countertop until my knuckles whiten. "I know that. You think I don't fucking know that?!"

"I don't know what to think! What if she tells someone? This could ruin your career, your life!"

"She won't tell anyone."

"How the fuck do you know? She's a teenager. She just gradu-ated from high school; she's been spoiled her whole life. Her father is the fucking president! Wasn't she pissed you left?"

"She won't tell anyone," I repeat. "I trust her."

Logan shakes his head. "Wow. She sure did a number on you."

"This isn't on her," I snap. "I wanted it too."

He scoffs. "Did you fuck her?"

I don't answer.

"Wow, you did. You probably had the president's daughter on her knees, begging to blow you. Pornhub should capitalize on that shit."

I breathe in and out of my nose, trying to keep my temper in check. "Talk about her like that again, and you won't be able to speak at all for a while."

"What the hell is going on in here?" Colby's voice joins the conversation, as he glances back and forth between me and Logan.

Logan has his arms crossed and is wearing an incredulous expression. I'm gripping the counter like I'm trying to pulverize it to dust with my bare hands.

"Nothing." I let go of the counter and straighten. "I'm heading out, and Logan wanted me to stay."

"Headed out? Where? There's a full period left, and you're my ride home."

Colby's lack of a car is a perennial thorn in my side.

"You can Uber," I tell him. "I got a better offer."

"A better off—oh." Colby grins. "About damn time, man. I was starting to get worried. Your side of the hall has been awfully quiet lately, if you know what I'm saying." He waggles his eyebrows.

Subtle, Colby is not.

He looks to Logan next. "Come on. You can't blame the guy. Every time I called him when he was out in California, he was on guard duty. Had to be hard to get laid with Georgie around all the time."

I'm not sure what it says that Colby—who will hit on any pretty woman with a pulse—hasn't so much as considered the possibility that some of the time I spent around Georgie was sans clothes. That she's the reason I left California and requested a reassignment.

I guess I should find it flattering. He's met her. Has commented on her attractiveness. He thinks it's a line I wouldn't cross, and I wish he were right about that.

I glance down at my phone, pretending to see a new text from my booty call. "Gotta go."

"All right. See you later," Colby heads back into the living room, leaving me and Logan alone in his kitchen again.

He speaks first. "I'm sorry. I shouldn't have judged."

"I would have done the same."

I used to shake my head at agents who missed a mark in training or used up all of their vacation time. If I'd heard a fellow agent was having sex with a member of the president's immediate family? I would have thought they were the poorest excuse for a public servant to ever exist.

"Still. You're one of my best friends. And because of that, you know all the stupid shit I've done."

I chuckle, because it's true. "Nothing this stupid."

"You never did *anything* stupid."

"Not true," I counter.

"It *is* true, Salisbury. You're always the DD. Mr. Responsible. Telling us all not to drink too much and wear a condom and set an alarm for work or for class."

"Someone has to."

"Are you in love with her?"

The question stalls me for a second. No one has ever asked me if I loved someone before. I've never asked *myself* if I loved anyone, let alone Georgie. I deflect, to avoid doing so now. "I should go."

"Sure. Go fuck your fake hook-up."

"How do you know she's fake?"

"Because..." Logan sighs. "Because you didn't answer the question."

He grabs his plate and walks out of the kitchen, leaving me standing here. I drain the rest of my soda, toss it in the recycling, and head for the front door.

The air outside is crisp and cool, holding the first notes of winter but not nearly there yet. I cruise through the streets of DC, glad I'm beating the flood of pedestrians that will be exiting the hockey arena soon. I'll be home before the game is over, at this rate. I'm not stopping at a bar or texting any of the numbers I have saved in my phone. My plan is to go home, have a beer, and go to sleep.

Logan was right that my hookup was fake. But that's all he was right about.

I hope.

———

Slouching on the couch with a cold beer gets old fast. I can't get the television to switch off the video game Colby was playing earlier to cable, so I'm stuck staring at a blinking *Game Over* message. It's only ten, which feels too early to go to bed.

I scroll through social media for a little while, then switch over to my messages. I should text some girl, force myself to move on.

Instead, I tap on Jeremy Owens's name. He answers on the first ring, before I can second-guess.

"Ethan! Good to hear from you."

His voice is upbeat and chipper, which is typical Jeremy. I don't think he's capable of anything but cheerful.

"Hey, Jeremy. I just wanted to check in. I know it was last minute, you stepping in out there. I'm sure it won't go unrecognized."

Jesus, I sound like I work for HR.

"No worries, man," he replies. "Happy to help. I mean, when the president asks you to do something, you do it, right?" Jeremy chuckles.

My "Right," is hollow.

Because I didn't. I cut and ran because I couldn't keep my emotions separate from the job.

Jeremy clears his throat, catching onto the subtext. "I didn't mean—"

"I know. It's fine." I hesitate, rubbing my thumb along the rim of my beer bottle as I debate what else to say. "How is she?" I finally spit out.

"Georgie?" Jeremy asks, sounding surprised by the question. "She's fine. Everything has been smooth and easy so far. I practically feel like I'm on vacation." He chuckles.

"She's been checking in when she's supposed to?"

"Like clockwork. Even when she's out at parties. Never forgets. Polite as can be."

Polite as can be? She's not giving him shit. I'm not sure if I should be annoyed or relieved that she's treating him differently than she treated me.

"That's great," I reply, in a tone more suitable for delivering bad news.

Jeremy catches it. "Everything okay with you, man?"

"Yeah," I reply. "Everything is fine, thanks." I told him personal reasons are why I requested a transfer back to DC, same as I told everyone else. It's a vague excuse sure to raise eyebrows. Requests for reassignments are usually reserved for major, life-altering, urgent emergencies. All I did was fail to keep my dick in my pants.

"Good. Glad to hear it." There's a rustling sound in the background, then I hear Jeremy say, "Yeah, sure," slightly muffled.

"If you need to go…"

"Sorry. No, it's fine. Kevin was just telling me he's going to the bathroom. We're both on duty tonight."

A car door opens and closes in the background.

"You're both on duty?" That means she's out, on a Saturday night.

It shouldn't surprise me. I shouldn't care. I didn't miss Jeremy's mention of parties earlier. But she's not at a party now. It's only a little after seven p.m. on the west coast. Practically the middle of the afternoon on a college campus. And the background noise is too quiet.

"Yep. We're chaperoning a date."

All I can manage is a "Hmm," as my insides churn with a mixture of rage and jealousy.

I'd think this was payback, her deliberately trying to piss me off, if not for the fact that she had no way of knowing I would call tonight. *I* had no idea I would call tonight, up until about five minutes ago when I tapped on Jeremy's name. And she definitely had no way of knowing Jeremy would mention it to me, if I did.

Jeremy clears his throat. "Um, while I have you, there is something I've been wondering."

I tense. "Oh, yeah?" He's going to ask why I left, I'm guessing. Since it's such a *smooth and easy* assignment, and all.

"How did you handle...*delicate* topics with Georgie? Would you mention stuff to her, or just pretend like you saw nothing?"

It takes me a minute to recalibrate and respond to the unexpected question.

"What sort of delicate topics?" There's a sharp, anxious edge to my voice that I don't bother to hide. Is she having issues with classes? Tennis? A guy?

"Never mind. I shouldn't have... Myles mentioned you had a good relationship with her, that's all. I thought you'd be most likely to know how to...handle it."

I don't let him backtrack. "What sort of delicate topics, Jeremy?"

He blows out a long breath, an audible whoosh that echoes on the other end of the line. "She bought a pregnancy test last week. I took her to the pharmacy after practice. I didn't see her buy it, but I found the receipt in the car a few days later."

Jeremy keeps talking but I'm no longer absorbing a single word he's saying.

Because *holy shit*.

I get why Jeremy is conflicted. Guarding someone inevitably includes private moments you're not meant to witness but can't avoid. No situation is the same and that makes it difficult to navigate. To decide whether to act oblivious or offer advice.

But, for me, I'm not the least bit concerned about propriety or the prospect of having to report to the president his teenage daughter might be knocked up. Of helping to cover up the scandal or come up with a positive PR spin.

I'm freaking out because there's an excellent chance that if Georgie *is* pregnant, it's with *my* kid.

"Jeremy, I'm sorry, something just came up. I'll think it over a little and let you know what I'd do, okay?"

His exhale is heavy with relief, letting me know how much this is weighing on him. It's nothing in comparison to the two-ton barrier it feels like I'm carrying now. "I appreciate it, Ethan, thanks."

We say goodbye, and then I'm left staring at a black screen. Did she know it was a possibility when I left? Would she have said something, if she did? I try to do the math, to figure out what date we had sex and work forward, but my head is spinning too fast to think straight.

My parents got married at twenty-two. Had Hudson a year later—when they were my age. Growing up, that sounded plenty old to have a kid. Now, I feel very different about it. I don't feel old enough to shoulder that responsibility, and I'm four years older than Georgie.

I can't call her now, because she's out on a fucking date.

And what does the fact that she's out on a date *mean*?

Jeremy said she bought the pregnancy test last week. She's taken it by now, presumably. Knows the results. And she went out with a guy.

Because she's not pregnant?

Because she's looking for a distraction?

Questions only she can answer buzz around in my head until I feel like it will explode.

I chug the end of my beer and stand. I'm wearing the sweatshirt and joggers I've had on all day. I grab my phone and keys, shove my feet into sneakers, and head out the door.

I run for over an hour. Until I'm soaked with sweat and my screaming muscles give me something else to focus on.

The apartment is quiet and empty when I enter. It's nearly midnight now, the game would have ended a while ago. Colby obviously decided to go out after, which I'm grateful for. This isn't a conversation I want to chance him overhearing.

I gulp down two glasses of water and head into my bedroom, flipping lights on as I walk. I yank my sweaty hoodie off, tossing it in the hamper and then stalking around my room to collect the other dirty clothes tossed around. By the time I'm finished, the hamper is almost full. I should do a load of laundry.

But there's a persistent, steady buzz under my skin. It flows over me like a constant thrum of electricity that doesn't allow me to sit still or to focus on anything else.

I need to know.

With a sigh that doesn't release much of anything, I take a seat on the edge of my bed and pull my phone out of my pocket. It's half past midnight here. Not even ten there. If it's a decent date, she'll still be out.

She might have blocked me. If she did, I don't know what the hell I'll do. Fly out to California, I guess?

I can't wait any longer.

I tap on her name and listen to it ring. Once. Twice. Three times.

"Hi." Silence follows the single word. Wherever she is, it's as quiet as an empty church.

The anger and resentment I'm expecting to hear is absent. *Everything* is absent—there's no emotion in her voice at all.

I cut straight to the chase. If I try to make small talk, I'm worried she'll hang up. I also don't want her to think I care by asking—about school, about her friends, about the guy she was out with earlier—which I'm aware is several shades of fucked-up. "I talked to Jeremy earlier."

"Great. Cool story." Boredom drips from each syllable.

She doesn't sound anxious. Doesn't sound like she misses me. I wish I could see her face, to try and match the words to her expression. To see if they line up.

I lean forward, pressing my elbows into my thighs and rubbing my face with my free hand. "He told me you bought a pregnancy test last week, Georgie."

"So *that's* what agents talk about when they're catching up, huh? Pregnancy tests?"

"You're going to make me ask?"

"Jeremy shouldn't have said anything to you. It's none of his business."

Is it my *business?*

I think the question but I don't ask it. Georgie knows exactly why I'm calling. "He's just worried about you."

"He shouldn't be. His job is to keep me safe, same as yours was."

I pinch the bridge of my nose and let a long exhale loose. "You know it wasn't that simple."

"According to you, it was."

My hand runs up my face and into my hair, tugging at the short strands so hard I wince. "Are you pregnant, Georgie?"

"No." Her answer is immediate. No hesitation. Then again, she knew I would ask.

I hesitate, knowing the next question will piss her off even more. "Would you tell me, if you were?"

She scoffs. "You think I'd lie to you about something like that?" There's annoyance in her response but also some hurt that makes me wince again.

"No. I just…I know you're mad at me right now. I want to make sure it's not—"

"I'm not mad at you."

"You're not?"

"No."

"Well, it sure seemed like you were, when I left."

"*Well*, I got over it."

"Georgie…" I scrub a hand across my face. "It wasn't—"

"You only called because Jeremy told you about the test, right?"

I sigh, knowing the truth isn't entirely accurate. "Right."

"Don't call me again, Ethan."

She hangs up. I toss my phone on the bed and press both of my palms against my eyes.

Fuck.

CHAPTER TWENTY-FOUR

GEORGIE

MY PERIOD ARRIVES the morning after my call with Ethan.

I complain loudly about my cramps and ask Jeremy to stop so I can buy some Tylenol, not missing the look of relief on his face. I wish I could be mad at him for saying something to Ethan, but I can't.

He didn't mean anything by it. He didn't know what it would mean to Ethan.

I almost wish I'd told him the full truth last night, that the test was negative, but I still hadn't gotten my period yet. He didn't give me any indication of his feelings before asking me point blank. No noble *I'll support whatever you decide* or comforting *We're in this together.*

He didn't ask about my date either. The only time Jeremy wasn't within hearing distance of me yesterday was when I was out with Jordan. If my potential pregnancy came up, I'm sure Jeremy mentioned my date to Ethan.

He probably doesn't care. Maybe he's happy to hear I've moved on. Except...there was something in his voice last night. Something that didn't sound like indifference.

I glance over at Jeremy as we walk across the center of campus. "How well do you know Agent Salisbury?"

He glances at me, surprise etched on his face. "Ethan? Um, not too well. We went through training together. He was…" Jeremy smiles. "Well, Ethan is pretty badass. Everyone was intimidated by him."

Nothing about what Jeremy says surprises me. "Do you know what he's doing now?"

"No. I don't. I talked to him yesterday, actually, but he didn't mention work. It could be administrative work on an old case. Giving up an assignment like this? Well…" Jeremy grows uncomfortable, remembering he's talking *to* the assignment. "But like I said, Ethan is good. He'll probably be back out in the field soon, if he isn't already."

"Oh. Good." My voice sounds flat, even to my own ears. It was one thing when he was here every day. I knew exactly what his everyday schedule involved. But not knowing where he is or what he's doing. What danger he might be in? It chafes at me in a way I wasn't expecting.

I've never worried about my dad's safety, even once he was elected, and arguably in constant danger. I trusted the protections that were in place would keep him safe, and so far they have.

But *Ethan* is part of those protections. There's no one keeping him safe, and that bothers me.

"You asking for any particular reason?"

I'm shaken out of my own thoughts by the sound of Jeremy's voice. For a minute, I forgot he was walking next to me. "I was just curious."

"Mm-hmm."

Silence falls between us as we near the building that houses the English department for my non-fiction class. The sun shines bright, illuminating all of campus. The palm trees and the row of sandstone buildings.

We're almost to the entrance when he speaks again. "He asked about you too."

I keep my gaze focused straight ahead on the building we're nearing. I'm worried what my face might give away, if I glance over. Worried that comment means Jeremy might have an idea of why Ethan really left.

⸻

I blink three times against the morning light, my eyes readjusting to the brightness as it takes in unfamiliar surroundings.

I arrived back in DC late last night, for the start of my Thanksgiving break. Part of me expected to see the light green walls of my bedroom at school when I woke up.

My alarm buzzes, so I roll over to shut it off. It took me a while to fall asleep last night. I'm tempted to pull a pillow over my face and try to go back to sleep. But the whole reason I left Stanford yesterday was so we could leave for Camp David early this morning.

I roll out of bed and head into the bathroom. I get dressed in jeans and a sweater, then pull my hair back into a French braid before heading downstairs and into the dining room.

Both of my parents have already eaten. I nibble on breakfast alone—scrambled eggs and fresh fruit—then head upstairs to finish getting ready. A few of the clothes I brought home get swapped for warmer ones, and then I haul my suitcase down the hall and stairs, depositing it next to the pile of luggage already waiting to get loaded.

Then, I head outside. It's a sunny day, with only the barest chill to the air. My dad's standing just to the right of the doorway, watching men in suits prepare and load the cars before we depart. He's wearing a navy bomber jacket with the presidential seal embroidered on the sleeve. I smirk when I see it. "Where did you get that?"

He smiles back. "It was a gift. What, you don't like it?"

"I think enough people know you're the president already, Dad. No need to be a walking advertisement."

"Oof." He grabs his chest like he's wounded. "I can always count on you to not pull any punches, Georgie."

"Maybe you're just getting soft, Dad, since everyone else is too scared to throw any."

He chuckles. "Maybe."

The smile from the easy interaction lingers on my face. It's been a long time since my dad and I had a light-hearted conversation, and I'm mostly to blame. Last summer was shadowed by the disagreement about my security detail, specifically Ethan. And I've treated my parents' check-ins since I left for college as an inconvenience, more than anything else. It's not like they weren't already receiving reports detailing my every movement.

I'm still smiling—when I see him. It freezes in place, right along with everything else.

Ethan is one of the agents inspecting the cars.

I don't know why this possibility didn't occur to me—that he might be here. When I asked Jeremy about Ethan's new assignment a couple of weeks ago, he made it sound like he was filing documents from a desk somewhere. I have no idea how the Secret Service chain of command really works. I asked my dad to give Ethan his first choice of reassignment, not because I was confident he had a say but because I hoped it would mitigate some of the fallout from his decision to leave. Turn the black mark a light shade of gray.

My father tracks my gaze to Ethan then glances at me.

Surprisingly, he doesn't comment. I'm sure he read into my request to grant Ethan his choice of reassignment. I'm not in the habit of asking my father for favors, and I didn't make my early disdain for Ethan a secret.

I don't meet my father's gaze. When I look back at Ethan, he's staring straight at me. Our gazes connect and hold. Neither of us are breaking eye contact, and I'm not sure if it's due to stubbornness...or something else.

"Okay, I'm ready." My mom's voice interrupts the staring contest. I look toward her automatically, and when I glance back where Ethan was standing, there's a different agent putting equipment in the trunk.

"Great!" My father says, his excitement on full display. This is the first trip the three of us have taken together in a while. Traveling anywhere as the president is a logistical nightmare, and so it tends to be limited for important trips like speaking engagements and meeting with world leaders.

I attempt to match his excitement by mustering a smile. But I keep glancing at each agent as they mill around and then start to load into cars.

Is he coming with us?

All three of us ride in the same car together—another rarity. Usually, my father is getting briefed on something important or preparing for an event with a member of his staff. Instead, my parents chat about a television show they're watching together, which is actually kind of sweet. If they weren't my parents, I'd probably find it romantic.

Camp David is sixty-eight miles outside of DC. We're about halfway into the hour-long drive when I cave and pull my phone out of my pocket. Our last messages stare at me.

Georgie: *I'm going to get a coffee after class.*
Ethan: *Okay.*

Georgie: *That's it? You're not going to complain?*

Ethan: *I'm going where you go regardless.*

I stare at the blinking cursor in the text box for another couple of minutes, then say an internal *fuck it.*

Georgie: *Why aren't you in Glenson?*

I begin gnawing on my lower lip as soon as I send it, second-guessing immediately.

There's no immediate response. No dots appear.

Maybe he blocked me.

But if I know Ethan—and I'm pretty sure I do—he didn't. I lean my head against the back of the car seat.

Ethan: *Didn't feel like it.*

An answer that tells me absolutely nothing. I chew on my bottom lip even more furiously, trying to figure out how to respond. *If* I should respond.

Before I can decide, dots appear again.

Ethan: *I knew you'd be here.*

And something that feels a little bit like hope flares in my chest.

＝＝＝

As soon as we finish lunch, my father suggests we head out to the tennis court tucked behind the house. The last time we played together was about ten months ago—the last time we were here. I inherited my love of tennis from my father. He played up through college, same as me.

Growing up, hitting the ball back and forth on a public court on a Saturday morning was a regular occurrence. It waned as I hit adolescence, then stopped completely when my father's political career hit new heights.

Watching his eyes light up with excitement as we walk along

the gravel path lined with trees boasting red, orange, and yellow leaves creates a warm glow in my chest.

It's a homey, comforting feeling perpetuated by the fact that it's been a while since my father and I had an easy, comfortable interaction like this. Here, it's easy to forget my father is the president. Even the airspace around Camp David is closely monitored. I know there are Secret Service agents all over the property, but none of them are visible right now.

It feels like a Saturday morning.

I grab a few tennis balls from the bucket beside the bin of racquets once we reach the court, tossing a couple to my dad. "You can serve first."

"Don't take it easy on me, Georgie," he says, pointing his racquet at me.

I laugh. "No promises."

My dad serves, and we start an easy volley back and forth that ends when I manage the game's first point. "Fifteen-love."

That's mainly what I associate love with—losing. And not just in tennis.

We play two more sets, both of which I win. My dad shakes his head with a rueful smile. "I promised your mom I would go for a walk with her before lunch. Maybe we can have a rematch after lunch?"

"Yeah. Sure," I agree.

"Ready to head back to the house?"

"You go ahead," I tell my dad. "I'm going to practice some more."

"You were taking it easy on me?"

I smile. "A little."

"All right, sweetheart. I'll see you a little later."

I nod, then lean down to pick up another ball. I send it over the net cleanly, smiling when it hits my favorite sweet spot just inside the line.

I run through the whole basket of balls before calling it quits. We're here for several more days, so I don't bother to pick them up. I'll serve from the opposite end tomorrow.

I turn to leave—and freeze in place.

Ethan is leaning against the fence, watching me. I tuck my racquet under one arm and brush the hair out of my eyes, feeling self-conscious.

He's changed out of the suit he was wearing earlier, into sweatpants and a hoodie.

I wait for him to speak first, since I texted him earlier and initiated the short exchange I'm not sure actually counts as a conversation.

"Tired?"

I grab my racquet again so I have something to fiddle with, tapping out a nervous beat against my leg. "No."

The infuriating smirk I love so much appears. "Wanna play with me?"

I chew on the inside of my cheek, trying to decipher any hidden meaning in the words. Is this an olive branch? The only way he could think to talk to me? "Play for what?"

"If I win, I want a date."

For a split-second, I think I must have heard him wrong. I was expecting something more along the lines of *one final game before you never see me again.* Surprise trickles through me. A little at first, then more and more as he holds my gaze. Not taking back anything he said, just waiting for me to react. Respond.

"A date," I repeat. "You left California—left me—and now you want to *go out on a date?*"

"We weren't going to work like that, Georgie. I needed to..." He sighs, then rubs his jaw. "It was hard, being around you, after.

274

Yeah, I left. But it wasn't because I wanted to. And it wasn't because I don't care."

"Careful, Ethan. You might make a *fool* of yourself."

He exhales, heavy and long. "I shouldn't have said that. I didn't mean it. I was just…trying to make it easier. I thought, if I left, things would go back to normal. But they haven't. And I don't want them to."

"What are you saying?"

"I'm saying—" He steps forward, grabbing a racquet from the bin of equipment next to the gate. "That if I win, I want you to go out on a date with me.

"And if I win?"

"You won't."

I battle an infuriating mixture of lust and annoyance, in response to his cocky answer. "Pretty sure of yourself, huh?"

"Against you, I'm undefeated."

"Once isn't much of a winning streak."

"Then give me another chance." This time, I'm not so sure he's talking about tennis.

"You're still an agent, Ethan."

He nods. "Yeah, I am. But I'm not *your* agent."

"Is there a difference?"

"To some people? Probably not. To me? Yeah, there is."

I say nothing, for a long minute. Then, finally, I walk over to the baseline, waiting expectantly for Ethan to walk to the opposite end of the court. He approaches me instead, holding a quarter. "Heads or tails?"

I call heads and lose.

We're evenly matched, to start. Ethan barely wins a set but then pulls ahead to a 40-15 advantage. He takes his time repositioning to serve again, keeping eye contact the whole time as he prepares for a match point.

It's a slow, easy serve, the kind you might send to a child. I could hit it easily, and I realize: he's giving me a choice. If I hit it back, the game will continue. But in one way, it will end.

I have to make a choice. There's no neutral option. Either I return the ball, or I let him win. Both decisions come with consequences. I'm at a fork in the road, with no decision to stay straight ahead.

I let it bounce. Once, twice, three times, until the ball is moving so slowly it's hardly leaving the surface of the court. Until there's no doubt I purposefully chose not to return it.

Ethan holds my gaze.

He smiles.

And the hope in my chest spreads.

CHAPTER TWENTY-FIVE

ETHAN

IT'S rare to become desensitized to entering the grounds of the White House. The building looks important. Decisions that change millions of lives are made within its walls. Not many structures hold that level of power. The grounds surrounding it are meticulously manicured. The fence and guards make it clear there's no open invitation for entry.

I wouldn't say I became desensitized, exactly, but I started viewing driving through the gate as commonplace shortly after I joined Georgie's security detail. It was a job; I made an effort to act professional and take it all in stride.

Tonight is personal.

I have my badge out and ready. But all I get asked for is my name and my driver's license. It takes me a minute to realize why —it's later than any agent would be arriving. It's obvious I'm not here to relieve anyone from duty.

Craig Neeson ambles out of the guard hut as my car gets checked. "Hiya, Ethan."

"Hey, Craig," I reply.

"You're the talk of this place, kid."

Great. I had a feeling that would be the case, though. You don't just casually date the president's daughter, especially when you're somehow involved in government yourself. It automatically involves a whole host of speculation. "Come on, Craig. Good lookin' guy like yourself? I'm sure you went out on a lot of dates."

He grins, flashing a gold tooth. "Sure did. Can't say I ever picked a young lady up from here, though."

I shrug. "What can I say? You know I like to live on the edge a bit."

Craig chuckles before shaking his head. "Good luck, Ethan."

"All clear," the other guard states.

I pull forward, driving through the open gate and curving around the drive toward the front of the residence. I park in front and climb out, well aware there are already eyes on me who would see if I hesitated now.

The walk up to the front door is mercifully short. It opens before I can reach it. A middle-aged man in a suit waits for me to walk inside the front hall, then closes it behind me.

Georgie is waiting, leaning up against the wall just inside the entryway. She smiles when she sees me, letting her crossed arms fall to her sides. I told her to dress casually, and she complied. She's wearing a pair of black jeans and a green sweater, her jacket tossed over the chair next to her.

"Hey," she greets.

"Hi."

We stare at each other for a few seconds. I count nine.

This feels familiar, all the way down to the energy humming between us. This past summer, I picked up Georgie dozens of times.

"Agent Salisbury." I glance up to see President Adams descending the central staircase, dressed smartly in a pair of charcoal-colored pants and a sweater vest. The First Lady is right behind him.

I've never met Georgie's mother, officially. In any capacity, let alone one like this.

I straighten instinctively, despite the fact my posture was already similar to a fence post. "President Adams. Mrs. Adams."

President Adams waits for his wife to greet me first. I shake her offered hand. "It's very nice to meet you, Ethan," she tells me.

Georgie mentioned her mother worked as a college professor before her father was elected. I can perfectly picture Mrs. Adams teaching a lecture. She's dressed semi-casually, just like her husband, in a sheath-style dress and matching sweater. She exudes an air of calm authority that is both intimidating and reassuring.

"You too, Mrs. Adams."

"Call me Ann, please."

President Adams steps forward. "Good to see you again."

"You too, sir."

He studies me with the uncomfortable intensity of an X-ray machine. The last time we had a one-on-one conversation, I told him I was too distracted by his daughter to do my job properly, so I can understand his hesitation.

There will be an official team of agents escorting us tonight, since not only am I no longer on Georgie's security detail, I'm not on duty tonight at all. "Should be an entertaining evening," President Adams comments.

Georgie glances between me and her dad. "You told him where you're taking me, but you won't tell me?"

"I didn't tell him," I answer. "He must have requested the security plan."

President Adams smiles. It turns a shade sheepish, when Ann elbows his side. *Like daughter, like father*, I think, knowing

Georgie has taken some liberties with requests herself. I had to report tonight's itinerary so the agents on duty could plan appropriately.

Georgie rolls her eyes, like she can hear what I'm thinking. "Okay, well..." She pulls her jacket on. "It was sort of sweet and super embarrassing that you both showed up, but we should get going."

"Have fun, you two," Mrs. Adams says, turning to head upstairs.

"Can I have a quick word, Ethan?" President Adams asks, earning twin glares from his wife and daughter.

"Joseph..."

"Dad—"

"It will only take a minute."

"Of course, sir," I say, leaving Georgie's side and following her father over to the right side of the staircase.

President Adams stops once we're out of earshot and turns to face me. "I'm trusting you with the most precious thing in the world to me, Ethan. Don't forget I have connections."

"I know, sir. She'll be safe with me. I promise."

He holds my gaze, testing my sincerity. It seems to hold because he nods. "Next time we talk, feel free to call me Joseph."

Before I can say anything in response, he's turning and walking down the hall and into one of the first floor sitting rooms.

Georgie raises both eyebrows as I approach her. "Did he threaten you?"

I smile. "Come on, let's go."

"Are you going to tell me where?"

"No."

She sighs, but it has an edge of excitement, not annoyance. We walk toward my car, an SUV parked right behind it. It's against protocol for a member of the president's family to travel without at least one agent in the same car. I'm pretty sure the only reason it was approved is because off-duty or not, I received all the training as any other agent and technically qualify.

We're almost to the car when she grabs my arm. I panic for a millisecond, worried I missed something she didn't. Heavily guarded or not, the White House is always a sitting target.

When I look at Georgie, I realize I should be worried for a different reason. She's wearing a sly expression that makes my blood pump faster. Her hand slips behind my back as she crushes her body against mine, smiling up at me.

"Georgie," I say.

Her smile grows. "I like when you say my name like that."

"Like what?"

"Like you're annoyed with me—but also like you're thinking about kissing me."

I don't disagree. "Lots of people are around."

"Does that bother you?"

"I wasn't sure if you'd..." I exhale. "I've never done this before, Georgie."

"It's a big relief, knowing you don't make a habit of picking up politicians' daughters." I roll my eyes at that response. "Are you embarrassed?" she asks, quietly.

I use the arm she isn't holding and tilt her head up with my hand. "No, Georgie. *No*."

"Then kiss me," she whispers.

So, I do. It feels like a New Year's Eve kiss, the sort with some special, assigned importance. Long before my lips touch hers, I know it will be more than an ordinary peck. That this will be a moment I think of and replay.

Our lips move together slowly at first. Then, gradually, the kiss deepens and quickens. I think—hope, assume—I'll have the chance to kiss Georgie Adams many more times. That tonight is a continuation of something that started between us a long time ago and never really ended. But I kiss her like it's the first and last time I'll ever get to do so.

I pull back first, ending the embrace before things get too heated between us. We're both inhaling and exhaling heavily, and for a minute, all I can breathe is her. It's funny, how you can miss *everything* about a person, all the way down to how they smell. Georgie's scent is a mixture of laundry detergent and citrus shampoo.

"We should go," I tell her. "Or we'll be late."

She smiles. "Late for what?"

I shake my head, silently letting her know I won't crack that easily. "Nice try."

Georgie laughs before climbing into the passenger seat.

Conversation flows easily between us as I drive off the grounds and head toward downtown DC. The past few weeks have been a regular back and forth between us, but I wasn't sure what to expect tonight. Since our tennis match at Camp David— when she agreed to tonight—I haven't talked to her in person. I returned to DC later that afternoon, my role fulfilled once the property was swept and secured.

A few days after her Thanksgiving break ended, once I knew she was back on campus, I called her. Partially under the pretense of checking and ensuring all was well with her new team—something I would have done as soon as I'd left, if we'd been on speaking terms—but mostly to test how things were between us. She answered, we talked, and then a day later Georgie was the one who called me.

We've fallen into a comfortable pattern since, which resulted in us talking every day of the past three weeks that were the tail end of her fall semester. She got back to DC yesterday and will be home for almost a month before returning for the spring semester early, to begin preparing for the start of the college tennis season.

Tonight feels tenuous. Big decisions and huge responsibility. An acknowledgment that I shouldn't be the one who makes all the choices. As the agent keeping her safe, it was one thing. As something else entirely—I can't think of one word that really applies—it's another.

I'm not being magnanimous, more selfish than anything else. Because I'm sick of fighting her on something I think we both want. That I know I want. Other people might respect me for never knowing I crossed an invisible barrier. But I'd respect myself less, for not having the guts to admit that I had.

I recognize the minute Georgie realizes where we're headed. She glances between me and the bright lights that cover Capital One Arena—twice. "How did you know I love the Jonas Brothers?"

A banner depicting three dark-haired men is hanging from the side of the massive building. I squint at the date, realize it's tomorrow, then glance back at Georgie. The only band she's ever mentioned liking is The Beatles, and I wouldn't place them in the boy band category.

I open my mouth, to tell her we're not seeing a musical performance tonight, and she's grinning. "Sucker. I'm going to see them tomorrow night, with Lucy. I figured *we* were going to see the Capitals play. Which is why I'm wearing this." She grabs and lifts the hem of her sweater.

I'm glad traffic around the arena has slowed progress to a crawl, because I'm not confident I wouldn't have swerved the car in an embarrassing—not to mention dangerous—response to the flash of bare skin and blue lace.

I glance back at the red taillights of the car in front of us. "It's been a while since I was out on a date, but I don't think flashing other guys is generally part of the package."

"The only guy I flashed was *you*," Georgie retorts. "And it was accidental. I was trying to show you this. It got stuck to my sweater."

I look over again. She's wearing a Capitals shirt under her sweater. "When did you get that?"

"After you asked me out."

"Pretty confident I'd bring you here?" I ask, as I drive into the garage

I'm surprised, because *I* wasn't confident I'd bring her here. Not only is Georgie not much of a hockey fan, but it's far from a low-key outing. It's a challenge from a security standpoint—the only reasons I was able to make it happen is Georgie can blend in better than her father and it wasn't an announced outing. A large part of me was sorely tempted to take her to a nice restaurant for a candlelit dinner, where I would have her to myself and not have to compete for attention against thousands of screaming hockey fans and the slam of bodies against boards.

"I asked you to," she answers. "And I think you're a guy who follows through."

I smile, savoring the warmth those words ignite. "I guess I'll have to make you more promises, and then you can decide for sure."

"Yeah. I guess you will," Georgie tells me.

⸺

It's usually easy to blend in when you are walking through a venue packed with people. Everyone is rushing. Trying to find their seats, trying to buy team apparel from the gift shop, trying to get food or drinks from a concession stand. Until they're waiting in line, no one is taking the time to look around and absorb what anyone else is doing.

Unless…you're walking around with an armed escort. That cuts through the noise. A literal hush falls, closely followed by whispers. And, once it registers that only people of importance travel with a security team, phones are pulled out to take photos.

Georgie—who I know hates the attention and the staring— appears oblivious to the scrutiny. She swings our joined hands together as we walk, occasionally glancing up at the declining numbers as we head toward our section.

Her jacket got left in the car and she took off her sweater before we entered the arena. There's a half-inch of skin showing between the waistband of her jeans and the bottom hem of her shirt. Each time I get a glimpse of the thin strip of skin, I'm reminded of how little she's wearing underneath the shirt.

After stopping for some popcorn and a soft pretzel, we reach the entrance to our section. I balance both snacks while Georgie carries two bottles of water. I thought there was a chance she'd try to order a beer, and I'm not sure what I would have done if she had.

I'm still navigating the gray space that's the transition between my former role as her head of security and this new relationship that's more of a partnership than me asserting authority and her pushing back.

Maybe Georgie is realizing the same, and that's why she didn't try to.

The usher blinks at the tickets, blanches at Georgie—I'm not sure if it's because she's hot or because he recognizes her—and then gestures for us to go ahead. I turn and give Archie, the head of Georgie's detail tonight, a questioning look.

He nods in response, letting me know we're good to proceed. The agreement was that unless there were any issues entering the building they would hang back at the top of the section for the duration of the game, giving us the illusion of privacy.

I doubt Mark—or whoever managed this week's schedule—was considering my love life while scheduling, but I'm relieved neither Myles, Kevin, Joey, nor Jeremy are part of Georgie's detail tonight. It would have served as a constant reminder of how I stood on the other side of this, not too long ago. How I was the one scanning the surroundings while some other lucky guy was getting to focus on nothing besides Georgie.

The players are just starting to file off the ice following warm-up. The Zambonis come out to clean the surface to a gleam, followed by the lights display projected on the ice of the season's most exciting plays. The National Anthem is sung, followed by Canada's. Two sets of colorful jerseys file back out onto the ice, the starting lineup is announced, and then the puck is dropped.

Georgie asks me questions about the game nonstop throughout the entire first period. I think I'm doing a terrible job explaining the rules of the sport—until she calls a tripping penalty on Donaldson seconds before the loudspeaker announces the same.

I feel like a proud coach.

Halfway through the second period, there's a television time out. Georgie glances at me. I think it's going to be another hockey question, until she asks it. "Did you mean what you said earlier, that you haven't been on a date in a while?"

I nod. "Yeah."

"How long?"

"Since before I met you." A lot longer than that, now that I think about it. Stella and I's brief shot at long distance didn't involve many.

"Anything else you haven't done, since then?"

"Anything specific you're asking about?" I ask, like I don't know.

Georgie rolls her eyes. "Have you been with anyone else since Stanford?"

"No. Have you?"

She shakes her head. "No. I did go out on a date though. With Jordan. It was...well, I had a lot on my mind."

I think back, to the call when Jeremy told me Georgie was out on a date and what else he shared in a short span of time. "You could have told me, Georgie. Before you knew for sure. I hope you know that."

"We were in a bad place, Ethan. I knew you regretted what happened between us. It made the most sense to say nothing, until I knew for sure."

I twist in my seat, so I can see her better. "Georgie, I don't regret anything that happened between us. I wish some of it had happened differently, sure. If your safety was ever compromised because I was too wrapped up in you, I never would have forgiven myself. That's why I got upset afterward. Why I left. But regret?" I shake my head. "Never, okay?"

"Okay," she says, then smirks. "Is this a bad time to tell you we're on the kiss cam?"

"We're what?" I glance up at the Jumbotron and—sure enough, there we are.

"Kiss me, Ethan."

My mom has always said *she knew*—when she met my dad. Knew they had something special that couldn't be replicated with other people. The sort of magic that some people never find.

I glance at Georgie, flushed and smiling beside me.

And I think, *I know*.

EPILOGUE
GEORGIE

I'M in the middle of another sea. This one is scarlet.

May sunshine streams down in strong rays, bathing the rows of folding chairs, podium, and stage in bright, golden light. I tug my gown up a bit, trying to readjust the polyester so it's not nearly as stifling.

This year's commencement speaker is an Oscar-winning actress. She's funny and quirky, delivering a speech filled with humorous anecdotes and advice far more profound than *your future looks bright.*

Stanford asked my dad to deliver the address, but he declined, saying he wanted to witness the ceremony the same as every other parent. I was relieved by the choice, even though the extensive security measures in place ensure my father isn't exactly blending in with the crowd in the back row.

The ceremony ends twenty minutes later, and I'm officially a college graduate. I file out with the rest of my row, saying a hasty goodbye to any friends or acquaintances I pass who I'm not sure I'll see later.

As always, my family is easy to spot. My father won reelection almost two years ago, meaning his security is for a sitting president, not a former one.

Déjà vu hits me in full force as I give my parents hugs and accept their congratulations, along with a bouquet of pink peonies. Only, unlike at my high school graduation four years ago, someone vital is missing. "Where's Ethan?"

My mom and dad exchange an amused smile. I roll my eyes. If it didn't make my life exponentially easier, I'd be annoyed by how thoroughly my parents approve of Ethan. Maybe I should have outgrown my rebellious phase a while ago, but it still pops up, now and again.

"Vincent wanted his input on something," my father answers.

"Huh." Vincent is part of my father's security detail. I'm not sure what he'd need Ethan for that another agent couldn't provide —especially at *my* graduation. Ethan is here for personal reasons, not in any official capacity.

Ethan never returned to my security detail after we officially began dating. It complicated our relationship significantly, since it meant I was mostly in California while he was working in DC. But we both agreed conflating the boyfriend and bodyguard titles were a bad idea.

Now that I've graduated, I'm doing what I always thought I never would: returning to DC. I'd be lying if I said Ethan hadn't played a major role in the decision. He's cagey with the details of his ongoing assignments.

I'm not sure if it's because he doesn't want me to worry, because it's confidential, or because of my proximity to the presidency. He tells me it isn't dangerous, but I don't think he would admit it to me, if it were.

Starting in the fall, I'll be pursuing my master's in social work, which is what I just received a Bachelor's degree in. While there are many parts of politics I don't enjoy, I've always appreciated the broad aim: to improve people's lives. I'm hoping to work as an addiction counselor or a criminal justice social worker once I'm licensed.

Ethan finally appears, pushing through the crowd of security that parts for him like the red sea I was literally just a part of.

I saw him just a few hours ago. Snuck him into my off-campus apartment last night instead of sleeping at the same hotel as my parents. I've known him for nearly four years now. And still, I feel the familiar flutter of butterflies in my stomach as he reaches me, and I'm enveloped in the arms that feel like the safest place in the world.

"Congrats, babe," he whispers to me, kissing the top of my head.

I loop my arms around his waist, not allowing him to move away any further. "Thanks." I tilt my head back, hoping he'll kiss me but knowing he'll probably wait until we're alone.

Ethan avoids PDA in front of my parents, which I get. I've never made out with him in front of his mom. Although I think all three of our parents have probably seen the clip of us on the kiss cam during our first official date, seeing as it amassed about fifty million views on social media.

It takes a while for our large group to migrate to the parking lot, between the crowds and the commotion. When we reach the asphalt, I automatically head for the SUV my security team brought here.

Ethan stops me with a tug on my arm. "You're riding with me," he tells me in a low, serious tone.

I raise both brows. "I am?"

"Yes." His voice returns to its usual volume. "Ann, Joseph, we'll see you at seven."

It took Ethan six months to start calling my dad by his first name, but now he does so with ease. My parents both nod and smile, their swarm of security hurrying them along toward the long convoy of cars waiting. In contrast, Ethan pulls me to the left, toward an identical black SUV, the standard sort I'm used to riding in. But no one else follows us, which isn't usual. Most of the time, even when I'm with Ethan, I have other security around as well.

"There's no car behind us," I state, after we've climbed into the car and Ethan is pulling out of the lot.

"Mm-hmm." He looks to the left, then flicks on a blinker.

I unzip my gown and slide it off my shoulders. My mom got plenty of photos before the ceremony, so I have no reason to wear it later.

Ethan glances over in response to the movement. His gaze heats as he takes in the navy dress I'm wearing. Not because it's all that revealing, but because he was there when I got dressed this morning and knows exactly what I'm wearing underneath it. I squirm in my seat, hoping wherever he's taking me is secluded.

The trip takes longer than I'm expecting. I glance over at Ethan a few times as we breeze along the highway, surprised he's taking me this far from campus. Dinner with my parents isn't for several hours. There's nothing to do until then aside from some packing I still have to do in my apartment, not that I'm overly eager to do that. I wasn't expecting a road trip though.

Finally, he pulls off the highway. We drive for another ten minutes, during which I sneak a couple dozen peeks at him. Sometimes, it feels like I'm seeing him for the first time. Like everything familiar is new and novel again.

I sort of hope I always feel that way. It makes me feel like falling in love is an endless process. Where you don't say you already fell, and it doesn't have a set destination. Where you keep tumbling, lost and powerless to stop it because the pull to the person is so strong.

When Ethan finally stops the car, it's at a short stretch of sandy beach. When he looks at me, I know my expression is confused. Because I have no idea why we just drove for close to an hour to end up at a small beach I've never seen before.

"Uh, this is nice."

Ethan cracks a smile. Then exhales. "I was going to do this on Nantucket. But they wouldn't let me take you, just the two of us, after what happened last summer."

I nod. The past few summers, my family has spent a week on the island. I told my dad it was a family experience I missed, and he made sure to make it happen. Last summer, there was chaos pretty much everywhere we went, like my dad was a movie star, not a politician.

"And then I was going to wait until Greece, which, yeah…you dropped enough hints. We're going this summer."

My smiles stretches across my whole face. I've always wanted to go to Greece and have been subtly suggesting to Ethan we make the trip for almost two years.

Ethan exhales again, and I realize: *he's nervous*.

He confirms it a few seconds later, with a low laugh. "Wow. So far, this has sucked. Maybe we should get out—yeah, come on. Let's go for a walk on the beach."

I crack open my door and climb out. Slowly, because something else is slowly dawning on me. Another realization I'm worried to devote any consideration to, in case I'm wrong.

Ethan starts down the beach, except there's not very far to walk. This seems like a private cove, nothing like the long stretch of shore near his mom's house.

We're both silent, and there's no one else around. Just seagulls cawing and surf pounding the shore.

"I've been putting off packing," I tell him, about halfway

down. "There's still a lot to do later. I haven't been feeling very inspired."

"Because you don't want to leave California?"

I shake my head. "No, that's not it. I mean, you know I don't love DC."

"I know." Ethan's smile is wry, probably recalling the times I've complained about the political bubble.

"But...you're there. So there's nowhere else I want to be."

He stops walking. "You mean that?"

"Yes."

"I brought you here for a reason, you know."

"I mean, we drove an hour to walk for fifty feet, so I figured."

"Smartass," Ethan mumbles. But he's smiling as he says it.

Then he sinks down onto one knee. And even though I had some idea it might be coming, even though I'm not completely caught off guard, my gasp is genuine. So is the way my hands fly up to my mouth and moisture pools in my eyes.

I don't have to think about my answer. It comes natural and easy, the way some moments feel perfectly scripted.

The way it feels when you're falling.

And all I can think, as Ethan promises me everything I've ever wanted to hear, is how I don't want to freeze this moment. I've imagined it before, plenty. I'm only twenty-two, but Ethan is twenty-six. We've been together for three and a half years. Our relationship has never been casual. It's always been consuming, and the intensity hasn't faded. I want to savor what's happening right now, but I'm mostly excited for what's to come.

I'm agreeing to spend my life with him. To share everything with him. It's the most important choice I'll ever make—and that's exactly what it is: a choice.

I start saying yes before he's finished talking. He laughs, slipping a ring on my hand before standing and kissing me. *Mine*, I think. Ethan Salisbury is *mine*.

Maybe we started with a thrill of the forbidden. But that would have worn off a long time ago, if that's all we were. I want to marry Ethan because he *gets* me, more than anyone else ever has. Because I love arguing with him and because I still get butterflies around him.

Ethan exhales, when our lips separate. "I was nervous," he admits.

"You thought I'd turn you down?"

"You usually surprise me in some way, so I figure there was a chance."

I kiss him again. "There wasn't." I admire the ring for the first time. It looks foreign on my hand, but also right. Like I'll look at it for a long time.

Ethan notices the direction of my gaze. "It was my mom's," he says, quietly. "She wanted you to have it."

Every time I've seen Ethan's mother, she's had a wedding band on, but not an engagement ring. Tears prick at my eyes as I realize this is one of the few reminders she had of her husband. Ethan's father chose this ring for her.

"I love it," I say, glancing up at him.

He holds my gaze, smiling slightly as he tucks a piece of hair behind my ear. "We have to go," he says, regret saturating each syllable. "I drove further than I should have."

"Why?"

"I wanted it to be just us. This stretch is a local secret, apparently."

I glance around at our surroundings, absorbing them more for the first time. The small cove is scenic, but I'd rather focus on him. My answer would have been the same, no matter where we were.

We walk back toward the car, hand in hand. Ethan opens the door for me. I climb back inside the SUV, alternating between looking at him and my ring as he rounds the front of the car and gets in the driver's seat.

"Do my parents know?" I ask.

"Yeah." He laughs. "I asked your dad for permission. Fuck if that wasn't intimidating."

"Yeah, right. My dad loves you."

"He loves you more. You're his only child."

"You're exactly the sort of guy he wanted me to end up with, you know." I lean across the center console. "Stubborn. Overbearing. Patriot—"

Ethan cuts me off with a kiss. This is different than the ones on the beach. There's an edge of lust that fills me with familiar heat. I kiss him back to a ragged, impatient rhythm, leaning across the barrier between us until I give up and crawl across the console.

He pulls back. "Georgie—"

"Don't you want to fuck your fiancée?" I whisper.

Ethan groans and says my name again. I love the sound of it, especially with the rasp of need. Our lips crash together again. I can feel him responding, the bulge of his erection obvious through the slacks he's wearing.

I love kissing him, but it's not enough. I fumble with his belt and zipper as best I can without looking down and am rewarded by the stiff length of his erection bobbing free.

Ethan looks around. The beach is still empty, there are no other cars or people in sight. I feel him acquiescence. Feel the tension drain from his body, to be replaced by a different sort of anticipation. His hands run up my legs, pulling my underwear to the side and discovering how wet I am for him.

"Fuck." Ethan growls the word into the hollow of my throat,

pulling my underwear to the side as I fist his cock and guide him inside of me. We both moan at the sensation that's amplified as I lift up quickly and slide down slowly.

It's difficult to move in the tight confines of the car, but it doesn't matter. I'm close already, based on nothing but the feel of him inside of me and the look of wonder on his face. I rise and fall in rapid succession, squeezing my inner muscles each time that he's fully seated inside of me.

The car is filled with the heavy sound of our breathing. The skirt of my dress covers his lap entirely. I can't watch him penetrate me, but I can feel it. The sensation is all I can focus on, as his hands fall to my hips, pushing up into me until everything else fades to the background.

"So fucking good." Ethan groans. "It's always so fucking good with you."

"I'm close," I tell him, my muscles tightening as I brace for the onslaught of pleasure.

He kisses me again. It's wild and desperate, and I'm so focused on the two spots where we're connected that I jolt when one of his hands leaves my hip and brushes me, just above where I'm bouncing on his dick.

It's too much. The way he feels. The way he looks, watching me ride him. Wave after wave of euphoria hits, as I clench around him and moan his name. Ethan spills inside me seconds later, his hands fisted in the folds of my dress.

"I'm going to have to change before dinner," I say, once I've regained the ability to form whole sentences.

Ethan huffs a laugh. "Are you complaining?"

"No." I run a hand through his hair, running my nails lightly along his scalp.

His eyes close, then slowly open. He's still inside of me, but it feels like we're even more intimately connected. "I love you," he tells me.

No matter how many times I hear them, those three words will never get old. "I love you too," I tell him, stealing one final kiss before I move off his lap and readjust my underwear. I settle back in the passenger seat, feeling the evidence of what just took place between us soak the fabric.

Ethan starts the car and pulls back onto the road. The windows are down, so a sea breeze blows between us, ruffling my hair and caressing my skin. Ethan fiddles with the radio, until the Beatles station I like comes in. "Blackbird" is playing. He glances over, a small smile on his face.

And it feels like the perfect start to forever.

THE END

ACKNOWLEDGMENTS

First off, thank YOU for reading *Serve*! I am so grateful to all of my readers, both those who recently discovered my books and those who have stuck with me from the very beginning. Your excitement is what motivates me through long days and late nights.

Britt, it was such a joy working with you. Thank you for all of your enthusiasm and support for this story. For helping it become the best possible version of itself. And, especially, for all the comments that made editing infinitely more enjoyable.

Alison, thank you for taking such a thorough final pass. It's always a pleasure working with you!

Sarah, thank you for another stunning cover. You captured exactly what I was picturing.

Autumn, I loved working with you. Thanks for helping me spread the word about this book and making sure everything ran smoothly behind the scenes.

ABOUT THE AUTHOR

C.W. Farnsworth is the author of numerous adult and young adult romance novels featuring sports, strong female leads, and happy endings.

Charlotte lives in Rhode Island and when she isn't writing spends her free time reading, at the beach, or snuggling with her Australian Shepard.

Find her on Facebook (@cwfarnsworth), Twitter (@cw_farnsworth), Instagram (@authorcwfarnsworth) and check out her website www.authorcwfarnsworth.com for news about upcoming releases!

CPSIA information can be obtained
at www.ICGtesting.com
Printed in the USA
LVHW111614310822
727185LV00005B/380